ZOMBICIDE
ALL OR NOTHING

A walker stumbled into him. A young man, in a polo shirt and chinos. Mostly in one piece, save for the hole where his jugular ought to have been. It rounded on him with a hiss.

Westlake flinched back, expecting it to lunge for him. Instead, it swayed for a moment, staring blankly at him. Then it continued on its way, as if nothing had happened. It hadn't attacked him. Why hadn't it attacked him?

He looked down. There was a broken tree branch sticking out of his abdomen. The larger part of him began to hyperventilate. Or he would have, had he been breathing.

He forced his way through the press of walkers, elbowing the slower ones aside. None of them made so much as a sound. They didn't care about him. They didn't care, because as far as they were concerned, he was one of them.

T0018449

More Zombicide

Zombicide
Last Resort by Josh Reynolds

Zombicide Invader
Planet Havoc by Tim Waggoner

Zombicide Black Plague
Age of the Undead by C L Werner

ALL OR NOTHING

Josh Reynolds

ACONYTE

First published by Aconyte Books in 2022

ISBN 978 1 83908 163 7

Ebook ISBN 978 1 83908 164 4

Cover art by Riccardo Crosa & Paolo Francescutto

Distributed in North America by Simon & Schuster Inc, New York, USA

Printed in the United States of America

9 8 7 6 5 4 3 2 1

ACONYTE BOOKS

An imprint of Asmodee Entertainment Ltd

Mercury House, Shipstones Business Centre

North Gate, Nottingham NG7 7FN, UK

aconytebooks.com // twitter.com/aconytebooks

For Derrick – gone but never forgotten.

CHAPTER ONE
Wreckage

Estela Ramirez sat on a mossy rock, studying the burnt-out wreckage of an off-road vehicle. The clearing still showed the signs of the crash, even now, months later. The bodies of the zombies were mostly gone, thanks to the local wildlife. Those that remained were little more than blackened bones with scraps of leathery skin fluttering in the chill morning air of the Adirondacks. Little by little, the natural world was reclaiming the spot. Soon, it would be nothing more than another bad memory, to add to the rest.

But until then, Ramirez intended to do what she did best. She studied the scene as she had every week for the past two months, with the eyes of a Quantico-trained investigator. She could replay the last moments of the crash in her mind's eye now.

The vehicle had not been going at its top speed when it crashed, but it had been going fast enough to rupture the gas tank and from there, one spark had been enough to turn it into a fireball. There had been no explosion – that happened rarely outside of the movies. Not that there were movies anymore.

Or, rather, there was only one movie left, of the post-apocalyptic variety, and they were living in it. With a sigh, she rose to her feet and put her hands in the pockets of her leather jacket. It was chilly this morning. The weather was cold and getting colder. Winter was rolling in over the mountains. She wondered whether that would hamper the zombies any. She doubted it. Nothing else seemed to. They just kept stumbling on, day after day, week after week, their numbers swelling and shrinking with no pattern that she could determine.

Ramirez slowly circled the burnt-out wreck, hands still in her pockets. The front of the vehicle looked as if it had been punched by a giant – not once, but many times. Impact points, from where it had struck trees on its way down into the clearing. The story she drew from the evidence never changed, no matter how many different angles she looked at it from.

The driver's last ride had been a short, eventful one. He'd headed downhill at an inadvisable speed. The zombies had given chase, some even managing to climb onto the truck as it slowed at points along the packed dirt trail. He'd spun out halfway down the trail, and the truck had plummeted through the trees before crashing down into the clearing.

She turned, surveying the area around the front of the vehicle. It was possible that the driver had been thrown clear during the crash. It was also possible, though unlikely, that he'd walked away from it. She'd heard stranger stories, even before the zombie apocalypse. In fact, these days it was more likely that he'd walked away – just not as a living, breathing person.

Ramirez flinched inwardly from the thought and paused. Frowning, she turned. A coyote sat at the edge of the clearing, watching her. It was big, but mangy looking. She studied the coyote, and it returned the favor, showing no fear of her. But why would it? Humans were no longer top of the food chain. They'd been supplanted by the dead.

The coyote tensed, nose quivering. It smelled something. Ramirez looked around, taking her cue from the animal's superior senses. There weren't many zombies in these parts, not lately. If the animals didn't get them, the mountains did. But that didn't mean there weren't any. Some managed to survive the natural hazards in order to make a nuisance of themselves.

The coyote rose to its feet, uncertain now. It turned as if to run, but too slowly. Something lunged out of the dark beneath the trees and collided with the animal. Together, they went down in a thrashing, snarling tangle. Ramirez took a step back, surprised despite herself. The two struggling forms collided with the front of the wreck, and she saw that the coyote's attacker was a zombie – a walker, she thought, though it was hard to tell.

The zombie was a leathery thing, its skin like jerky, its face nearly a skull. It was so withered, she couldn't tell whether it had been a man or a woman, but it wore the filthy remnants of a park ranger's uniform. The walker clutched the coyote's throat with its claw-like hands, as if attempting to throttle the writhing animal, and snapped ineffectually at its prey with brown, broken teeth.

Ramirez's first instinct was to go for her sidearm. The Glock had been her constant companion both before and after the apocalypse. But ammunition was getting scarce, and the sound of the shot might well draw more nearby walkers down on her. She decided not to chance it. Instead, her hand went to the hunting knife on her hip. She drew it and crept toward the distracted zombie. It wasn't going to be easy. The coyote was putting up a desperate fight. It snapped and snarled, biting chunks out of the walker's arms and chest. Whatever else, the animal was keeping its attacker occupied.

When she'd gotten close enough, she reached out and caught hold of what was left of the walker's scalp, jerking its head back. The scalp began to tear away in her grip, but it held long enough for her to drive the hunting knife up through the base of its skull and into whatever calcified lump passed for its brain. She gave the blade a practiced twist and then wrenched it loose. The zombie slumped sideways with barely a twitch. The coyote twisted free of its loosening grip and darted away into the undergrowth.

"You're welcome," Ramirez called after it, as she wiped the knife clean on the back of her jeans. Behind her, a branch snapped. She whirled, the knife slashing out in a tight arc. It caught the zombie beneath the chin, opening its throat to the bone. Unfortunately, that didn't do much to alter its momentum. It crashed into her and drove her back against the wreck. Like the other, it was shrunken, withered; it too wore the remnants of a park ranger's uniform, in somewhat better condition than the other.

It hissed at her through tombstone teeth as she tried to

push it away. Her knife had been knocked from her hand, and it was all she could do to keep the walker from tearing her throat out. Even so, she didn't panic. Panic killed you quicker than any zombie.

She struck at its elbows and shoulders methodically, trying to break its hold. When that didn't work, she started on its knees. One of her awkward kicks finally connected, and she heard the telltale snap of bone. The zombie sagged, suddenly off-balance, but not giving up. She hit it in the face with a fist, and its head snapped back.

Momentarily freed from its grasp, she dove for her knife. There was still a chance to do this without noise. If she had to shoot it, there was no telling how many more might show up. Its hands fumbled at her jacket even as her fingers closed about the hilt, and she was yanked roughly backwards. She twisted in its grip and attempted to drive the knife into its head, but it caught her wrist. That shocked her into a moment's immobility. That hesitation almost cost her.

Its teeth were almost at her throat when a hunting arrow sprouted from its skull. The walker rolled away from her with an ugly gurgle. A second arrow joined the first, knocking it down completely. It thrashed for a moment, then lay still.

Panting slightly, Ramirez turned. Elizabeth Sayers stood at the top of the slope that led down into the clearing, a camouflaged longbow in her hands and a matching quiver on her hip. Lean of build with a sharp face, her shaggy hair was tied back and out of her eyes. She had the look of someone who spent most of her time outdoors. She lowered the longbow and gave Ramirez a stern look. "That was stupid. Letting it sneak up on you like that."

"I was distracted, dealing with the other one," Ramirez said, defensively. She didn't like Sayers and the feeling was mutual. Though they'd been forced to work together of late, their dislike of one another hadn't dwindled so much as simmered.

"You shouldn't have bothered. Coyotes can handle themselves."

Ramirez grimaced. "You saw?"

Sayers wasn't looking at her now. Instead, the former park ranger's eyes were on the trees. Scanning. "I saw enough," she said, absently. "You weren't paying attention."

"You could have warned me!"

"I saved you."

"If you'd warned me, you wouldn't have had to." Ramirez went over to the zombie Sayers had dispatched and quickly retrieved the arrows with the help of her knife. It was important to save every type of ammunition.

. "I wouldn't have had to do either if you didn't insist on coming out here every chance you get." Sayers glanced at her. "Westlake is dead. Whether he walked out of here or not, he's dead and you know it."

"Maybe." But Ramirez knew she was right. There was no way Westlake could have walked away from the crash alive. He'd already been hurt, and between the wreck and the zombies, there was no way he'd have made it. But there'd been no sign of him – no sign that he'd turned, even. Walkers could travel for miles, but only if they had a reason, and a zombified Westlake would more than likely stay in this area. There'd been no sign of him among the walker herds they'd thinned out in the weeks that followed. It was as if he'd vanished. She stood and looked down at the zombie. "It grabbed my hand."

"They do that."

Ramirez turned. "No. It… it stopped me from stabbing it." The moment played out again in her head. The shock of it. They'd never really fought back, not in a way that implied they actually understood what was happening. They just kept trying to take a piece out of you, whatever you did to them. "Since when do they have anything approaching an instinct for self-preservation?"

"Muscle memory," Sayers said, but she didn't sound like she believed that.

"Maybe." Ramirez climbed the slope. She offered the arrows, and Sayers took them without comment. "I owe him," Ramirez said, after a moment. "Westlake, I mean. I owe him. I told him – I promised him I wouldn't let him become one of them. That I'd put him down." She spoke slowly, afraid that the words would overwhelm her.

Westlake had been a hardened criminal before the dead rose, and the end of the world hadn't done much to change his outlook. But even she had to admit that he'd come through for them when the chips were down. When they'd needed him, he'd been there. She still wasn't sure why he'd done any of it. At first, she'd thought it was purely self-interest; nowadays, she wasn't so sure. All she really knew was that she'd made a promise, and she wanted to keep it.

"The dead don't keep debts or hold grudges," Sayers said.

Ramirez nodded. "But we do."

Sayers grunted, clearly not buying that line of logic. She stiffened, then reached for an arrow. A moment later,

Ramirez heard it. A groaning, far off and faint. "How many?" she murmured, her hand resting on her sidearm.

"Enough to warrant leaving before they get here," Sayers said. She slid her arrow back into the quiver and turned to head back up the slope. "Let's go."

"Yeah. Right behind you." Ramirez followed the other woman up the slope but stopped at the top and looked back. The wreck sat still and silent, two new bodies added to its resting place. And one body still missing.

"Where are you, Westlake?" Ramirez murmured.

CHAPTER TWO
Mishegas

On hands and knees, Rabbi Saul Blum carefully examined the tripwire he'd strung between the display windows of two high-end clothing outlets two days before. The tripwire was connected to the pin of a grenade he'd scavenged from a low-end pawn shop a few weeks earlier on a supply run. He'd had no idea whether it still worked when he pocketed it, but figured at the time it was worth a try.

He gave a sigh of relief as he saw that it was intact and untampered with. He rose creakily to his feet, and his kneecaps clicked unhappily. The apocalypse was hard on a man's knees, especially one on the wrong side of fifty like himself.

"Well, Rabbi?" Amos called out from behind him. The younger man – no more than a teenager really – crouched nervously in the doorway of the storefront opposite Saul, a heavy sledgehammer clutched in his hands.

Saul himself was armed with a snub-nosed .38. It only had three in the cylinder and he'd never so much as fired a gun before, but he felt better with it than without it. God provided for his chosen, though of late he was being a bit stingier than Saul would have liked. Saul gave Amos a thumbs-up and said, "Still intact, this one."

"That makes for a nice change," Ruth said, as she hurried down the corridor towards them. Amos's sister could have been his mirror image; fraternal twins, Saul thought, though he'd never asked. Apparently, they'd been on *Rumspringa* when the dead rose. It was like an old Catskills club joke: a rabbi and two Amish kids walk into a bar.

The world ends.

Ba-dum-tish.

"I found two more cut up there, past the juice bar," Ruth continued. Like Amos and Saul, she'd armed herself with whatever had been to hand the day the world had gone *mishegas*. In her case, a fire axe, its blade a vibrant red. She'd put it to good use more than once since Saul had met them.

"Cut or torn?" Saul asked. He'd set those two as well, though they'd been connected to empty cans rather than a pawnshop grenade. As early warning systems went, it was a bit crude, but better crude than nothing. He and the others in their small group had strung wire throughout Playground Pier once they'd cleaned out the majority of walkers clogging the corridors – a nasty schlep that he wasn't eager to repeat.

"Cut. Clean." Ruth glanced over her shoulder, as if expecting a zombie to come pelting around the corner at any moment. "No telling how many of the undead have gotten in since it was done. Who would do that?" she asked, looking to Saul for answers, or maybe just comfort.

Saul patted her shoulder with paternal affection but

shook his head. "Questions for another time. Right now, we should check in with the others." He fumbled for the brightly colored walkie-talkie clipped to his belt. Kid's toys, but useful. Moments later, he heard the telltale roar of a shotgun echoing up from the bottom floor of the pier. "Never mind," he said.

More gunfire followed. A piecemeal fusillade. Their group only had a handful of firearms, and ammunition was at a premium. A gun was good for killing a zombie, sure, but guns made noise, noise drew zombies, and soon you were out of ammunition and up to your *tuches* in walking corpses. So, if someone down on the first floor was shooting, that could only mean things had gone from bad to worse.

"Should we go help?" Amos asked. He was frightened, but willing. A good kid; Ruth too. Saul considered it, but shook his head.

"If they're smart, they're already falling back to the third floor. So that's what we'll do." He clapped his hands. "Hurry, please." Ruth hurried past him, and Amos fell in beside her. Watching them, he felt a sudden rush of sadness on their behalf. They didn't deserve this. No one did. Well, maybe some people, depending. But it wasn't for him to judge.

They hurried through the darkened husk of the second floor and past silent stores that had been emptied of everything useful long before the zombies showed up. The pier had been in steady decline since the early part of the decade. By the time the first zombie had staggered across the boardwalk, the pier had been down to only a handful of stores and the motley collection of restaurants on the third floor. A veritable ghost town. Funny that it had ended up as a sanctuary. Though from the sound of it, possibly not for long.

The second and third floors of the pier were clean of walkers. Saul and the others had made sure of that. It was the bottom floor that was the problem. Zombies, like in-laws, apparently saw closed doors as an invitation to visit. They'd tried chaining the entrances, but one brute later, there'd been no doors to chain. Being quiet and keeping to the upper floors had seemed to do the job after that, and enabled them to sleep at night, but maybe they'd been fooling themselves. Or maybe it was simply God's way of telling them to get a move on.

Saul's reverie was broken by the slap of bare flesh against tile. He whirled to see a zombie dressed to the nines but for lack of shoes racing towards them. He snatched his revolver out and shouted a warning. The zombie leapt onto a plant stand and vaulted towards him, arms extended and jaws wide. Saul's eyes widened. He'd never seen one jump before.

Amos's hammer snapped out, catching the zombie in the skull. The young man was fast, when the occasion warranted it. The dead man went down in a heap but was still twitching. "Ruth, if you would?" Saul asked, politely.

"A pleasure, Rabbi." Ruth brought her axe down on the zombie's head, splitting it. It flopped limply for a moment and then went still. Saul nodded in thanks.

"Why isn't it wearing shoes?" Amos asked, looking down at the body.

"More to the point, how many more are up here?" Ruth asked.

"A good question, best asked elsewhere. Go, go." He flapped his hands at them, hurrying them away. They quickly made their way to the nearest stairwell and headed up to the third floor. The restaurants had been converted into a communal living area. Big windows and easily barricaded doorways made it the safest spot in the building.

Two men with rifles were waiting at the top of the stairwell, near the doors leading the restaurants. One wore a battered tracksuit, the other a policeman's uniform. Saul nodded to them in greeting. "Theodore. Markus."

"Rabbi," Markus – the policeman – said. "Lot of noise down there."

"We should close these doors," Saul said. "The others will be coming up the stairs on the other side." He and the others left them to it. It was a familiar routine by now. The doors to the third floor would be shut and chained, providing some slight defense against any zombies that managed to make it up the stairs. Most of the dead couldn't quite manage the steps, but the fast ones could do so with ease.

Through the doors, the restaurant area was largely empty save for tents and boxes of scavenged supplies. Most of the tables and chairs, as well as the odd kiosk, had been shoved against the glass partitions or arranged to make improvised kill boxes near the entrances. The theory was that the kill boxes would slow the zombies long enough for the survivors to deal with them, but it had never been put to the test. Saul hoped it never would be. There were around thirty people holed up in the pier – men, women and children.

He heard a shout and saw a heavyset figure in ill-fitting army surplus fatigues hurrying towards them. "Well?" the big man demanded. McCuskey was built like a linebacker running to fat, unshaven, his eyes perpetually hidden behind a pair of aviator sunglasses. He liked to wear fatigues, but to the best of Saul's knowledge had never served in the military, American or otherwise.

"It was as we feared. Someone cut our alarms," Saul said.

"Sabotage," McCuskey snarled, thumping his beefy fist into his palm. "It'll take weeks to clean them out, if we even get the chance."

"That might be the point," Saul said. He bit a knuckle, thinking. "When was the last time you spoke to the Duchess?"

The Duchess was an oddity. Whereas most survivors hid in one spot, she and her small group of miscreants moved around constantly. They were scavengers, mostly, trading supplies for ammunition or intelligence. Saul had only met her once, and she'd struck him as someone with an excess of chutzpah.

McCuskey grunted. "A week ago. She brought us some boxes of canned food." He paused, a terrible look dawning over his face. "You think she was scoping the place out?"

"Maybe not," Saul said. "She was the one who showed it to you in the first place." Another of the Duchess's talents was finding safe places for survivors to set up camp. She'd done it for others across the city, or so she claimed. "Either way, perhaps we should have your brother get on the radio and see if we can find some help. A few extra hands on this particular deck wouldn't go amiss. Perhaps the Duchess could swing by–"

"No. No outsiders." McCuskey pounded fist into palm again. "I'm not putting this place even more at risk."

"Maybe it's not up to you, McCuskey," Ruth said. Amos nodded. "We should all have some say." She glanced at her brother. "That's the way we do it back home."

"Well, this ain't Amish country," McCuskey said. He poked a finger in her face. "I'm in charge. What I say goes – got that?"

"I don't recall agreeing to that," Amos said, tightening his grip on his sledgehammer. For all his natural diffidence, he was big; strapping. Saul had seen him pulverize a zombie's head with one swing of his hammer. McCuskey looked him up and down, and his hand fell to the Desert Eagle holstered on his hip. Saul had never seen him use it, but he had no doubt McCuskey had experience with firearms.

The confrontation had drawn an audience. McCuskey wasn't popular, but he was the sort to take the initiative – even if what he said made no sense half the time. But no one really wanted the big man in charge. McCuskey had finally started to realize that, and he now spent most of his time reasserting his assumed authority. Eventually, someone was going to shut him up. Markus, maybe. But today, McCuskey's unpopularity was a distraction they couldn't afford.

Saul cleared his throat. Everyone looked at him. "While I enjoy a good argument as much as the next person, now is not the time. The others will be coming back here with a whole bunch of unwelcome guests looking for something to nosh on. I'd rather that not be me if it's all the same to you." He looked around. "We have good barricades, but they won't hold forever. We need reinforcements – or rescue. And we need it soon."

He paused, about to add to his statement, then turned

towards the big windows that lined the shorefront side of the pier. "Anybody else hear that?"

It was a high-pitched whine, like a fan. He squinted and spotted a small, black and silver shape hovering outside the restaurant. But only for an instant.

The explosion knocked him and the others off their feet. Glass rained down. People screamed. Through smoke-stung eyes, Saul saw that whatever it was had exploded, taking out the windows. More small, black shapes, highlighted in red and blue and purple, shot through the broken windows and buzzed towards the front of the restaurant area. Three of them – no, four. They split up, moving in different directions.

"What…" Saul coughed. He saw Amos and Ruth picking themselves up, and felt a flash of relief, followed by confusion.

McCuskey hooked Saul's arm and hauled him to his feet. "Drones," he grunted. There was glass in his cheek and scalp, the wounds leaking thin rivulets of blood. Saul stared at him in incomprehension.

"What?"

"Drones," McCuskey said again. He had his pistol in his hand. "They're heading for the steps. This was all a plan. A set up." He was rambling, his voice disjointed and dull. He let go of Saul. "Someone cut the wires, let in the zombies…"

Saul shook his head. His thoughts rattled loosely as he tried to make sense of it. Drones? Who used drones during a zombie apocalypse? "Where did the others go?" he asked, dully. The rest of the drones had headed somewhere – but where?

The subsequent explosions answered that question. Smoke boiled through the restaurant area as the pier shook. Saul felt his heart drop into his stomach as he realized what had happened. "The barricades," he whispered. "They've blown the barricades."

CHAPTER THREE
Playground Pier

Westlake heard an empty can crumple beneath his foot and looked down. The can was a flat splat of tin, its branding faded past the point of recognition. He stared at it for long moments, uncertain. Something told him that noise – any noise – was bad, but his brain was having a hard time coming up with reasons why.

Was someone after him? That was always a possibility. But Playground Pier was noisy enough that one can crumple shouldn't matter. He looked up slowly. It was crowded today. It was crowded every day. The neon interior of the four-story pier was akin to a vibrant tunnel, lit by strings of lights and shimmering storefronts that rose in gaudy stacks. Ten different kinds of music made the air throb and his teeth itch. Someone bumped into him, and he muttered an apology before moving on.

Why was he in Atlantic City? The question nagged at him. It wasn't a bad thing. But he felt sick. Stuffy. Like he'd taken a bad hit of something inadvisable, and now everything was topsy-turvy. How had he gotten here? Had there been a car? Must have been. He'd been in New York, hadn't he? The thought seemed wrong somehow.

He stopped and leaned against an ornamental pillar fronting a clothing store. Mannequins stared down at him judgmentally. He made a pistol out of his fingers and pointed it at the row of empty faces. "What are you looking at?" he croaked. His voice sounded wrong – raspy. Like he'd swallowed battery acid.

Westlake shook his head. Nothing was making sense lately. He knew he'd driven because he'd suddenly remembered where he'd parked his car. He'd managed to get a spot near the pier, wonder of wonders. Which meant it was the off-season... wasn't it?

He watched the people puttering past. Elderly tourists on unsteady legs; early morning drunks, drawn by the light and noise; joggers pelting along, getting in everyone's way. A real microcosm of humanity. He closed his eyes and clutched his head. A dull ache reverberated through his frontal lobe. His sinuses felt clogged, but he wasn't having any difficulty breathing. Maybe the sea air would do him some good. Maybe that was why he was here. For his health.

He opened his eyes. The world spun for a moment and the faces around him ran like water down glass. He smelled something sour, like spoiled meat, but then it was gone and the only smell was that of the restaurants that girded the pier, hogging the ocean view. He paused as a thought surfaced out of the murk. Maybe he was meeting someone; maybe that was why he was here? A job. That had to be it.

He frowned and pushed away from the pillar. Glass

crunched beneath his feet, and he saw that the window was busted. No wonder the mannequins were angry. He hunched his shoulders and dove into the stream of bodies. He was meeting someone – fine. Who did he know in Atlantic City? Lots of people. Some of them even liked him.

But some of them didn't. Maybe that was why he was feeling woozy. Maybe someone had slipped him a mickey. Wouldn't be the first time. His stomach gurgled, as if for emphasis. He touched his midsection and experienced a moment of disorientation, as if his abdomen wasn't where it was supposed to be.

Westlake froze and looked down. He wiggled his fingers in empty space. There was a hole where his stomach ought to have been. Why was there a hole? A sudden flash – the crunch of metal and glass – something sharp – a tree branch? – ramming into him, then… what? His knees threatened to buckle as he clutched at his head. He didn't fall, but instead remained on his feet, swaying.

A body bumped into him. Then another. A jogger collided with him, sending him staggering back, into an old lady. She hissed and groped at him, her eyes like watery sores. He grunted and shoved her back. She caromed off a display window and went down in a heap. There were no shouts of alarm, no sign that anyone had even noticed. He watched, uncomprehending, as the old woman rolled onto her stomach and pushed herself up onto all fours and scuttled away like a cockroach in a pink cardigan.

Westlake wanted to laugh, or maybe scream, but all that came out was a soft, ragged exhalation of air. He turned, wanting to see if anyone else had seen what he'd seen. No one was looking at him. No one was looking at anything. Not the shops, not the lights. Not even each other. But they were still moving. All in the same direction.

His face twisted up in a smile. Maybe a new restaurant had opened up. He paused. The music had changed. Not a jumble of songs now. Just the one song. Some techno nonsense. The bass sounded like gunshots. The repetitive nature of it made his head ache. Maybe he was seeing things. Maybe that old lady hadn't crawled off. Something that might have been panic buzzed at the base of his skull. He turned away from the crowd, wanting to go. Whoever was waiting on him could keep waiting. He needed to go, until he figured this all out. He had to get out, away from the pier.

Westlake took a step against the flow of the crowd. There were too many people and none of them were moving out of his way. They just kept going, ignoring him. He started to get angry. Anger turned to shoving. They barely responded. They just pressed against him. That only made him angrier.

He had always prided himself on keeping his cool. You couldn't pull a job with a temper. Anger made you sloppy and being sloppy led to mistakes. Mistakes got you dead or in prison. But he was angry now, and it growled up in him like a long-simmering fire. He grabbed the nearest person – a heavyset man in a suit. The guy smelled like warmed-over death. He pawed feebly at Westlake's wrists. "Look at me," Westlake snarled. "Look at me!"

The man looked at him. Eyes like poached eggs rolled sloppily in dried out sockets. The fleshy ridges of a cavern where a nose ought to have been twitched. A lipless mouth champed mindlessly. No teeth – just jagged stumps.

Westlake shoved him back with a cry. The big man wobbled for a moment, and then lurched forward, stumbling past Westlake as if nothing had happened. The bass continued its beat.

Westlake shook his head. He rubbed his eyes, trying to process what he'd just seen. As he did so, the world spun, twitched, and shattered. The storefronts crumbled – display windows broke and the mannequins toppled. Lights hung like jungle vines, bulbs black and burnt out. He could hear the remorseless drone of flies and smell the rotting meat stink of the people wandering in and out of the looted stores. No, he realized. Not people.

Not living ones, at any rate.

Westlake turned slowly, not quite able to believe what he was seeing. Zombies shuffled aimlessly past him, wearing the tattered finery of their former existences. What was left of an elderly man in a violet tracksuit crawled past, dragging the shattered remnants of an electric mobility scooter in his wake. The corpse of a woman in a badly torn business suit lurched along, the snapped handle of a briefcase still gripped in her hand. Walkers. That was what Ramirez had called them.

Ramirez. He shook his head, feeling like a punch-drunk boxer. Ramirez, the FBI agent. Ramirez – where had he seen her last? Not Atlantic City, that was for sure. A zombie, a walker, stumbled into him. A young man, in a polo shirt and chinos. Mostly in one piece, save for the hole where his jugular ought to have been. It rounded on him with a hiss.

Westlake flinched back, expecting it to lunge for him. Instead, it swayed for a moment, staring blankly at him.

Then it continued on its way, as if nothing had happened. Westlake stared at its back. It hadn't attacked him. Why hadn't it attacked him?

He looked down. "Shit."

There was a broken tree branch sticking out of his abdomen. He gave it a tentative tap. From the way it felt, a small, calculating part of him thought it must have been lodged between his lower ribs somehow. The larger part of him began to hyperventilate. Or he would have, had he been breathing.

When he realized he wasn't, he spent a few panicked seconds trying to remember how. Questions rattled through his head, a trickle at first and then a torrent. One after the next, all tumbling over one another until his head felt like it was fit to burst. He forced his way through the press of walkers, elbowing the slower ones aside. None of them made so much as a sound. They didn't care about him. They didn't care, because as far as they were concerned, he was one of them.

That thought drowned out all the rest. He reached the wall and slid down. He felt stiff, off balance – possibly because of the branch. It twisted as he sat, angling upwards. It wasn't large; part of it had been snapped off, leaving a chunk mostly inside him.

Westlake closed his eyes. He wanted to sleep, but the dead didn't sleep. Instead, he turned his mind inwards. He was close to full on hysteria, closer than he could ever recall getting. Even when a job had gone bad, he'd never panicked. But this wasn't a silent alarm going off, or a cop showing up out of the blue. This was a bit more serious.

He almost laughed but squelched the urge. If he started, he might not stop. Eyes still closed, he forced himself to relax. To think. It was hard. He felt sluggish, and his thoughts ran like sand, sifting away before he could focus on them.

First things first. He opened his eyes and looked down at the branch. The blood – his blood – was crusted on it. Almost black. It was an old wound, then. Not days, but weeks. He'd been wandering around for weeks with a piece of wood shoved through his stomach. Time to fix that. Slowly, carefully, he began to work it out of his flesh.

It wasn't easy. It was definitely caught on the bone, and his fingers didn't respond with anything approaching his usual dexterity. He gave a wet chuckle. He probably wouldn't be cracking safes anytime soon. His patience wasn't what it had been either. He gave up on careful and finally settled for just wrenching the wood free. He felt something give in his chest but experienced no pain. That was something, at least.

Westlake tossed the wood aside and examined the hole. It was a puckered rupture, and as he probed the edges, he felt something move beneath his skin. He found the first maggot a moment later. He dug the squirming thing out and eyed it before flinging it aside. He spent the next ten minutes plucking maggots and flicking them at any zombies that got too close. It was childish, but emotionally satisfying.

When he'd finished, he tore several strips from his shirt and carefully wound them around the hole in his torso. It wasn't necessary; he wasn't bleeding. But it made him feel better. As he did so, he heard the staccato *crack-crack-crack* of gunfire. He'd been hearing it all along, he knew, but his addled mind had decided it was music.

There was someone alive in Playground Pier, though possibly not for long. Westlake sat back and looked at his hands for the first time. Bloody, grimy, the flesh torn; they looked more like slabs of meat than human hands. He doubted his face looked much better, though he wasn't in any hurry to check out a mirror.

More gunfire. He could hear shouts as well. Whoever it was, they were in trouble. That explained where the walkers were heading. "Not my problem," he said, out loud. He was dead, after all. The affairs of the living were no longer his concern. The thought brought with it a sudden flicker of panic, but he crammed it down, cutting it off before it could fully emerge. "Not my problem," he repeated.

He thought about Ramirez again. Then, with a coffin-rattle sigh, Westlake forced himself to his feet and headed in the direction of the gunfire.

CHAPTER FOUR
Ptolemy

Aliens.

Calvin Ptolemy stared at the topographic maps he'd scavenged from Saranac Lake rangers' station. He'd pinned them to the walls of what he'd come to think of as his office. In reality, it was an insulated outbuilding, with its own generator. The generator was his, as was the dwindling store of fuel he used to keep it running. He slept in his office, ate in his office, and generally didn't leave his office, unless it was absolutely necessary. He found the claustrophobic interior soothing.

Between each map was a row of newspaper clippings, internet printouts, and sheets torn from notebooks. Some of those sheets were covered in notes he'd made. Others bore diagrams copied from various books. An intricate, if somewhat confusing network of strings and pushpins connected all of it together.

Ptolemy was the only one who could make sense of this web of confluence. And for him, what it all added up to was: aliens.

It was the only possible explanation. Yet something in him, the practiced skepticism of a hardened conspiracy theorist, refused to believe it. Alien technology, perhaps. In the hands of unscrupulous government officials – or perhaps operatives of the neo-capitalist dark state, acting on the orders of the Knights of the Golden Circle or one of the Baphometic orders. That seemed more plausible.

Yet – aliens.

A part of him, that remaining flicker of childlike innocence, desperately wanted it to be aliens. If aliens were behind it, then humanity was not, in fact, responsible for its own inevitable extinction.

He sat back in the leather office chair, listening to the springs squeak. He'd purloined it from one of the offices inside the large, nearby stronghold-mansion, called the Villa. No one seemed to mind.

Slowly, he spun around, hands clasped behind his head, wondering what Charles Fort or Richard Shaver would make of it. Shaver, of course, would blame his underground race of monsters. Fort would be more philosophical about the matter – "science is a turtle that says its own shell encloses all things." Fort would not volunteer an answer, because answers were anathema to the true Fortean. Only questions mattered, in the end.

Ptolemy spun back around to stare at the maps. They covered the entirety of New York state. He had other maps as well, encompassing the rest of the United States, but these were the ones that concerned him at the moment, due to what they did not show. It had become an obsession with him, and he had duly added it to the pile.

He thought he could be forgiven a few obsessions. The world had gone dark almost two years earlier. Governments had fallen. The internet had collapsed under the weight of silent server farms. All that remained were a few, tiny points of light, scattered across his maps. A part of him wondered if that was all there ever would be.

Maybe it was meant to be. Maybe humanity's time had passed. He had no answers. Answers were anathema. But the questions kept coming.

There was a knock at the door. "Enter," he said, without taking his eyes from the maps. He smelled woodsmoke and leather, and relaxed almost against his will. His guest had had that effect on him since the first time they'd met. "Elizabeth."

"Calvin," Sayers murmured, as she shut the door behind her. Her voice was husky and pleasant. "Have you eaten today?"

Ptolemy paused, trying to recall. "Yes. Jerky."

Sayers grunted. "There is enough food that you could eat a proper breakfast."

"Jerky contains all the necessary vitamins." Ptolemy glanced at her. She was lovely, albeit in the same way a good knife or a well-designed rifle was lovely. He felt a twinge of regret and forced it down. Their relationship had ended almost a year ago, but they were tentatively feeling around the edges of something new, but both of them were wary about moving too fast. "You told me that, remember?"

"I do. And I regret it. Have you been staring at these maps all day?" Sayers leaned past him to peer at his careful work. She tapped one of the pushpins. "This one is new. What's it marking?"

"The same thing as all the rest. Blank spots." He gestured about himself. "Just like this place." The place in question was colloquially known as "the Villa." Formerly a five-star hideout for organized crime figures, it was now a refuge for survivors of the zombie apocalypse. The Villa had been hidden by people who knew what they were doing; it wasn't on any map or record owned locally or by the government. They only way he, Ramirez and the others managed to find it had been due to the aid of someone who knew it was there – a former thief named Westlake. Westlake had died helping them.

Sayers shook her head. He'd expected that. He had a theory, and she thought it was merely another of his obsessions. Perhaps it was. Regardless, her reaction was one familiar to him. Disbelief was an old friend.

Ptolemy knew that his views were regarded as irrational; he also knew that rationality was an external social imposition. Rationality was defined by the majority. If the majority believed that rain fell up, rather than down, anyone who said otherwise would inevitably be regarded as a fool at best and a lunatic at worst.

"You still think there are more places like this, hidden out there?" she asked.

"Like this? Possibly not, though we should not discount the idea. Criminal organizations have a long history of creating caches, hideouts, and secret bases. But they are not alone in this compulsion. Others do so as well."

"Doomsday preppers," Sayers said, studying the map more closely.

"Among others. The world ended according to schedule.

Not ours, perhaps, but someone's. And they are out there; we just have to find them."

"Why?"

Ptolemy blinked in confusion. "Why what?"

"What's the point?" She gently turned his chair around so that they were facing one another. "Why go looking for trouble?"

Ptolemy hesitated. "One cannot win a war, if one does not fight."

Sayers frowned and stepped back. "What war, Calvin?"

"The one we are waging even as we speak. The war between the living and the dead. A war I believe to have been instigated by a third party."

She shook her head. "It always comes back to aliens with you, doesn't it?"

Ptolemy acknowledged the point gracefully. "Because I find the idea of outside intervention preferable to the alternative. If this – all of this – was done by a man in a lab somewhere, then there is truly no hope for us as a species."

Sayers sighed. "Or maybe it was all an accident."

"Even worse. An accident still implies the human factor. Better it be some natural event, like a volcano erupting, than that." Ptolemy scrubbed a hand through his thickening hair. He hadn't trimmed it in weeks, and it was growing unruly. "Kahwihta agrees with me. She believes the causative element to be designed, rather than naturally occurring."

Sayers snorted. "Last I checked, she was still a graduate student, not a scientist."

"Her observations have been invaluable, Elizabeth. Without her findings, I would not have been able to predict the timing and location of the last two hostile surges." He indicated one of the maps, where he'd made a number of notes relating to zombie numbers. Their population swelled and shrank according to some as-yet unidentified pattern.

Every few weeks, hundreds of zombies would stagger down the interstate and into the mountains, before the number would thin once more as many wandered away or vanished into the wilderness, only to pop up later. There was no way to tell what was driving the dead, though both he and Kahwihta were working on the problem, albeit from different directions.

"I suppose," Sayers allowed and then her voice softened. "You should get out more. Fresh air would do you good."

"There are zombies outside."

"Fewer now," Sayers said, mildly. Ptolemy looked at her. Sayers had adapted unsettlingly well to the end of the world. Sometimes he suspected that she'd been waiting for it. Before the zombies had showed up, she'd been a weird, anxious woman. Part of that, he now knew, had been due to her relationship with the former notorious owners of the Villa. But not all of it. Now, those anxieties had dried up and blown away.

In contrast, Ptolemy felt that he'd acquired far more worries than he'd had before. Even in his wildest prophetic imaginings, he'd never dreamed of having to cobble together a functioning civilization from the cast-off remnants of its predecessor. They had been lucky so far. Things could have been worse. There had been no outbreaks of disease, no starvation. The immediate area had been largely cleared of zombies.

Sayers emphasized the point, "I've put down maybe five zombies in the past two weeks. All walkers, alone or in pairs. No more hordes."

"Around here," he countered. "There are plenty everywhere else." He lurched to his feet and went to the smaller of the two work benches that crowded the outbuilding. It was covered in CB radios, a ham radio set up, and boxes of radio parts. Some of them were his from before things had gone bad; the rest of it had been scavenged from nearby towns.

Several smaller state roadmaps overlaid the topographic ones on the wall here. A wealth of notes, mostly concerning radio frequencies, covered them. He picked up a small, battered notebook and flipped it to the first page. "These numbers correlate to radios in survivor camps in the first week after the zombies showed up." He turned the page. Fewer numbers. "Third week." He flipped through half a dozen more pages until he reached the most recent. The numbers had shrunk to a bare handful. "Yesterday."

Sayers took the notebook from him. "So?" she said, at last.

"The number of zombies is constantly increasing. There were seven camps within walking distance of Saranac Lake at the beginning. By the time we found this place, there were three. Now there are none. We are alone in the wilderness."

"Because everyone is here," Sayers protested.

"Not everyone," he said, pointedly.

"That's their bad luck."

"Ours as well. We are safe in the mountains, but for how long? How long can we stretch the fuel for the generators? How long will it take to get a dependable hydroelectric generator set up? Or convert our existing ones to ethanol?

Do we have anyone capable of doing that? How long will our other supplies last? Long enough to get us through one winter – what about two? We need arable land for crop production. We need access to water not infested by floaters. These are all things that could be provided by other camps, other kinds of skilled people, with access to resources we do not have the capacity to exploit." He realized he'd raised his voice and forced himself to calm down. He took a deep breath. "I apologize."

Sayers dismissed his apology with a gesture. "Say you're right. What do we do about it? What can we do about it?"

Ptolemy hooked his chair and pulled it over to the workbench. He sat down. "Since we made our catabasis–"

"Our what?"

"Our march inland," he clarified. He gestured to the maps. "Since we came here, I have attempted to make regular contact with other camps in the New York state area. To date, I–" He was interrupted by a sudden squall of sound from the ham radio. Both he and Sayers stared at it in startled shock.

"Is that … ?" she began.

"It is." He snatched up the microphone and fiddled with the tuner, trying to sharpen the signal. His heart was pounding and his mouth was dry. "Hello? This is Saranac Lake. Is anyone there?"

At first, a buzz of static. Then, a voice. It burst, broke, and faded, before returning at full volume. The voice was unfamiliar, someone he'd never talked to before. As words continued to spill across the static-riven line, Ptolemy gestured frantically to Sayers. "Get the others," he hissed. "Hurry!"

Sayers stared at him for a moment, then nodded and rushed out the door. Ptolemy turned his attentions back to the radio and what it was telling him. The same old story, but maybe, with a bit of luck, they could give it a different ending.

CHAPTER FIVE
Horde

Westlake found it hard to focus, even as he followed the echoes of the explosion. Even though he hadn't immediately recognized what it was that he'd heard, he'd been drawn to it nonetheless. It was like being hypnotized, like he was a passenger in his own body.

It was odd. He could barely feel anything, and he was fairly certain that his sense of taste had gone the way of the dodo. But his eyesight was still sharp, as was his hearing and his sense of smell. The things he needed to hunt with. At times, he felt as if he were trying to swim through molasses. His ability to see colors came and went; half the time, the world was a sludge of gray shapes. Only instinct kept him from bouncing off display windows.

He shook off the distractions and forced himself to move in step with the horde. Mostly walkers, though he'd heard a dull, bass groan that he thought marked the presence of a brute. He'd spied a runner earlier, in full evening wear, heading off at full pelt.

It was difficult to think. His brain had been chugging along in neutral for weeks. Maybe if he exercised it enough, some of the old flexibility might come back. That was his hope, anyway. But if he was being honest with himself, his brain was probably in as bad a condition as his body. But then, where had honesty ever gotten him?

He flinched as a second runner darted past him, weaving through the horde with inhuman instinct. Walkers fell in behind the runner, filling the gaps before Westlake could take advantage. His reaction time had slowed to almost nothing; for every upside, there was a downside. Still, he would make do.

He ran his hands over his head. Bits of his scalp flaked away, and he grimaced. There was no telling how long he had left before he was just another walker – or worse. Maybe he'd never lose his sense of self, just everything else. Maybe he'd just keel over and rot, conscious the whole time. He shied away from the thought, tried to focus on the sound ahead of him. The echoes of the explosion had long since faded, but the horde was still heading in that direction. And why not? It wasn't like they had anything better to do. Even the echoes of the sound compelled him towards it.

The horde had aimed itself at a set of security doors at the far end of the corridor. There was smoke boiling out of them, but someone was still putting up a fight. Probably not for too much longer, though. The zombies didn't care about casualties. They just kept going until something stopped them or – well... He pushed the thought aside and tried to come up with a plan. Something. Anything.

He wasn't sure how much help he was going to be to

whoever was shooting. He doubted they were going to welcome him with open arms, not looking like he did. In fact, they'd probably shoot him on sight. But if they didn't, if he got close enough to say howdy – what then? The thought was knocked from his mind by the boom of a shotgun.

His head whipped around, almost against his will. The sound was closer than the doors. Someone had gotten cut off; isolated. It was easy to do when a hundred zombies were pressing towards you. The sound had come from the display window of a high-end clothing store. Whoever was in there had thrown shelving, mannequins, and whatever else they could find in front of the window as a barricade. He heard shouting from inside, but he couldn't make out what they were saying.

He realized they were making a break for it when part of the barricade fell out of the window. Zombies pressed forward, converging on the first man out – a muscular man in a fireman's jacket. He swung a fire axe with ruthless precision and a zombie's head spun off its neck. The fireman called out to the others and started fighting his way towards the security doors. Two more survivors followed him, guns blazing. They were covered by someone still inside.

Unfortunately, whoever they were, they were a bad shot. For every zombie that fell, two more pressed on without slowing, all of them trying to get through the now useless barricade.

"Might as well get started," Westlake muttered. He grabbed a handy walker, gently swung the zombie in front of him like a shield, and started moving. If he could get close enough, get inside – what? Talk? It didn't matter. He'd figure it out when he got there.

But first, he needed a weapon. He wasn't certain what would happen if he decided to play hero; the zombies were ignoring him at the moment, but if they decided he was food, he didn't stand much of a chance.

He scanned his closest neighbors until he found what he was looking for on the belt of a nearby zombie – a cop, still wearing the helmet and jacket of the mounted division. Westlake snatched the dead man's service weapon from its holster. He ejected the pistol's magazine and checked the clip. There was enough ammunition to get to the stairs, maybe. He nudged the walker, forcing it to pick up its pace.

When he got to the display window, he shoved past his meat-shield and made to clamber up through the window. He was almost inside when a bullet hummed into his thigh, and he nearly fell. "Hey, I'm on your side!" he shouted – or tried to. His voice came out as a hoarse whisper. He spotted the gunman a moment later – gunwoman, rather. She was dressed in frayed flannel and denim, a ski-cap messily planted on her head. She backed away from him, tears streaking her soot-stained features. She raised her weapon. He raised his hands, slowly. "Can we talk about this?" he croaked.

Her eyes widened in shock. Before she could speak a runner made to dart past him, teeth clicking like loose stones in a can. Her eyes widened now in terror, her weapon gave a sad click, the runner hissed.

Westlake brained it from behind. The zombie whirled, and Westlake caught its skull and struck it again with the pistol. The blow propelled it backwards, into the edge of the display window, hard enough to split its rancid skull. He slung the body into the nearest walkers and turned to the young woman. "Run," he croaked.

She stared at him for a moment, then did as he'd advised. She sprinted away as Westlake turned to face the closest walkers. They came at him from all directions, clawing, biting. They'd decided he was a threat. That was fine. Part of him preferred it this way.

Teeth clamped down on his shoulder and he savagely hammered at his attacker with the butt of his pistol, reducing its skull to the consistency of a deflated soufflé. The walker fell, but left its head attached to Westlake's shoulder, still gnawing away.

Westlake punched a walker away and kicked another down. Teeth sank into his shoulders, his wrist, his thigh. He caught a zombie by the head and drove it face-first into the floor. "Come on then," he hissed. "Come on." Rotting flesh came away in his hands. Brittle bones splintered and cracked. The world became shadows and sludge.

Then, all at once, it was over. The rest of them were backing off, turning away. Maybe they'd realized he wasn't alive. Or maybe they were afraid of him, the same way they were afraid of runners and brutes. He wished Kahwihta was around, so he could ask her for her opinion. She'd have a hundred theories.

Westlake paused. Kahwihta. Ptolemy. Hutch. Ramirez. Names flooded into his head, followed by faces; the sound of voices. Memories, formerly disjointed and fragmentary, shuddered into semi-cohesion. He felt sick as the flood of information threatened to overwhelm him. Still clutching his head, he sank to his knees. The world spun like a flock of butterflies all winging in different directions.

He saw Ramirez in the rear view, watching him as he edged the truck out of the Villa's hangar-like garage and led the zombies infesting the compound on a merry chase. It shouldn't have worked. A one-in-a-million chance. But it had. He'd saved the day, his pockets full of money and his skin burning with fever. He felt the jolt of the truck as it went careening down the mountain trail, slamming into trees. Dead faces pressed to the windshield, the smell of rot in his nose, the taste of the grave in his mouth.

A good death. A better one than he'd been destined for. But he wasn't dead. Why wasn't he dead? Why was he like this? No answers came. He glanced at the zombie head still chewing on his shoulder. A trickle of sour blood spilled from the head's mouth as it redoubled its efforts to bite through his shoulder ligament.

"Persistent, ain't you?" he muttered. He pressed the muzzle of his pistol to the spot between the chewer's eyes and fired. When he'd pried what was left of it off him, he checked the wound. No blood, but plenty of mess. He rotated his shoulder gingerly. He was going to have to be careful. Just because he couldn't feel pain didn't mean he couldn't be hurt, and badly. He didn't feel like seeing if he could walk on a broken leg.

There had to be a way... He paused in mid-thought. A coppery odor filled the air, accompanied by a scream. Westlake's head turned automatically, searching for the source of the sound. He cursed when he saw it. One of the other survivors was down.

Unlike the young woman, he'd been a half-second too slow, and now he was being swarmed by walkers. They clung to him, their teeth sunk into his flesh. The other survivors either hadn't heard his cries, or had decided to cut their losses. They'd finally gotten the security doors open. If they were smart, they'd chain the doors behind them.

Westlake rose slowly, not wanting to draw fire. The smell was getting stronger. He took a step towards the fallen man and shot one of the walkers. Then another. The others ignored him, intent on their meal. The survivor had stopped screaming, but he was still alive. His struggles were weakening. Westlake looked down at him and felt a roiling in his gut.

The survivor was middle-aged. A stockbroker perhaps, playing survivalist. He wore camo hunting gear over what was left of a business suit and had been carrying a hunting rifle with the price tags still attached. He reached up, snagging Westlake's shin with bloody fingers. He gurgled something unintelligible. Westlake stared down at him, unable to look away. The sensation in his gut was getting stronger, or at least harder to ignore.

It took him several long moments to identify it, and when he did, he wished he hadn't. It was hunger. A gnawing, bone-deep hunger that clawed at the underside of his mind. It forced him to look at the dying man, and instead of a human being all he saw was… a meal. Meat on the hoof. He felt what was left of his lips split and peel away from his teeth. The world shrank to a red tunnel, and he felt a black heat boiling within him. A fire that demanded feeding, and right now.

His muscles cramped and he felt himself sinking to his knees, to take his place with the others, even as his rational mind screamed in horror. He stretched out his free hand, to sink his fingers into that warm, red, meat. To tear it away, to eat and eat and eat and–

The pistol boomed and the dying man went still. Westlake shoved himself upright, turned, and fired, emptying the weapon into the walkers hunched over the body. He flung the empty weapon away with a guttural moan and clutched at his head. The hunger was still there, crouched in the pit of his stomach, waiting for its chance. He looked at his hands: torn, ragged. He curled them into fists and felt the skin of his knuckles pop. No blood. No pain. Just hunger.

He'd never been so hungry in all his life. It gnawed at him like acid, suffusing his thoughts, drowning them in need. He wanted to eat and eat and eat until his belly burst and then eat some more. But first, he had to find food.

He sniffed the air. He could smell… blood. Viscera. The stink of death.

It smelled wonderful.

His jaw sagged. He gave a rattling hiss. He took a step back towards the body. He needed to feed. His memories shrank to pinpricks; his thoughts turned to dust. Schemes and plans rattled in the hollow of his skull like shards of broken glass.

"Got another one."

The voice cut through the sludgy haze in his head. Something looped around his neck and slid tight. He clawed at it, snarling in frustration even as his conscious mind took in the figures in black surrounding him. One of them came towards him. "He's in good condition. He'll make perfect fodder for the arena. Get him into the truck with the rest."

Westlake reached for the speaker, but thanks to whatever was around his neck he couldn't get to them. Instead, he was yanked around and shoved forward, to stumble away from the horde. More black-clad men and women trotted past. They carried firearms, wore riot gear and black fatigues, and used a bulwark of riot shields to part the sea of zombies. Every so often a long cattle prod would slip through a crack in the square and tap a walker, knocking it to the floor.

Behind them came others carrying capture poles; the sort you used to nab stray dogs. Like the one they had around his neck. They snagged the downed walkers and dragged them back, out of the way. Westlake couldn't fathom why they didn't just shoot them. Or him. But he wasn't going to complain.

He was forced away and out of Playground Pier, stumbling on the pulped remains of walkers. He saw dozens of zombies, most of them in terrible shape, being herded towards the rear of what looked to be an industrial livestock hauler. One by one, the zombies were sent up the ramp by application of catch pole and cattle prod. Any that resisted were shot or otherwise dispatched without any undue hesitation on the part of their handlers.

The hunger was receding, and his focus was returning. A mixed blessing. He doubted his captors would wait to hear what he had to say. Better to keep quiet and let it play out. They obviously wanted him in one piece for this arena of theirs, whatever that was. That meant there might be a chance to escape, if he could keep it together long enough to do so.

When his turn came, he went up the ramp quiet as could be. The hauler was crowded; the dead were jam-packed, cheek to jowl. He took his spot and was relieved when the walkers paid him absolutely no mind at all.

After a few more walkers were herded inside, the ramp was closed and locked. A moment later, he heard an engine rumble to life. One of the nearby walkers stirred and gave a thin whistling moan of complaint. Westlake laughed softly.

"You and me both, pal. You and me both."

CHAPTER SIX
Contact

Kahwihta Trapper tapped the glass of the pickle jar with a forensic probe. The severed hand floating in the formaldehyde solution twitched like a spider. She continued tapping, following the circumference of the jar. The hand thrashed, chasing the vibrations.

"Well, that answers that," she murmured, as she sat back on her stool and made a notation in her notebook. "Of the tested subjects, around thirty percent continued to remain active after being reduced to component parts." She looked down at the lean, brown and black dog laying on the floor at her feet. "We definitely need to start burning them – just to be safe, don't you think?"

Attila gave a lazy *woof* in reply, and rolled over onto his back. Kahwihta idly used one foot to scratch the offered belly, as she turned her attentions to the rest of her collection. A dozen jars of various sizes occupied the salvaged storage shelving that stretched along one wall of the outbuilding. She hesitated to call it a laboratory – though that was what everyone else called it – because labs were well-equipped. Hers was just a whitewashed cinderblock room with some shelves, jars, and a ping-pong table she used for dissections.

It had taken some convincing to get Ramirez and Saoirse and the other survivors at the Villa to agree to set aside the space for her, though the Villa wasn't that crowded. Mostly, they just didn't want a room full of chopped up zombies in their sanctuary, which was why she'd agreed to set up in one of the unused outbuildings, though it was less convenient.

Kahwihta didn't blame them, but they needed any edge they could get over the dead. That meant they needed to know everything there was to know about them. That had been her pitch, at least. In truth, it was proving a lot more difficult in execution than she'd hoped.

She had some decent equipment, rescued from the Saranac Lake coroner's offices, but it wasn't enough to do much more than take a body apart and clean up afterwards. And taking zombies apart to see how they worked wasn't getting her anywhere.

There were precious few answers to be had from the dead. She'd spent the better part of a year observing them, noting their behavior, but so far all she really knew was that they were invariably attracted to areas with high populations of living humans. The average walker would travel miles across the worst terrain imaginable just to stand outside a fence and moan aggressively. What she hadn't yet figured out was how they knew. How did they know what direction to travel in? They hunted by sound – what about scent?

Her working theory was that zombies didn't follow humans so much as they followed other zombies. Some sort of herd instinct, or maybe they were still social animals on some level. That made as much sense as anything else.

The crushed remnants of a head stared blankly at her from one of the largest jars. Wispy strands of hair floated around the mangled skull. One eye remained and most of a jaw. It twitched slightly as she watched. It never did anything more than twitch. But the twitching itself interested her because it implied the nerves were still functioning somehow, though that should have been impossible. Then, some might say that impossible had gone out the window the day the dead rose and started to eat the living.

She sighed and ran her hands through her short hair. "Why am I doing this again?"

"Because someone must," a deep voice rumbled. Attila's tail began to thump against the floor. Kahwihta turned as El Calavera Santo stepped into the room. Even if his sheer size hadn't immediately identified him, the black and white mask he wore would have. The mask resembled a stylized skull – appropriate, given his name.

The big man was dressed, as ever, in loose clothing that had been fashionable prior to the end of the world. It turned out that the luchador, besides being the sort of guy who thought nothing of fighting zombies barehanded, was something of a clothes horse. Any supply run he accompanied was guaranteed to stop at one clothing outlet, at least.

Calavera sank to his haunches and fussed over Attila for a moment; the dog returned the favor with a regal bout of licking. The big man stood and looked down at Kahwihta. "Any new discoveries?" he asked, with genuine interest.

"We need to start burning them," she said, tapping the

jar with the hand. Calavera watched curiously as the hand twitched and flapped in its murky solution.

"A good suggestion. For the sake of hygiene, if no other reason." He looked at her. "Ptolemy has made radio contact with someone. A group of survivors."

It took Kahwihta a moment to wrap her head around the idea. She'd started to think they were the only survivors left, when she let herself think about it at all. "Do we know where they are?"

"No. Ptolemy is still trying to talk to them. His enthusiasm is infectious. I thought you might like to know."

"Definitely, thank you." She leapt from her seat, startling Attila and Calavera both. "Let's go and see what all the fuss is about."

Attila led the way, eager to get outside and into the gray drizzle of the day. Kahwihta paused, as she always did. The Villa was impressive, even after all this time. High security fences with reinforced foundations rose on three sides, stretching from the shore and up along the slope of the mountain, creating a horseshoe courtyard twice the size of a campground parking lot in front of the entrance to the building. Multilevel outbuildings of various sizes and makes clustered along the fence-line, including her own. Ptolemy's lair was at the far end, away from hers.

Opposite the lakeside doors was a large quay made of quarried stone, with an attached boatshed. The quay had an old-fashioned timber roof and heavy support beams connecting the two. The Villa itself was a three-story building with a peaked, split-frame roof and dozens of windows that had been built into the slope of mountain.

It had been a mine, once. Then a speakeasy. Then a hideout for criminals. Now it was the last bastion of humanity – at least, that portion of humanity in the Adirondacks. She heard the crunch of treads on loose gravel and spied the squat, black shapes of the Villa's unsleeping defenders doing their daily rounds.

The four were autonomous tracked military robots – Foster-Miller TALON SWORDS, or so Ptolemy insisted. They resembled squarish steel boxes with heavy caterpillar treads, and each of the four was topped by a different weapon assemblage, including machine guns and grenade launchers, as well as solar batteries.

They prowled a circuit of the courtyard, including the fences and the quay. Whoever was on guard duty at the time controlled them from the largest of the outbuildings. Ramps had been built so that the robots could roll up and over the tops of the outbuildings, if needed.

Outside the main gates, an old logging trail led down the mountain. Sometimes the robots patrolled it as well, though it hadn't been necessary in days. Winter was rolling in and tourist season was over.

There were people everywhere. Several of the outbuildings had been converted to living quarters or crude gardens. Nothing fancy and not nearly enough to sustain everyone, but it was a start. A group of children of varying ages played kickball nearby, but quietly. Children learned quickly that noise attracted unwanted attention. A lot more quickly than adults did, come to that.

On the other side of the quay, motorized rafts rolled across the lake, fishing for floaters. They'd dispatched most of the submerged zombies weeks ago, but every now and then, one surfaced. Fences were being slowly erected on the far shore, when there was time. The Villa had a store of chain-link fence, posts and cement, as well as a few small unassembled outbuildings. Not enough to cover the entire shoreline, but enough to make getting off the rafts less dangerous.

It wasn't perfect, Kahwihta reflected, but it was a damn sight better than it had been. But it all hinged on keeping things controllable. Manageable. If the dominoes of their operation started to fall, things would descend into chaos quickly. It was one of the few things everyone agreed on.

They reached Ptolemy's "office" a few moments later. A small crowd had already formed. People eager to hear voices from somewhere – anywhere – else. Proof of life. Kahwihta knew that feeling herself. She nodded to Ramirez and Sayers, both of whom stood just inside the doorway.

Ptolemy sat hunched over his equipment, wearing a pair of headphones. She watched him fiddle with the knobs, and static skirled up then evened out into a voice. A murmur ran through the crowd, but a look from Sayers shut everyone right up. The voice crackled and popped for a moment, then "…*eed help, please,*" a man's voice said. Kahwihta knew that voice; not the person behind it, but the sound of it. Hoarse. Ragged. Tired. They'd all had that same voice at one time or another, when pushed to the breaking point.

"This is Calvin Ptolemy with the Saranac Lake survivor camp. Who am I speaking with?" Ptolemy's voice didn't crack or falter, but she could tell he was as excited as anyone. It was in the set of his shoulders, the way his leg bobbed.

"*Manny, my name's Manny, we need help, please, oh God,*" came the reply. There was something else audible in the background. Something familiar and awful: the moan of the hungry dead. The sound rose like a musical note, and a woman in the crowd turned away, hands over her mouth. People looked at one another and Kahwihta read the resignation in their eyes. No hope. No way to help. All they could do was bear witness.

"We can help. We have a safe place in the mountains that we can guide you to. What is your location?" Ptolemy asked, voice level, expression set.

"*Playground Pier! We- we're on the third floor! Someone took out the barricades – we're under attack. We need help, please…*"

Ptolemy looked at Sayers, who shrugged. Ramirez answered his question. "Atlantic City," she said, softly. From her tone, it might as well have been the moon. Kahwihta turned away and looked towards the lake. The groaning on the radio was getting louder. She wondered whether it would attract any zombies that were nearby. Maybe, if it was recorded and played through speakers.

She filed the idea away as a sudden thought occurred to her. She turned back. "What does he mean someone took out the barricades?"

Ramirez looked at her, and then at Ptolemy. He waved them to silence. The signal was going screwy again. "Is there anywhere you can go?" Ptolemy asked. "A fallback position or a safe place? Someplace to hide until we can get to you?"

"*We can – the freezers,*" Manny panted. He sounded frightened. Kahwihta didn't blame him. Attila whined and she scratched his head. "*But they – what?*"

A second voice intruded. "*Turn the radio off and put your hands over your head.*" Manny blubbered something, a protest perhaps. Then a gunshot.

The radio went dead.

CHAPTER SEVEN
The Duke of Atlantic City

Rupert St Cloud kept count in his head as he swung the kettle bell up and down. He'd been at it since he'd woken from his afternoon siesta. Two hours of physical exercise, every day, like clockwork. Routine was important, especially these days.

A timer beeped and he set the kettle bell down. He turned, examining himself in a nearby full-length mirror. He was classically handsome, thanks in equal part to genetics and a bit of pre-apocalypse nip and tuck. He flexed, watching the play of his muscles beneath his dark skin. He had a body Charles Atlas would envy, not that anyone remembered who Charles Atlas was these days.

St Cloud sighed and reached for a monogramed towel hanging from a nearby drying rack. The rack, like much of the furniture in his penthouse, was an antique. It had been professionally refinished so that it might last another century. Money well spent. Only the best for Rupert St Cloud. That was his guiding mantra.

Come to it, it was probably why he was still alive. He'd hired the best security people money could buy, and given them access to the latest technology. The night the dead had risen, it had been his people that had locked off the building and ensured the survival of the majority of his employees and his customers. Without his foresight in the matter, everyone would have died that night. All hope for the future would have been lost.

He took in his penthouse as he toweled off. The windows were reinforced glass, capable of withstanding both high winds and a sniper's bullet. The furniture was top end, stylish and expensive. Artwork, purchased at no small expense and bought solely for its likelihood to increase in value, hung from the walls. All of it had been arranged by his personal assistant... back when he'd had a personal assistant.

He paused, trying to recall her name. Beryl? No, that wasn't it.

A single bookshelf occupied one wall. The books were arranged neatly by size and coloration. That he'd done himself. He'd never let... Sheryl? Carol?... touch his books. They were first editions, after all. Only the best for Rupert St Cloud.

He followed the same philosophy when it came to clothes and shoes. Everything he owned had been made to fit him, so that he looked his best whatever he wore. Standards had to be maintained, even amidst the apocalypse. His people could look at him and be reminded of better days, and what might be again, if they all worked hard enough.

St Cloud was no stranger to hard work. It had taken effort to turn the few paltry millions his parents had gifted him into something substantial. Something useful. He'd sweated over investments and buyouts, waging wars in boardrooms and country clubs, all to ensure that his empire was not built on a foundation of debt and sand.

Through sheer will – as well as that endowment from his parents – he had made himself into one of the richest men in the world. His penthouse sat atop a monument to human greed – a casino. A symbol of his will, surmounting the weaknesses of others. It hadn't been hard to acquire one, either.

Atlantic City was full of casinos, or had been. Prior to the apocalypse, the city had been in financial free fall. New businesses had closed almost as soon as they'd opened, as the rich sought newer playgrounds and the middle classes stopped spending as much. A few of the older establishments had hung on, more out of inertia than anything else.

He'd bought the casino cheap, after its previous owner had declared bankruptcy for the fifth time, and renamed it the Elysium. A grandiose name, but one had to begin as one meant to go on. In Greek myth, Elysium was paradise for the deserving. It was a fitting name.

He'd intended the casino to be a place where the deserving few were granted a glimpse of heaven. He'd spared no expense in refitting and refurbishing the building to his own exacting specifications, down to the dessert menu in the restaurant. Solar panels, on-site generators and professionally designed indoor gardens with experimental built-in aquifers kept some of his costs down.

Even so, his financial advisers had screamed bloody murder for the first year, until the casino had turned a profit.

He'd fired them after that. If they couldn't see what he saw, what good were they? His sister, Ariadne, had been much the same – denying his obvious superiority, even as she proclaimed her own. As if what went for one did not go for both. They were twins, for God's sake.

But, as with the advisers, she'd soon been hoist by her own petard. Another obscure phrase, but one he thought fitting, given her love of sailing. Of course, his advisers had taken the hint, but his sister had never been one to willingly cede the stage. Despite his best efforts, however, she had persisted and forced his hand.

He paused, remembering. The dead had risen that night, but his mind had been on other matters. Securing his empire, for one. Tossing his sister off of her own damn boat for another. He recalled the look on her face – not betrayal, or fear, but cold, ruthless admiration. It had startled him, for he'd never seen such an affectionate look on her face before. The moment before she'd gone under, he'd known that she'd intended a similar fate for him.

In the end, they'd both gambled on an all or nothing chance. He'd won, she'd lost, and that was all there was to it. Except it wasn't, because Ariadne hadn't had the good grace to die, like he'd hoped. She'd survived, somehow, and was haunting him like an exceedingly irritating ghost. But not for long. Soon enough, she'd make a mistake and he'd have her. And when that time came, he planned on making certain she was dead. For good.

Pushing all thought of his sister from his mind, St Cloud went to his bedroom and dressed with brisk efficiency. The bedroom window looked out towards the boardwalk and the ocean. There was smoke on the horizon. That was a good sign. It meant things were going according to schedule. Schedules were important. Without a schedule, a man was adrift, a castaway on the seas of fate.

St Cloud kept to his schedule, come hell or high water as the saying went. His days were parceled out, and each parcel maintained down to the minute, to the second. Six hours of sleep. One hour for breakfast. Another hour for ablutions. Two hours for exercise. So on and so forth. He watched the smoke corkscrew into the gray skies above Atlantic City and fiddled with his cufflinks. Mr Keates would be calling soon.

As if on cue, the satellite phone in the living room buzzed. St Cloud made his way to it, counted to five, and picked up. "Well?" he said.

"It's done," Keates said.

"Just like last time?"

"Just like last time. Simms went in, disabled the boobytraps, and we set the dogs loose. Place was like a damn funnel. Once they caught wind of fresh meat, there was no stopping them."

"All survivors accounted for, then?"

"Yessir. Though it took some convincing to get them to come out of the freezers."

"No permanent damage, I hope," St Cloud said, examining his fingernails. He couldn't recall the last time he'd had a proper manicure. He hoped one of the Playground Pier survivors was a manicurist. That would be a fine stroke of luck.

"Not from us. Kid gloves, like you said."

"Good. What was the material take?"

Keates grunted, and St Cloud heard the rustle of paperwork. "A few firearms, some ammunition. They didn't have much of an armory. Lot of canned goods though. Also camping supplies, the usual sort of thing. Medicine as well. They must have raided a pharmacy. A bunch of its expired, but when has that ever stopped anyone?"

"Enough to make it worthwhile, then. And the dead?"

"Full cattle car. Best haul yet."

"Excellent." St Cloud went to one of the windows. It faced the same direction as his bedroom window. He took in his reflection and adjusted his necktie. "ETA?"

"Half hour, if we're careful."

"Take an hour," St Cloud said. "No sense risking yourselves." He paused. "Is there anything else I should know?"

He could almost hear Keates's hesitation. "What is it?"

Keates sighed. "They had a radio setup. A good one."

St Cloud frowned. That was unfortunate. He didn't like his pigeons squawking to one another without his say-so. People got funny ideas about who was in charge when they were allowed to speak freely amongst themselves. "And?"

"They might have been talking to someone, before we arrived."

Filled with a sudden anxiety, St Cloud began to gnaw on a thumbnail and stared at his reflection. It seemed to be smiling at him. "Was it her?" he asked, softly.

"They wouldn't say."

A twinge of pain made St Cloud look down at his thumb. He'd drawn blood. He pulled his thumb away from his mouth. Until he had secured a manicurist, he couldn't afford to chew his nails. Chewed nails were a sign of anxiety. Anxiety was a sign of a lack of control. Lack of control led to death – or worse.

Rupert St Cloud was always in control. He was the axis upon which the world spun. Without him, the world would collapse. The best would become the worst. He took a steadying breath, wondering whether Keates could hear him. Then, pushing the thought aside, he said, "The radio setup. Is it salvageable?"

A moment of hesitation. "Nope. I made certain of that."

"Fine. We'll talk when you return." St Cloud cut the conversation and set the satellite phone down in its cradle. He wondered how much longer it would be viable. How long could satellites remain in orbit, without humans to look after them? Years? Months? Not long, probably. He'd recalled reading about something called a degrading orbit – eventually, all the satellites currently orbiting the planet would tumble earthwards, burning up in the atmosphere. Then, no more satellite phones. One less thing.

The world was fast running out of things, St Cloud feared. Soon, there'd be nothing left but dirt and the dead. Unless someone did something about it. Someone had to take charge, had to run what was left properly.

"Why not me?" he asked, still looking at his reflection. He asked himself that every morning. It had become one of his daily affirmations. Reminders to himself that he was special. That without him, the center could not hold. He was the bank, the man who ran things. He was the house, and the house always won.

He straightened his tie for a second time and turned

towards the door. In the hall outside stood two of his security people, both anonymous in black riot gear. The casino's security force had been twenty strong at the beginning of the apocalypse. Now it was easily double that, though only a fraction were professionals. All of them handpicked by Mr Keates, of course.

Keates had come with the casino. He'd been the head of security under the previous management. A steady middle manager with a good head on his shoulders. Not the sort to take undue initiative, but neither was he one to willingly go along with a bad idea. The perfect man to have in your employ during the apocalypse.

Only... well. The world had changed, hadn't it? St Cloud wasn't worried about Keates's loyalties, but neither was he so foolish as to assume that the situation was inviolable. At some point, it might become necessary to terminate Mr Keates's employment and find a replacement. Someone more pliable, perhaps.

He adjusted the hang of his jacket, surreptitiously touching the specially tailored holster in the lining. Inside the holster rested a Walther PPK. A present from his father, with a childhood's worth of lessons to ensure he knew how to use it. He was fairly certain that Keates didn't know about the gun. Another ace in the hole. Another bit of insurance against future unpleasantness.

He started towards the private elevator at the far end of the hall and the two security guards fell into step behind him. The on-site generators kept the lights on in the building and the electricity running, but only just. Elevator use was reserved for a select few individuals, himself included. This one went all the way down to the subbasement. He'd taken to calling it Tartarus. No one else seemed to get the joke.

The first thing on today's docket was the daily visit to Elysium's resident mad scientist, a gentleman named Harvey Brewer. Dr Harvey Brewer. A doctorate in engineering was still a doctorate, or so Brewer insisted – often at substantial volume. He was something of an acquired taste. Even Keates, normally a byword for stoicism, found it hard to stomach Brewer's more unfortunate quirks of personality.

Still, the man was useful. Without his skills, St Cloud would never have been able to host the games which gave his people so much entertainment and helped them forget about the tribulations of the outside world. Bread and circuses, as one of the Caesars had put it. St Cloud could provide the bread easily enough, but it was Brewer who was undisputed master of the circus. The problem was, he knew it – and took every opportunity to show that he knew it. Not a subtle man, Brewer. But clever. Too clever. He thought he was untouchable.

St Cloud did not think of himself as clever. But he knew how to handle clever people, and he knew that sometimes they needed to be reminded of their proper place in the grand scheme of things. The elevator door opened, and he stepped inside. His guards followed.

It was time for Brewer's daily reminder of just who was in charge in Elysium.

CHAPTER EIGHT
Convoy

It wasn't a pleasant trip. The cattle truck hit every bump, and every time it swayed it set its unliving cargo to moaning or clawing at each other. As near as Westlake could figure, the convoy was six or seven vehicles in total. The livestock hauler was at the back and trailing some distance behind. He wondered if that was planned or just because it was hauling a heavier load.

He made it to a window with some jostling and held tight, keeping his eyes fixed on the street. The last time he'd been in Atlantic City was starting to come back to him. He and a few others had met at a restaurant on the pier. There'd been a job on offer from some foreign investor from across the pond. They'd wanted a crew to hit one of the remaining casinos in the city, no reason given, and Westlake was too experienced to ask. A tough job, but not impossible. Atlantic City wasn't Vegas, after all, for all that it had a special place in his heart. The job had gone off without so much as a hitch.

He'd done the bonds job for a mafia leader, Sal Bonaro,

not long after that, trying to build up his savings for another well-deserved vacation. But… things had gone from bad to worse. The job had been blown… Westlake's bad, he'd admit it. He'd been arrested by the police, and then escaped, breaking his promise at taking Bonaro down for a reduced sentence. But then he was abducted by a couple of Bonaro's henchmen ready to make him pay. Then the apocalypse had happened. Now he was sitting here in a cattle trailer, penned up with a bunch of deadheads. Some days it was like he couldn't catch a break.

"Story of my life," he muttered, feeling at his cheek. One of the walkers had clawed open his face, right to the bone. It didn't hurt, but he wasn't going to be winning any beauty contests. He looked at his wrists and hands. They were still wet with gore. Idly, he sucked on one of his fingers before he realized what he was doing and stopped himself.

It didn't taste bad. It didn't taste of anything at all. It wasn't like his taste buds were working, or his stomach. He didn't need it. But God, he wanted it. He wiped his hands on the back of his trousers and looked up. Someone had welded a roll cage to the top of the trailer, and he could hear people walking around above him. He could smell something like gasoline, and hear it sloshing around in tanks.

The convoy didn't move very fast. The streets were crowded with burnt-out cars, barricades, and rubble. A few of the buildings near the boardwalk looked as if they'd been caught in a fire or ruptured from within or both. Maybe a gas main had exploded. Frankly, he was surprised the city was still in as good a shape as it was.

Every so often, a jet of flame would streak down from

above and lick across the zombies that lurched too close to the convoy. That explained what the gasoline smell was; someone had rigged up some sort of flamethrower and mounted it atop the trailer. Smart.

Westlake leaned his head against the side of the window and looked out at the zombies clustered in the streets. There were a lot of them, packed cheek to cheek in places, almost all of them old – or they had been, before they'd died. Some dragged oxygen tanks, or mobility walkers. Once he spied a mobility scooter turning slow donuts at a barricade, its rider flailing mindlessly at the passing convoy. Snowbird tourists, he thought, come to enjoy some fun in their twilight years.

But it wasn't just oldies; there were dancers in spangled, blood-spattered costumes and men and women in ragged business suits or casual wear. He saw dogs, too. Lots of them. Some were alive, but others not so much. Big dogs and little dogs, toy breeds and mongrels. Both the living and the dead canines went after the walkers, harrying them and dragging them down. Eating their fill as the walker struggled and snapped uselessly at them.

Westlake watched it all, but without paying much attention. Mostly he noted the way the barricades had been placed. Someone had created a semi-safe corridor from the boardwalk to wherever they were going, blocking offside streets where possible with concrete barricades or chain-link fencing. Some zombies still got through, but not many. Most walkers weren't clever enough to deal with obstacles that couldn't be pushed out of the way. But walkers and dogs weren't the only things running wild in the streets.

The truck rumbled to a halt, and Westlake staggered. He

tried to get a look at what had brought them to the sudden stop, but couldn't see anything around the walkers pressed against the barricades. A low groan settled on the air. Once, that sound had irritated the hell out of him. Now, he found it almost soothing. It agitated his fellow captives, though. They raised up their own hue and cry, thrashing against the sides of the trailer in agitation.

Westlake tensed as someone opened a hatch set into the roof. Black helmet, black goggles, black bandanna – nothing to be seen of the face. Even so, Westlake could smell the anxiety leeching off of them, whoever they were. The hatch clanged shut after a moment; obviously they were satisfied that their cargo wasn't getting out.

He studied the hatch. The hinges were on the inside. Given how quickly they'd gotten it open, it probably wasn't locked. Latched, possibly. No easy way up, but he could possibly get a hand from one of his fellow prisoners – even if they weren't aware they were being helpful. But even if he got up there, and outside, what then? He didn't particularly like his chances against whatever hardware they were packing. He might be… God, could he say it? He might be undead, but he didn't want to be fully dead.

Not to mention, he was curious. He wanted to know where they were going. The barricades, the flamethrowers, the attack on the pier – it all spoke to long-range planning. Something was going on, something big. Besides, it wasn't like he had anywhere to be. And Ramirez was in his head. Making him feel like he should *help* people.

A thunderous, guttural groan erupted from somewhere up ahead. He knew that sound: a brute. One of the big ones.

He heard the chatter of gunfire and the thud of running feet overhead. The barricades wouldn't have been any trouble for a brute; they could plow through almost anything, including concrete.

Another bellicose groan-roar echoed over the street, momentarily drowning out the walkers. The ones in the cattle car had fallen silent. He'd noticed that before, when he'd still been breathing. The walkers shut right up when a brute was nearby. Maybe it was some sort of weird herd instinct, or maybe it was self-preservation. Given that the brutes would happily eat a walker if they were in the mood, he figured it was probably more the latter than the former. This one sounded real close.

The front axle of a car punched into the side of the trailer like a javelin. Westlake was knocked sprawling, as were most of the walkers. One wasn't so lucky; the chunk of metal had pinned it to the opposite side of the trailer. He dragged himself to his feet and felt the metal vibrate beneath him. Through the window he could see that the fencing was down, and the walkers were scattering as something lumbered swiftly towards the convoy.

The brute was bigger than the others he'd seen, and clad in the remnants of police riot gear. It didn't so much shuffle as bound forward, moving like some demented circus ape. He could hear it slobbering as it galloped over the fallen fencing and launched itself at the trailer.

A gout of flame caught it in midair and sent it floundering backwards. It didn't fall immediately. Instead, it howled and came back for another try. More fire solved the problem. At least, that particular one.

He could hear someone shouting up above but couldn't make out what they were saying. Probably something about the walkers that were now flooding through the broken fences. He expected another gout of flame, but all he heard was a sloshing sound. Out of fuel, or maybe there was a clog in the line. It didn't matter, the result was the same either way. Lots of unburnt walkers edging up against the trailer, and the ones inside were getting worked up again. Maybe it was time to go after all.

He pushed his way to the rear of the trailer. No point in going up and out. Better to go out the back. These trailers were meant to keep in animals without opposable thumbs. If he popped the bolt on the rear gate, he could get out and vanish in the crowd. Not the best plan, but it had the benefit of being simple.

He had the bolt half out when he heard the sudden chatter of a machine gun. A big one, something belt-fed and mounted. He didn't see where it was coming from, only that the shots scythed through the walkers with the expected results. Then, car doors slamming. Westlake hurriedly withdrew his arm as several black-clad people picked their way through the fallen. "Get anything in one piece into the back of the trailer," a man yelled. Something about his voice was familiar.

Westlake spotted him a moment later. He was short, shaped like a fireplug, but with an undeniable air of authority. He was the only one not wearing a helmet, which made him easy to pick out of the crowd. Older. Gray hair cropped close – high and tight. Military then, or a cop. Why was he familiar? What was it about him? Westlake stared, trying to jostle something loose from the morass of his memories.

All in a rush, it came to him, and the name came unbidden to his lips. "Keates," he hissed. The sound must have been louder than he thought, for the guy turned slightly, a quizzical expression on his blunt features. He knew that face. The guy had been wearing a suit last time, a good one. Expensive, but not tailored. Off the rack. Cops and mob guys had the same problem; neither knew how to dress. They could pick out a good suit, but they didn't know enough to get it fitted.

The casino. Westlake had seen him on the casino floor. Doing what? Had he worked for the casino? Keates. Keates. Who was Keates? The guy was still looking in his direction, but with no sign of recognition. Even so, Westlake turned away before the guy decided to take a closer look. Whoever Keates was, he didn't think they'd parted as friends.

After a few minutes, the back of the trailer opened and half a dozen more walkers were shoved inside. The back banged shut before the others could react. Westlake risked a glance back out the window. Keates was nowhere in sight, but he heard a car door slam. Then they were moving again – but to where?

He found out a moment later, when the casino hove into view over the tops of the surrounding buildings. He gave a short grunt of laughter, glad the rumble of the engine covered up the noise. "Well, well, well," he rasped. "It's a day for coincidences, don't you think?" He nudged a nearby walker, and it moaned in what he took to be agreement.

It had been called the Amphitheatre by its former owner, but the name had changed to something else after a buyout by an overseas firm. He remembered reading about it online, and wondering if their robbery had had something to do with the change of ownership. It looked like Keates had held onto his job, whatever had come of their previous encounter.

The convoy passed through a bulwark of concrete barricades, broken down cars and chain-link fencing. There were people on guard inside and on top of makeshift pillboxes, made from tin siding and repurposed storage containers. Not quite an army, but close.

Westlake glanced at the walker beside him. "I don't know about you, but I'd say that's pretty interesting."

The zombie grunted noncommittally. Westlake turned back to the window. The convoy was heading around to the loading dock. He remembered it from the last time he'd visited. Why were they bringing a bunch of zombies into a place like this? He settled back to wait. He had a feeling he was going to find out sooner rather than later.

CHAPTER NINE
Preparations

"Have I mentioned that this is a stupid idea, Calvin?" Sayers asked as she looked around the Villa's armory. Guns, many still shiny with packing oil, had been set out for ease of access on a random assortment of shelving. Most of them were military surplus, bought bulk from overseas dealers. No serial numbers or other identifying markers.

She wasn't certain what the Villa's previous owner, Sal Bonaro, had intended to use them for, and didn't particularly care. She had her bow, after all, and the Mauser C96 holstered at her waist. Her fingers tap-tapped against the pistol. Her father had been an avid collector of firearms. The C96 was the last of his collection; the only piece she'd been unable to part with. It was running low on ammunition, but she couldn't bear to be without its weight. One day, maybe. But not right now. "Just give me a reason, Calvin. Why?"

"Human decency is not enough?" Ptolemy asked.

"We've had this argument before," Sayers began, in exasperation.

"But this time it isn't a hypothetical; someone is asking

for our help," Kahwihta said, from across the room. The young woman looked through the scope of a hunting rifle. "Granted, they're pretty far away, but they're the first survivors we've heard from in – what? – months? That alone ought to pique your curiosity some."

Sayers turned. "Shouldn't you be somewhere, making notes in your little book?"

Kahwihta met her glare placidly. "Shouldn't you be hiding in a tree somewhere?"

"Ladies," Ramirez called out, from across the room. "Save your hostility for the walking corpses, please." She twitched her wrist, and the collapsible baton she held hissed to its full length. "I have a feeling we'll need it."

"We don't even know who these people are," Sayers said.

"All the more reason to find out," Calavera said. He sat on a table near the door, perfectly at ease. "Caution is wise. But too much caution is nothing more than cowardice."

"Maybe so, but Sayers is right," a woman in a wheelchair said, as she rolled herself into the armory. "I'm all for extending a helping hand and all, but Atlantic City is a bit further than across the bloody table," she continued, her words tinged with a soft lilt. She was middle-aged, her red hair streaked with white.

"I agree with Saoirse," the big man who followed her added. He was dressed in flannel and a puffer vest with a faded company logo on it, and had a battered ballcap on his head. "I'd hate to lose you all on something this risky. Especially when we're not exactly getting anything out of it."

Sayers gestured. "See? Saoirse and Dunnigan agree with me."

Saoirse snorted. "I didn't say I agreed with you, just that you were right."

Sayers glared at her. "What's the difference?"

"The difference is not all reasons are practical ones, and what is smart is not necessarily what is right," Ptolemy said, softly. "But if you insist, I can name you three practical reasons for the journey. Number one: supplies."

"We have supplies," Sayers protested.

"Enough to get through winter, maybe," Saoirse said. She was the camp's quartermaster. She kept count of every bullet and can of beans in the place. "But we'll run out eventually. Especially if hunting proves as sparse as it has of late."

Sayers frowned. She didn't like to admit it, but Saoirse was right. The zombies had practically denuded the mountains of deer and smaller animals. And the living had done the same to all of the nearby towns and villages. The shelves of every grocery store and gas station for thirty miles were bare. She glanced at Ptolemy. "What are the other two reasons?" she demanded, stubbornly.

"Intelligence," Ptolemy said. "The gunshot, remember? Who fired it and why?"

"Why does it matter?"

"Because whoever did it might well come for us one day. We cannot – and should not – fight against zombies and our fellow man."

Sayers grunted. She didn't think that was likely, but she could see that the others were worried about it. "Fine. And the third?"

"The zombies are the least of our concerns. A hazard, but a controllable hazard."

Sayers sighed, recognizing where he was headed. "Not this again."

"Yes, this again. The zombies are not a natural occurrence. Something instigated the apocalypse and the only way to find out what or who is behind it, is to go out there and look." He frowned. "It could be the Deros, you know. Shaver's theories were discredited, but that does not mean they were incorrect. A race of subterranean sadists might well find it amusing to unleash a biological plague on the upper world."

"I thought you said it was aliens?"

"According to Shaver, the Deros do have regular contact with certain extraterrestrial species," Ptolemy began, but Sayers raised her hands in surrender.

"Never mind. Fine. That still doesn't change the fact that we have no way of getting there." She looked at Saoirse and Dunnigan for backup. Before either of them could speak, however, Ramirez's voice beat them to the punch.

"I have some thoughts on that, actually." Ramirez set a black Benelli M4 semi-automatic shotgun on the table in front of Ptolemy. "Speaking of which, I found this. Remember how to use it?"

Ptolemy smiled thinly. "Indeed."

Ramirez looked at Sayers. "Did you bring the map, like I asked?"

Sayers frowned but pulled the folded map out of her pocket. "Of course. I don't see what good it'll do us, though."

Ramirez unfolded the map across one of the tables. She found a Sharpie in one of the nearby boxes, pulled off the top with her teeth and began to mark a route. As she did so, she asked, "Who can tell me about the Adirondack Regional Airport?"

Ptolemy blinked. "It is little over five miles northwest of Saranac Lake. It covers little under fifteen hundred acres, with two runways and parallel taxiways. At any given time, there were around sixteen aircraft based there…"

"Seventeen," Sayers interjected, quietly. Ramirez smiled and nodded.

"Exactly."

"Exactly what?" Kahwihta asked, as she joined them. "What am I missing?"

Sayers pinched the bridge of her nose. Of course Ramirez knew. "Sal Bonaro had a private plane. Private hangar too."

Ramirez's smile widened at Sayers. "And I bet you know which one it is."

"Yeah." Bonaro had once asked her to guide some of his guests from the airfield to the Villa, just prior to the end of the world. Russians, she thought. Eastern European, definitely. Mobsters, just like Bonaro. Sometimes she wondered whether they'd been among the zombies infesting the place, their sanctuary having become a tomb. "You can't be serious, though. Can you even fly a plane?"

"In fact, I can." Ramirez said it with an air of mild conceit. Sometimes Ramirez could be so annoying. "There's no way of knowing if it still works."

"Only one way to find out," Calavera rumbled. He leaned over the map, balancing on his scarred knuckles. "How long will it take us to get there?"

"It depends," Sayers said, as the others looked at her. She ran her hands through her hair, studying the map. "If we take the safe route, a day, maybe a bit more, on foot. We hike up towards Lake Clear, stay off the roads, keep to the trail. We could start in the morning, be there by nightfall. Hole up in a hangar and fly out the next day."

"How long by car?" Ramirez asked, stroking her chin.

"A half hour, maybe less," Sayers said. "Why?"

"We've got a few vehicles here. Why not use one?"

"It makes noise, for one thing," Sayers said, pointedly. "We'd be alerting every zombie for miles to our presence. Might as well ring a dinner bell."

"That might be a good thing," Kahwihta said. She leaned down to stroke Attila's broad head. The dog thumped his tail, pleased with the attention. "We've cut down the local population up here significantly, but there's still plenty of them wandering around down there. If we did it right, we could pull a bunch of them away from the mountains and get them moving down the road. Remember, once they start moving, they don't stop." She gestured lazily. "They just… keep going, until something gets their attention."

Ramirez nodded. Sayers shook her head, appalled at the thought of even attempting such a stunt. She'd found that the problem with other people was that they were idiots – often selectively and unpredictably. Generally attracting the attentions of the walking dead was a bad thing. But here they were, discussing it as if it were a strategic master-stroke.

"So… what?" she asked. "You want to just lead them all to the airfield? How does that help us?" She looked at the map again. "We should go on foot. It's safer."

"Why exactly?" Ramirez asked, studying her coolly.

Sayers hesitated. The truth was she'd been to the airfield just the once after things had gone sour. She still wasn't certain what she'd hoped to accomplish; it wasn't like she could fly a plane, and siphoning fuel was a fool's errand. Maybe she'd just hoped someone might take her away. "People… tried to get out. After things went bad. The airfield wasn't safe."

"How many?" Ptolemy asked, softly.

Sayers looked away. She hadn't been there when it happened. She'd arrived a day later, maybe two days. It had all been over by then. "Sixty. Maybe seventy. There might be more now, or less." She glanced at Kahwihta. "Depending on whether or not something caught their attention."

The young woman smiled slightly, and Sayers felt a flicker of something that might have been unease. Something about Kahwihta bothered her, although she couldn't say what. Maybe it was as simple as her abiding interest in the dead. Whatever it was, it made her uncomfortable around the young woman.

"I see now why you are so reluctant to go there," Ptolemy said. "If it is occupied territory, so to speak, then our plan might not be the best one." He looked at Ramirez, who shook her head and frowned, clearly still digesting what Sayers had revealed.

"I ask again, what's the point?" Sayers asked. Ramirez's frown deepened. Before she could speak, Sayers went on. "Why are we doing this? And I don't mean Calvin's pie in the sky idealism. I mean what do you expect to happen when we get there?"

"It's not quite an hour to Atlantic City from here, by

plane," Ramirez said. "We could be at Playground Pier by tomorrow afternoon."

"So?"

"So, we find out what happened. Someone might have escaped. Maybe there are other camps in the city. Other people."

Sayers stared at her. "It's all very well and good to talk about riding to the rescue, about supplies and all that, but what can the five of us do for these people, even if we find them? What's the plan?"

"We won't know until we get there," Calavera said, in his deep voice. It reminded Sayers of someone calling up out of a grave.

"That is the opposite of a plan," Sayers said.

"You don't have to come," Ramirez said.

"Of course I do," Sayers snapped. "If I don't go, who'll keep Calvin alive? You? No."

Ramirez was silent for a moment. Then she smiled thinly and said, "You know, I've been thinking about this almost since we found this place. The real problem is that people have nowhere to go." She looked around, as if taking in the walls and the guns.

"There's no place to hole up, to catch your breath," she went on. "Exhaustion, fatigue, it wears you down. You start running on autopilot. All you can do is survive – until you can't. Until your instincts let you down. But we can change that."

"With a plane?" Sayers asked, her voice like acid.

"If we can fly a plane in, then we can fly one out." Ramirez gestured for emphasis, mimicking a landing plane with her hand. "A bigger one, from the Atlantic City airport. We can get people to a safe location and ferry them. With supplies to support them here, where it's safe for the most part. It's not perfect, but it's workable."

Sayers shook her head. "You're just going to fly people back and forth?"

"I'm not the only pilot in the world, Sayers."

"And if we don't somehow stumble across another one?"

"Then we make do," Ramirez said, firmly. "The airport will have fuel, vehicles and supplies, if it hasn't been picked over. We fly in, we load up, we ride the ten or so miles to Atlantic City. We know we're heading for the Playground Pier, which is easy enough to find. And we start at the Adirondack Regional Airport." She tapped the map and looked at Sayers. "We can do all of this in a few hours, especially with your help."

"You've got it all figured out," Sayers murmured. She had to give Ramirez credit, it was starting to sound like a decent plan. It wasn't going to work, but as plans went it was solid, even though it relied on everything working in predictable fashion. Sayers had lived in the wilderness long enough to know that the world was anything but predictable.

Ramirez stepped back, arms folded. Defensive. "You wanted a plan. That's a plan."

Sayers looked at Ptolemy. He met her gaze, and she saw no doubt, no hesitation. Of course not. Whatever else, he was an idealist. An optimist too, in a strange sort of way. It was his way of coping with the state of the world. Rather than just accepting that the world had ended and nothing more needed doing, he insisted on making more work for himself. For her as well. It was one of the reasons she loved him – even now.

"Us humans must help each other," he said softly.

She sighed and looked back at the map. "Fine. We'll need something heavy-duty. We won't have much fuel, but we won't need it. I suggest we use the vehicle to draw away any unwanted attention while the rest of us approach from the tree line, across the runways. The fencing is all chain-link, so we should take something to cut it with. Bonaro's hangar is at the far end of the parking lot. If we can get the plane onto the runway, and get the engine started, then we'll be in business."

Ramirez nodded, and looked at the others. "I guess we just need to figure out who the best driver is."

"I will do it," Calavera said, with what Sayers found to be a disturbing amount of confidence. He cracked his knuckles. "I may even dispatch a few on the way."

"Why not?" Sayers muttered. "It's not like we're in a hurry." She looked at Ptolemy. "Are you absolutely sure about this?"

He nodded. "I believe it will work."

Sayers found herself wishing, not for the first time, that she'd just taken to the timber the way she'd intended to, all those weeks ago. She smiled sourly.

"People say Atlantic City is nice," she said. "Guess we'll find out."

CHAPTER TEN
Tartarus

It was hot in Tartarus; appropriately so. Brewer liked the heat, or so he'd claimed to St Cloud. But it made everything in his fiefdom stink of rotting meat and spoiled blood. Attendants in scavenged and much-patched hazmat suits hurried past St Cloud and his guards, on errands for the ruler of the underworld.

Brewer's laboratory had once been the laundry facilities for the casino. Four large concrete rooms just below the ground floor, reachable only by a quartet of elevators and a single set of fire stairs. The area was isolated and ignored by most of Elysium's population, just the way both St Cloud and Brewer liked it. The fewer people who knew exactly what went on down here, the better, as far as St Cloud was concerned.

Originally, he'd intended to turn the facilities into a secondary stockpile – a final redoubt for himself and a few others, in case of disaster. Potable water was at a premium after all, and no one was using the machines. Brewer had convinced him otherwise. At the time, the other man had seemed perfectly sane, if a touch cold-blooded. In the months since, St Cloud had come to doubt his initial assessment. Brewer was utterly insane, but useful.

St Cloud pulled out a scented handkerchief and pressed it to his nose as they reached the doors that led to the central lab. There was an armed guard in a hazmat suit on duty, as was procedure. Couldn't have any lost souls getting out and making a nuisance of themselves. He would have preferred a hazmat suit himself, if only to cut the smell, but he couldn't be seen to be wearing one. It might provoke the wrong sort of talk among his people, and there was enough of that to worry about as it was.

Things were becoming tense on the lower floors. Food was in short supply, and the gardens weren't producing anywhere near the proper quantities yet – not to keep both his guests and his workers fed.

The guests resided on the uppermost floors of the hotel, beneath the penthouse. He'd made the decision early on to establish a well-to-do class. Every society needed its middle-managers. They'd been corporate royalty and celebrities.

Now they were overseers, in charge of the gardens, the water, the waste disposal facilities. He delegated the business of the day to day to them. Others bought their status with access to homes and businesses, selling him their worldly possessions just to keep themselves from having to grub in the gardens with everyone else.

The problem was, the more camps he co-opted, the more mouths there were to feed. But he needed strong backs and steady hands if he was going to accomplish anything of value. All progress required sacrifice. Hence, the arena. Entertainment kept his subordinates happy. And happy subordinates were productive ones.

The guard saluted awkwardly, the seals of his hazmat suit flexing against the duct-tape. Steeling his gag reflex, St Cloud entered Tartarus, his guards at his heels.

Inside, it looked to him like so much controlled chaos. There were work benches situated along the walls, cooling units liberated from restaurants and hospitals, racks of equipment scavenged from pharmacies, as well as hardware and electronics stores.

A dozen makeshift pens, crafted from chain-link fencing and bulletproof glass, were strategically arranged near the drains. Each one contained an examination table and restraints of various makes and models. Three of the pens were currently occupied by listless walkers; the other seven needed washing out. They were the source of the smell.

The walkers shuffled to the fronts of their pens, glaring at the newcomers. All had mesh cages fixed to their heads, preventing them from biting. Their hands had been cut off, and their stumps thumped against the pens in futile aggression.

Brewer went through a dozen walkers a week, easily. Some he vivisected, others he simply observed for a time before having them destroyed. The rest went to the arenas. Through his observations, he'd managed to identify the areas in the city where runners and brutes congregated in great numbers, the movement patterns of the local walkers, and other such useful information.

He'd even devised several methods of repelling the

occasional mob of walkers that tried to breach the casino – from recorded brute groans to using ichor, gleaned from the more aggressive types of zombie, to scent mark certain buildings.

On one of the examination tables, trays of zombie body parts waited patiently for their turn under the knife. The walls were decorated with photographs, drawings and crude schematics. Brewer was an inveterate doodler.

St Cloud's eyes were immediately drawn to the far end of the space where a larger cage, far sturdier than the others, sat. The cage had belonged to a novelty act at one of the other casinos – something to do with tigers. But the monster the cage now contained was no tiger.

It crouched at the center of the cage, dozens of lengths of chain extending from it to rebar anchors sunk into the floor and the nearby walls. It was a zombie, but unique in its physiology: a hulking tower of muscle, covered in slabs of what look like bone or fossilized keratin beneath the tattered remnants of a gray-green boiler suit. Its big hands were clawed, and its legs were jointed like an animal's. Its face was thankfully hidden beneath a bright crimson mask. The mask had been stitched to its head, so that it couldn't remove it.

El Gigante.

The zombie stared incuriously at the newcomers from beneath half-shuttered eyes. Another of Brewer's contributions to the cause – something the doctor also insisted on referring to as a *he*. Brewer had figured out how to keep their prize asset doped up and docile after a few weeks of trial and error. A good thing too, since the creature was exceedingly dangerous in its natural state.

St Cloud strode towards it, his hands clasped behind his back. "Magnificent," he murmured, looking up at the creature. It never failed to take his breath away, seeing it up close. El Gigante was truly a sight to behold. With a dozen like it, he could easily take the city. Maybe even the state. For now, he just had the one.

"Yes. Isn't he just?"

St Cloud frowned and turned. Brewer stood beside him, eating a somewhat bruised apple. His hands were bloody, but he didn't seem concerned. Unlike his staff, Brewer didn't bother with a hazmat suit. Instead, he dressed like an old man at the track. He was round and shiny with sweat, a grizzle of white on his cheeks and chin, and thinning hair the same color. He was in his fifties, or maybe his sixties.

He took a bite of the apple, chewed methodically, clearly in no hurry, and then looked up at St Cloud. "You took your time getting down here today."

St Cloud ignored the comment. "How is he? Ready for tonight?" He'd wanted something special to celebrate the first step in his plan. El Gigante was to be that something special.

Brewer frowned. "He's getting hungrier. It's getting harder to keep him under."

"You assured me that he was under control."

"He is. For the moment. But I wanted you to be aware in case the situation becomes… untenable." Brewer dropped his apple into the pocket of his sport coat.

"It would be a shame to put him down, given your hard work," St Cloud said, letting a little acid creep into his voice. "Especially before we have a chance to watch him."

"You wanted a monster for your circus, I gave you one," Brewer said, wiping his hands with a cloth procured from one of the examination tables. "But value is often finite and always debatable. If you were that worried, you should have used him before now."

"I wanted to save him for a special occasion." St Cloud looked up at the somnolent creature, who had been a member of the casino's custodial staff originally. Then, during the first week of the zombie apocalypse it had changed into… whatever it was now. Not a brute or a simple walker, but something far more monstrous.

"You ran a casino, Mr St Cloud. You of all people should know that what you want and what you get are not often the same."

St Cloud brushed the statement aside. "We had a good morning. Supplies are coming in. More warm bodies for the gardens. You know what that means?"

Brewer grinned. "More test subjects."

"A celebration," St Cloud corrected. "As I said, tonight will be special."

"Well, you know best." Brewer knelt and clucked his tongue gently. A heretofore unseen shape rose on unsteady legs and lurched into view. It had been a dog once, a stubby faced little Pekinese. Brewer had arrived with it in his backpack. It had already been a zombie by then, and he'd kept it muzzled. But it wasn't muzzled any longer. Instead, it had a black collar with a small box mounted on it.

Brewer murmured softly to it in what St Cloud thought was Polish, and stroked its ravaged skull. "And how is the little fellow?" St Cloud asked. It was the dog that had convinced him of Brewer's claims. There were plenty of zombified dogs wandering around the city, but only one seemed inclined to listen to its owner.

"Pierogi is quite cheerful, as one judges such things," Brewer said, still stroking the dog. "He is safe and well fed. More than can be said for most."

"I notice you've stopped using the muzzle."

Pierogi looked up and gave a guttural sniff. The dog's eyes were the color of pus, and its tongue was black. Something oily dripped from its frayed jowls. It growled softly as its eyes fixed on him. Brewer turned. "I've installed a small inhibitor chip in his head." He rummaged in his pocket and came out with a remote. "A tap sends a signal to the receiver on his collar, which then passes it along to the chip." He tapped a button on the remote and the dog stiffened, its eyes rolling. Then it subsided and laid down.

"Well, that is something," St Cloud said, grudgingly.

Brewer stood and indicated a cardboard box on a nearby workbench. "I've made a few, and converted the receivers to go with them. I'll begin inserting them in some of the new test subjects this afternoon. If I am right, they'll work the same regardless of the difference in size of subject."

St Cloud considered this. There were definite possibilities there. Especially in regards to El Gigante. "Is it programmable? Or simply on/off?"

Brewer smiled grimly. "The latter, at the moment. But the former is a possibility, given time and resources."

St Cloud nodded. "Can you… make more?"

Brewer gave him a sly look. "Enough to control a horde, say?"

St Cloud didn't reply. Brewer gave a little laugh. "I'll need supplies. I can provide a list. Most of it can be found in any electronics or pet store. And I'll need test subjects, of course. No more than a dozen, ideally. Walkers, for preference." He looked at El Gigante. "I've already put one in him. My prize test subject." He turned his gaze back to St Cloud. "That should make tonight very special, eh?"

"Yes, it might just. Very good, Doctor. I am suitably impressed with your progress. I no longer doubt my wisdom in giving you sanctuary." He smiled. "Is there anything else?"

"Some food for Pierogi," Brewer murmured, his attentions drifting back to El Gigante. He scooped up the dog and scratched it under the chin. St Cloud looked at the dog, and grimaced. The wretched thing let its tongue loll as it snuggled into its owner's arms.

"Pierogi and I thank you," Brewer said. Something came away on his fingers as he scratched it and he idly wiped them on his sport coat. The dog didn't seem to notice. Indeed, its cheerful smile widened unhealthily. A surge of bile threatened to well up and overcome St Cloud, and he quickly pressed his handkerchief to his nose and mouth as he turned to go. He was nearly running by the time he reached the doors.

"I'll send the list up later, Mr St Cloud," Brewer called after him, as he fled.

CHAPTER ELEVEN
Prisoners

Saul squinted as a short, stout woman in black fatigues and body armor shined a penlight into his eyes. "Open your mouth," she said, curtly. He did so, and gagged slightly as she used a tongue depressor to rummage around in his mouth. He wasn't sure what she was looking for, but it probably wasn't buried treasure. "Clean," she said, and picked up a clipboard from the tray table beside her stool. "Name?"

"Saul Blum," he said.

"Occupation?"

"Survivor."

Her gaze hardened. "Before that."

"Rabbi." His eyes slid around the loading dock as he spoke. The survivors from Playground Pier were all here, divided into two groups.

One group, composed of those who'd already been processed, milled about inside a chain-link enclosure. The other group waited in an orderly line, watched over by the armed guards who'd herded them out of the vans that had brought them here. One by one, they were escorted up to the checkpoint, where one of the half-dozen people on duty would give them a thorough once-over.

"Are we prisoners, then?" he asked, rubbing his wrists. It certainly felt like it. He and the others had been zip tied until they'd been escorted out of the vehicles that had brought them. Not to mention being herded onto said vehicles at gunpoint in the first place.

She ignored the question. "Joe, put this one with the rest and send up the next applicant," she said, not looking at Saul.

One of the guards loitering nearby caught Saul by his elbow and dragged him towards the rest of the processed prisoners. Saul knew better than to resist. They had guns and cattle prods and weren't shy about using them. That hadn't stopped some fools from trying, of course. Nobody was dead – yet – but they probably wished they were.

He caught sight of Ruth and Amos as he was pushed into the pen. "You are well?"

"In one piece," Ruth said, glancing at her brother.

Saul nodded. "We appear to be in a casino. Do either of you recognize this place?"

Again, they looked at one another. Both shook their heads. "No," Amos said. "Though I heard one of the guards call it Els-y-something. A funny sort of name."

Saul grunted and looked around the pen. Playground Pier had been home to around thirty survivors; men, women and children. Of that number, only a few seemed to be missing. "McCuskey?" he asked.

Amos shrugged. "The last I saw of him he was heading for the stairs." His shoulders slumped slightly as he continued. "We lost Lonnie and Mrs Bridgeman as well."

Saul nodded. "I saw. They were too close to the doors when those *farkakte* drones hit." Lonnie had just turned twenty, and Bridgeman had been a mother. Thankfully, her children had already been in the freezers with the others when the drones arrived. He paused. "I do not think McCuskey is the sort to be taken alive."

Amos looked towards the guards and kept his voice pitched low. "They used the zombies like... like shock troops. Who does that?"

"Someone who is not our friend," Saul said. He closed his eyes and rubbed his face. He was tired. It had been a stressful morning. "Oy vey. Like we didn't have enough tsuris." He looked around again and felt a sudden wave of sadness.

Men, women, and children. Less than twenty, now. Makeshift families, absorbing the casualties and sorrow. Readying themselves for tomorrow. There was a grim resilience to those who'd survived this long, even the children. And, to go with it, an awareness that life was all too brief. That every moment was to be enjoyed.

He wondered what the next generation would be like, if there was one. Would they even recall the way it had been before? Would anyone be left to tell them, or would the past be cast aside as all useless things were?

He pushed the thought aside. "Where's Manny?" Manny was McCuskey's brother, and their resident radio expert. Or he had been.

"He's not here. They separated him from the rest of us as soon as they arrived." Ruth frowned. "He was talking to someone on the radio before that big guy, the one in charge, shot it. The radio I mean."

Saul nodded. In the confusion after the drone attack, he'd managed to convince McCuskey to send out a mayday on the radio. Manny had managed to contact someone. "Were you with him when he made contact?"

Ruth nodded. "Just at the end. He was talking to someone. A man with a Greek name." She paused and snapped her fingers. "Ptolemy – that was it."

"Greek?"

"He didn't sound Greek," Amos said, doubtfully. He paused. "Then, I've never met a Greek person, so I'm probably not the best judge."

Saul dismissed this with a twitch of his head. "What exactly did he say?"

"Just something about there being a safe place. A refuge. Hidden in the mountains. We told them our situation, and he said – he claimed – they would send help. That they would send people to guide us there, if we wanted to go. That they'd help us in whatever way they could."

"And you believed them?" Saul asked.

Ruth hesitated. "Yes. I think so." Amos nodded in agreement.

Saul studied them. Both the young woman and her brother were remarkably good judges of character, considering their otherwise sheltered upbringing. He was about to ask them more about what they'd heard when he heard a loud whistle from outside the pen. He turned and saw the man called Keates standing in front of the pen.

Keates was built low and wide, like a bulldozer. He had big shoulders and a stump of a neck, atop which was perched a flat head. His silvery hair was clipped high and tight, like a marine – which he probably had been, given his posture.

"All right, listen up," he said. "You've all been processed. Good news, nobody has any signs of infection or illness other than malnutrition. Congratulations. Now you're free to hear the pitch. Mr St Cloud?" He turned as if to welcome someone.

Saul looked past Keates and saw a dark-skinned, handsome man striding towards them, flanked by a pair of guards. The newcomer wore a suit and fiddled with his cufflinks as he walked. "Hello, I'm Rupert St Cloud. The owner of this establishment." He spoke with the trace of an accent; like an extra off one of those British shows about the landed gentry. He spread his arms in a gesture of greeting. "Welcome, one and all, to Elysium."

He came to a halt beside Keates and continued. "What you have experienced today was a hostile takeover. As in any hostile takeover, some of you will be retained in your current positions. Others will be reassigned. The remainder will be let go."

"Somehow, I don't think you mean that in the literal sense," Saul said, speaking up.

St Cloud looked at him. "Sadly, no. Not my call, but, well, these are hard times and they require hard methods, Mister…?"

"Blum. Rabbi Blum."

St Cloud nodded. "A rabbi? Wonderful."

Saul frowned. "Are you a religious man, Mr St Cloud?"

"I prefer to think of myself as spiritual."

Saul snorted and looked around at the pen housing them. "This doesn't seem like the work of a spiritual man."

"We all express our faith in different ways," St Cloud said, with an edge in his voice – a warning that Saul thought he'd best heed. St Cloud straightened his tie and went on. "I am a businessman. And right now, my business is mankind. Specifically, it's survival." He extended his hands, as if to encompass all of them.

"Elysium is humanity's last redoubt," he continued. "A fortress to withstand the end of the world. Or it will be, when we're finished. But to accomplish that, I need people. Good people. People willing to work, to share." He paused. "Willing to follow orders. My orders. Willing to do what it takes to save the world."

"Starting with Atlantic City," Saul said.

St Cloud nodded but didn't reply. Instead, he scanned the faces of the survivors. Saul had the unpleasant thought that they were being weighed and judged. Saul cleared his throat, drawing the man's gaze back to him. "You might have asked first, before you sent in the Gestapo." He used the word intentionally, emphasizing it. St Cloud didn't so much as blink, but the heavyset man beside him, the one who'd been in charge of the raid, flinched.

St Cloud pressed his hands together. "As I said earlier, this was a hostile takeover. I would have preferred to do things diplomatically, but sadly these are not civilized times and discussion is an extinct method of conviction. I cannot afford to let you make the wrong choice. I cannot afford to let you make any choices at all, frankly. Free will is a thing of the past, like Chinese takeout and reality television."

Saul made to speak, but St Cloud spoke over him. "That you have survived this long is a sign that you are the type of people I want in Elysium. But not every survivor understands that we must do more than scavenge the ruins of the world we have lost. That we must build a new society from the ground up, if necessary."

It sounded good. But Saul didn't buy it. He could tell Ruth and Amos didn't either. But there was uncertainty on the faces of some of the others. After all they'd endured, the need for safety, stability, even when it came at the end of a gun, was a lure too strong to ignore. Saul couldn't find it in him to blame them.

"Playground Pier was hardly conducive to long-term survival," St Cloud continued. "More hands make for swift work. The more of us who are together, the greater our chance of survival…"

Saul grimaced. "You sent drones to blow up our defenses and an army of zombies to devour us. That doesn't sound like you had our survival in mind."

St Cloud looked at him. "You are here, aren't you? In one piece. Safe and sound."

"Not all of us," Saul countered.

"Collateral damage," St Cloud said, flatly.

"You attacked us, kidnapped us, and now tell us we are to – what? Be slaves?" Saul scoffed and shook his head.

"I prefer the term employee." St Cloud paused. "You will be assigned to a type of work that best fits the skills you bring to the table. If you have no useful skills, well, we're always in need of people to carry night soil to the gardens. Everyone here has a job to do, and so long as they do it, things will run smoothly."

"And you're the boss at the top," Saul said.

"Someone has to keep their eye on the big picture. Someone has to be in charge. Why not me?" For a moment, Saul almost believed he expected an answer. The moment passed and St Cloud continued. "I don't blame you for your skepticism. I would be skeptical myself, were I not the one in charge." He frowned. "But you bring me to my next point. Mr Keates, would you bring out Mr McCuskey?"

Keates turned and barked an order. Two of his people went to one of the vans and brought out someone with their hands zip tied and a bag over their head. It was obviously McCuskey. He was struggling, but not much. Hurt, Saul figured, given the state of his clothes and limbs. When they reached St Cloud, Keates pulled the bag off McCuskey's head and exposed his bloodied features.

"You fu-" McCuskey began. Keates hit him with a rabbit punch and McCuskey sagged, the obscenity turning into a pained wheeze. St Cloud studied the injured man with a neutral expression.

"Mr McCuskey here was your leader. He was bad at it. I say this with no ill will. It is simply fact. He had you hiding in freezers and chaining doors. Scuttling about the city like rats. He had no plan beyond living to see another day. Shameful." He turned to Saul and the others. "Under his leadership, your numbers would have dwindled with every passing day, until – well... Mr Keates?" He held out his hand. Keates hesitated and then drew his sidearm and handed it to St Cloud.

St Cloud shot McCuskey in the chest. The big man folded over without a sound. The guards let him fall and stepped back, as did St Cloud. They knew what was coming. Saul did, too. He'd seen it enough in recent days. McCuskey began to twitch and jerk. Maybe he'd been bitten. Maybe it didn't matter. No one really knew.

The newborn zombie heaved itself up, like a snake rearing to strike. "This is what awaits anyone not under my aegis," St Cloud said loudly, as he circled the zombie. It tried to get to its feet but failed. "Death, followed by undeath. If you are not with me in Elysium, you are nothing more than fodder for the armies of the dead. That is why you no longer have a choice, because there are no more options."

St Cloud pressed his borrowed weapon to the side of McCuskey's head and pulled the trigger. McCuskey toppled once more and lay still. St Cloud handed the weapon back to Keates, who grimaced slightly as he took it.

"The worthy will join me in Elysium. The rest will join Mr McCuskey in oblivion." St Cloud smiled and clasped his hands behind his back. He looked at Saul whose mouth was open in horror.

"I trust no one has any questions."

CHAPTER TWELVE
Zombie Corral

Westlake shuffled along the edges of the pen, gauging the dimensions of his new prison as surreptitiously as he could. It wasn't hard. The other zombies were doing much the same. They had that in common. Zombies incessantly tested barriers. It was like they couldn't help it. They were like yardbirds on the wrong end of their second dime, always pressing their faces against the fences.

In a way, he was starting to feel sorry for them. They wanted, without knowing what it was that they wanted. They were driven by an incessant and all-consuming need. He knew something about that. Most professional thieves did. There was always one more score to be had, one more job to pull. One more and I'll retire, that was the inevitable refrain.

But you never did. Not really. Because the need was a fire in your belly, and it grew with every passing day until you found yourself sitting outside the local branch of your bank, making notes about times and alarms and all the other minutiae that went into planning a clean heist. There were no retired thieves. Just old ones, and dead ones.

He pushed the thought aside. It was getting harder to stay on target. His mind kept taking little rambles off into the weeds of his memories. It was like he was losing cohesion. His body was rotting; maybe his mind was too. Not a pleasant thought. Nothing he could do about it, though. He forced himself to focus on the job. The job that the Ramirez in his head was saying: *help others*.

The pen was situated in what had been the parking garage of the casino, behind the loading dock. The exterior of the pen was made from stalled cars, chain-link fencing, barbed wire and repurposed wooden pallets. It occupied almost the entirety of one level of the garage, making efficient use of the pillars and walls. From the scratch marks on the floor and the drill holes in the concrete pillars, it looked as if it had been expanded more than once. Given the number of zombies crammed into it, it was probably due for another expansion in the near future. He wondered what anyone needed with this many zombies.

Another thing he noticed was the lack of anything other than walkers. No runners, no brutes. No crawlers, no floaters. All in good shape as well. Nothing missing more than one limb, nothing too desiccated. That implied something more than a random collection. There was a purpose behind this. Maybe someone was cultivating another assault force, like the one that had hit the pier. But why bother housing the dead when you could just round them up in the wild a few hours ahead of time?

As he prowled the edges of the fence, he kept an eye out

for weak points – places where the anchors were loose, where the metal was weak, where the wood was cracked. There were a lot of them. But there were also people with flamethrowers standing on the other side. Whatever they wanted the zombies for, they weren't taking any chances. The moment the dead got too rowdy, the result was a lick of flame and some crispy walkers.

Not enough guards, though. Only a handful. Why? Not enough troops to spare? Maybe. There had seemed like a lot earlier, but maybe that explained the zombie blitzkrieg on the pier. Maybe that explained keeping the undead within easy reach as well. Safer to cull a few from a pen than capture ones in the wild, perhaps. He filed the thought away.

A sudden disturbance on the opposite side of the pen caught his attention. The walkers were getting riled up. Something was going on. He sidled towards the noise, making sure to stay well back from whatever was going on. He paused when he realized that someone had come into the pen through the only gate. Said gate was set up facing the stairwell that led into the casino proper.

A phalanx of riot shields pushed through the wall of dead flesh. Cattle prods, batons and baseball bats darted out intermittently to clear the newcomers some space. The zombies retreated before this onslaught, but never for very long. Long enough, though. Catch poles slid out from behind the riot shields and snagged a trio of walkers. One, in a bedazzled cowboy outfit, tried to pull itself free and a cattle prod caught it in the spine.

The phalanx retreated, dragging their captives in their wake. Westlake followed, with the rest of the dead.

Something was definitely up. He paused, letting a zombie dressed like a Roman centurion in tacky casino plastic armor surge ahead of him. There were a lot of them, almost a full legion.

He watched as the gates were slammed shut and padlocked. On the other side, the phalanx had opened up. The zombies were hogtied by a crowd of guards in black. Keates stood nearby, smoking a cigar and watching. Westlake studied him, trying to recall more about who the man was, and why he knew him.

He'd worked for the casino; that much Westlake was certain of. Maybe he'd been the inside man for a con job – though why they might've needed one, he couldn't say. Up close, Keates looked older than he remembered. But then the apocalypse wasn't particularly good for anyone's health. Like earlier, he was dressed in paramilitary gear, the sort you could find in any police station in these United States of America. Tactical fatigues, body armor and weapons. The same gear as his people. If they were his people. The Keates he remembered, however fuzzily, hadn't been a leader – a natural second in command. A born number two.

Keates turned. Westlake followed his gaze. An older man, round and dressed like one of those retirees who haunted the boardwalk, approached. He was accompanied by several people in patched hazmat suits. They didn't look like guards so much as attendants. From the look on Keates's face, he didn't like the new arrival much.

"Only three," the old man said, loud enough to be heard over the groaning of the zombies. He looked at Keates, who shrugged.

"You asked for a sample, Brewer. I got you a sample."

"Are they fresh?"

"As daisies," Keates said. "Though I don't see why it matters."

"I don't expect you would, Mr Keates." The old man gestured to one of his assistants and they brought forward a tray of instruments. "You do not strike me as a man with much curiosity about the world or his place in it."

"Are you calling me stupid?"

Brewer shook his head. "No. You aren't stupid, Mr Keates. Merely ignorant, and intentionally so." He selected a syringe from the tray and gave it a few flicks. Then he went to one of the zombies, caught it by the chin and forced its head to the side, exposing its neck and the black veins that crawled there beneath its tattered skin.

He plunged the syringe into one of the veins without hesitating. When he'd extracted enough, he set it down on the tray. "Label this one with the date," he said to one of his assistants, as he selected another syringe. The process was repeated twice more. Westlake couldn't find any sense in it. What good was zombie blood except as a sure route to infection? "The drones worked then?" Brewer asked.

"As you promised." Keates blew a plume of cigar smoke into the air. "Gonna need more. Especially if Himself decides to take on you-know-who."

"Then you'll need to procure them for me. Or at least the correct parts, this time."

Keates grunted. "You asked for parts, we got parts."

"The key word in that sentence was 'correct'," Brewer said. Westlake noticed Keates's look of anger, and he couldn't help but let loose a raspy chuckle. He regretted it immediately, as Keates turned at the sound, one hand on his sidearm. "Did you hear that?"

"Hear what?"

"Sounded like someone laughing."

Brewer frowned. "I assure you, that is not likely."

"I know what I heard." Keates strode towards the pen, tapping his pistol with a finger. He peered at the milling zombies with a flat, keen gaze. Westlake kept himself from freezing only by a sheer effort of will. If he stopped, or moved back, Keates would notice. Something told him that wouldn't be optimal.

Instead, he allowed the other zombies to jostle him aside as they forced their way to the fence. Keates studied them all, blowing cigar smoke into their faces with studied disdain. His eyes reminded Westlake of gunsights. Brewer joined him, wiping the blood from his hands with a handkerchief. "It was probably nothing more than a necrotic exhalation – gas escaping from a corpse."

"You're telling me I heard a zombie fart?"

"I'm saying zombies do not, as a rule, laugh."

"You'd know, I guess."

"I would know, yes. You heard nothing, Mr Keates. I promise you." Brewer paused. "I heard they had a radio."

Keates stiffened. "Did you now?"

"I did."

"You hear a lot for a guy who spends his days dissecting zombies."

"I keep my ears open. Did they?"

"Not that it matters, but yeah."

"What happened to it?"

"I shot it," Keates said. He paused. "They made contact with someone."

"Was it the Duchess?" Brewer asked, his tone mocking. Keates rounded on him.

"You know better than to ask that," Keates said. He looked at Brewer like he wanted to murder him. Westlake wondered what that was about. Another thing to file away. A zombie bumped into him, and he instinctively shoved it aside. Keates didn't notice, but Brewer did. The old man's eyes fixed on Westlake with startling speed. Westlake paused, and he saw Brewer smile. Westlake tried to sway zombie-like and blend in. The old man said nothing. Instead, he turned away. A cold rush of fear filled Westlake.

"My mistake. Forget about it. We need to get these three downstairs anyway." Brewer turned to go, but Keates didn't move. He was still scanning the zombies, searching every rotting face the same way he'd searched the faces of people coming into the casino. The thought popped unannounced into Westlake's head and brought with it a memory: Keates, standing above the casino floor, watching him like a hawk. Finally, he flicked the bum-end of his cigar into the pen.

It struck Westlake in the chest and fell to the floor, trailing sparks. He watched it roll, coming to rest atop the faint outline of an access hatch. Another memory sparked in the recesses of his brain. Access hatches. Tunnels. There were maintenance tunnels running underneath the entire casino.

He looked up. He hadn't spotted any cameras, but that didn't mean they weren't there, that they weren't remotely working on whatever power remained. But if they were, they were likely aimed at the gates and walls, not into the pen itself. He shuffled over to the hatch and sank to his haunches. Milling zombies protected him from view as he brushed filth from the hatch, uncovering its shape. There was no way to open it from up here. Not without a screwdriver. Or a knife.

Westlake spied a walker with a shard of bone protruding from its leg. He reached out and carefully yanked it loose. The walker grunted, but didn't otherwise react. He scraped the sharp edge of the shard against the floor until it had come to a wicked point. Using the point, he attempted to unscrew the hatch. It was hard; more than once, he feared he might snap his improvised tool. But finally, the first screw gave way.

He didn't pause to celebrate before starting on the second.

CHAPTER THIRTEEN
Airfield

Calavera cracked his knuckles as he studied the airfield through the spiderweb of cracks that marked the truck's windshield. He'd brought the truck to a halt outside the gates, waiting for his pursuers to catch up.

A great number of zombies stumbled aimlessly across the airfield, many of them making a circuit and winding up back where they started. Almost a hundred, he judged, if his count was accurate. From what he could make out, they had come from all walks of life. Some wore the weather-frayed remnants of uniforms; others wore suits and dresses. A few were, or had been, ground crew.

He felt a ripple of sorrow as he considered the horde. Young and old, rich and poor, they'd all come looking for sanctuary and escape. Instead, they'd found only the worst sort of death. The zombies were not the enemy, whatever Ptolemy and the others thought. They too were victims of a great evil, a warping of the natural order. Their suffering was no less than that of those they devoured. That was why he sought to give them peace.

He and the others had made it to the Adirondack Regional Airport in good time, courtesy of one of the Villa's collection of vehicles, a late model Chevy truck with four-wheel drive. Unfortunately – or, fortunately as it went according to their plan – the truck was loud. But then, any vehicle was loud, when it was the only one on the road. Walkers prowled along the road, hunting for the source of the noise. A great number of them had pursued the truck as it neared, leaving a horde of zombies following them as they rushed to get to the airfield.

He was waiting for them to catch up now, occasionally honking the horn to keep them going in the right direction. His companions had bailed out up the road and headed into the trees. The zombies were fixated on the truck. So long as they stayed that way, Ramirez and the others could get to the plane without incident. If Santa Muerte was with them.

He glanced in the rearview mirror. A walker, still some distance behind, staggered towards the bed of the truck, hands reaching. More followed. Not so many as they'd feared, but enough to be troublesome if he let them swamp the truck. He cranked the engine. It stuttered and, for a moment, he was afraid it wasn't going to turn over. But the hand of Santa Muerte was upon him, and the truck roared to life.

He paused and retrieved a tiny icon from his coat. It depicted a woman's well-dressed skeleton: Senora de la Noche, Our Lady of the Night; also known as Nuestra Señora de la Santa Muerte – Our Lady of the Holy Death. He raised the icon to his lips and kissed it reverentially. "Watch over me, Lady of Shadows."

He placed the icon back into his coat and looked at his reflection in the rearview mirror. Carefully, he straightened his mask. As he did so, he was tempted to lift it, to view his face. But he resisted the urge. That man was a stranger.

He put the truck into gear. Moments later, he was barreling for the main gate to the airfield. Idly, he fiddled with the radio dial. As far as he knew, there were no radio stations left, but one lived in hope. He'd always preferred to exercise to music. To his surprise, he caught a snatch of voice, the end of a sentence. Then, music began to play, something released just before the apocalypse. He laughed in delight and turned it up.

He got the truck up to eighty by the time he hit the gates. He didn't slow down. The walkers between him and the parking lot either scattered or were run down. The truck fishtailed slightly as skulls and torsos were pulped beneath his wheels. He pushed open his door and caught a walker in the head, smashing it from its feet.

He spun the wheel and took the truck in a tight circle, hammering the horn with his fist as he did so. More walkers lurched into view, boiling out of the main building and the hangars. Others came from across the runways, all zeroing in on him, just as the survivors had planned. He reversed the truck and peeled out, leading them away from the parking lot.

Several of his pursuers darted ahead of the pack. The closest of the runners was dressed for the gridiron, complete with pads and helmet. A high school football player, maybe. Before he'd become something else. The runner charged towards the truck like an enraged bull.

Calavera kept it in reverse, but slowed slightly so the runner could catch up. It leapt and clawed at the hood of the truck, trying to clamber up. He stomped on the gas and sent the truck hurtling forwards. The runner went down with a crunch, under the wheels, and was gone. Calavera clucked his tongue, hoping for more of a challenge.

The driver's side window exploded inwards and a rotting hand shot through, clawing for his face. He laughed and turned, driving his fist into the walker's face, knocking it off of the truck. "That's more like it," he shouted. "Come on, come and get me!"

He brought the truck to a halt in the middle of the smaller runway and began to hit the horn as hard and as often as possible. At the same time, he turned up the music as loud as it could go. Walkers converged on him from every direction. Time was of the essence. His energy called to the dead, bringing them to him.

He felt no fear at the sight of them. Fear had been burned out of him well before the world ended. Or so he thought. In truth, he could barely recall the time before Santa Muerte had pressed her cool lips to his brow and claimed his soul. He remembered only the sound of the bell, and the myriad smells of bingo halls and bars. The faces of the crowd, staring up at him. Watching him rise and fall. Again and again.

The old aches hummed through him; a hitch in his rotator cuff, a persistent pain in his left knee. How old was he? He couldn't recall. The life he'd chosen aged a body ahead of its years. Had he been a good man, or a bad one? Virtuous, or venal?

He glanced at the rearview mirror again, but only the

empty sockets of a skull looked back at him. The eyes of Santa Muerte. And her eternal, unflinching smile. He nodded. "Yes, I hear you," he murmured.

Whoever he had been was gone; lost to the conflagration of the world's end. She had raised him up from the ashes of his former life, so that he might fight in her name.

She was angry, was the Lady of Death. She could not accept the loss of what was hers, and so she had gifted him the strength to send her stolen souls back to her. One at a time, if necessary. A task he was only too happy to accomplish.

When he judged he'd made enough of a spectacle of himself, he started to move. Not fast, just enough to keep the interest of the undead. The walkers could overturn the vehicle with enough time. But if he kept moving, they wouldn't have the opportunity. He craned his neck, trying to spot the others from where they should have emerged from the trees. He saw a flash of movement on the other side of the parking lot. He wasn't certain that it was his companions, but he had faith. Santa Muerte had extended her protection to them all, for they all did her work.

A soft, feminine whisper, in his ear – a warning. A ponderous movement, out of the corner of his eye. A brute, forcing its way through the crowd. It was clad in the tattered remnants of a dress, its face a stretched and swollen mess. He spun the wheel and the truck slewed about, out of immediate reach of the hulking zombie. The brute kept coming, shoving aside the walkers in its eagerness.

He popped the horn again, keeping its attention. Keeping all their attentions. Beyond, his companions darted across the sidewalk as a low, fast moving line, heading for the hanger. The brute's fists slammed down onto the tailgate of the truck, causing the front wheels to lift off the ground for a few moments. He stamped on the gas and the truck jolted forward, leaving the brute to sprawl on the ground in an ungainly heap. It wouldn't stay down long.

He heard the sputtering growl of what could only be a plane engine and smiled. Santa Muerte smiled upon them once more. As he had told Ramirez on many occasions, all things were possible with faith. He laughed out loud and threw the truck into reverse. It collided with the brute, just as the creature got to its feet.

The brute fell backwards and the truck stalled – but only for a moment. He saw the plane in his rearview mirror, taxiing down the second runway. He turned the truck around and headed in a wide circle around the airfield. The zombies followed.

Calavera made a hard circuit, crossing around behind the main building and the hangars. Zombies stumbled out from between the buildings, reaching vainly for the truck as it passed them. He turned the music up as loud as it could go and tore the knob off. An old song this time, one he thought he recognized. He hummed along, tapping the wheel as he drove, until Santa Muerte murmured in his ear. He looked back and saw a trio of shapes sprinting after him. More runners.

The truck began to slow and sputter. It was running low on fuel. He aimed for the runway and the blue Pilatus PC-12 rolling down it, the propeller on its nose spinning. The runners were closing in; so close now that he could make out the highway patrol uniforms they wore. He veered onto the runway, the truck jolting as it left the dirt and hit the tarmac. The runners followed him. The plane was gaining on him. The fastest of the undead leapt onto the back of the truck. Calavera ignored it, even as he ignored the other two as they drew up alongside him.

He honked the horn, and the hatch behind the wing began to lower. He swung the truck closer to the plane. The runner on the back hammered at the rear windshield. The glass was reinforced, but it was starting to crack. The other two were clawing at the doors. He had to slow down to make the jump to the plane, but if he slowed down too much, they'd be on top of him. He grinned and glanced at the broken cement block he'd tossed into the passenger seat. Luckily, he'd come prepared.

One hand on the wheel, he grabbed the block and rolled it over onto the gas pedal. It was heavy enough to depress it, but not heavy enough to press it flat. Even as he did so, the rear windshield collapsed into the backseat and the runner squirmed through, gory moustache bristling above a lipless, ravenous mouth.

Calavera kicked open his door. The plane was nearing the end of the runway. The wheels were lifting away from the tarmac. He was almost out of time. A runner leapt and he twisted aside. It collided with his door, tearing it off. Zombie and door fell away. Calavera clambered onto the top of the truck. It was difficult, but once a man had walked a ring rope, balance was rarely an issue.

A runner leapt onto the front of the truck and scrambled up towards him. Calavera waited until the last moment and then clapped his hands against either side of its skull. The runner's head came away in his hands and its body tumbled into the back of the truck.

He tossed the head over his shoulder and leapt for the open hatch of the plane, even as it left the runway. For a moment, he thought he'd missed. But then his shoulder connected with the steps and his flailing hand found the rail. He hauled himself into the plane as the hatch closed behind him.

Calavera looked up into the astonished faces of the others – save Ramirez who was at the controls, and Santa Muerte, who had never doubted him. He laughed and pushed himself into a leather seat. "What?" he said, rubbing his shoulder. "I told you it would work."

CHAPTER FOURTEEN
Interrogation

Harold Keates rubbed his forehead and wished that the casino hadn't run out of aspirin. He'd left Brewer to play mad doctor after helping him with wrangling the samples. He hated the old man with a passion; he still wasn't sure why St Cloud had decided to bring him into the fold. Sure, he was smart. But it was an ugly sort of smarts. The kind that only made trouble for everyone. But what St Cloud said went. For now.

That was his mantra these days. Sometimes though, he wondered if his new boss was playing with a full deck. The drones, for instance. He'd thought it was a good idea at first. But after seeing the devastation, and the consequences thereof, he wasn't so sure. They hadn't meant to kill anybody, but people had died nonetheless.

Keates wasn't sure how he felt about that. There were plenty of people he wouldn't hesitate to put a bullet in, but killing some random schmuck wasn't the same thing. They were supposed to be helping people, after all. Blowing them up seemed somewhat contrary to that. Then, maybe that was why St Cloud was the one in charge of the big picture and Keates wasn't. For now.

He pushed the thought aside as his prisoner gave a hitching moan. "Quiet," he said. "I've got a headache." He glanced at the man tied to the chair in the center of the old jacuzzi and then quickly away. No water in the jacuzzi now. Just a drain.

The room had three jacuzzis in it, and was tiled in alternating bands of chalk blue and pastel pink. Some of the tiles were missing, leaving bare patches of old plaster visible. It was a storage room nowadays, and an interrogation room.

St Cloud stepped into the room, closing the door behind him. "This is him?" he asked without preamble, looking down at the man tied to the chair.

"It is," Keates said, studying his employer. The owner of the Elysium looked as well put together as a male model. St Cloud knew the value of appearances, even in the apocalypse. Then, St Cloud was a classy guy. Or at least, that was how he presented himself.

Keates had his doubts. St Cloud, like a lot of men with too much money, struck him as being largely artificial. He'd seen a lot of that, before the world had ended. Men who hired people to dress them, to choose art for them, to schedule their days. Even to choose their vices for them. Keates kept his own vices simple – a bit of gambling, a bit of booze. Or he had, back before everything had gone wrong.

St Cloud's voice was always mild, his expressions barely there at all. He might as well have been a mannequin. But he had good ideas. That put him a step above most people in Keates's estimation. The way the world was, they needed ideas.

"He looks rough."

"He resisted."

"Must have been quite the tussle," St Cloud said, somewhat disapprovingly. "He must weigh – what? – a hundred pounds, soaking wet?" He turned the prisoner's head, exposing a bruise-like mark. "Is this a bite?"

"He came at me with a wrench," Keates said, defensively, ignoring the question. He'd nearly gotten his skull cracked. The raid had gone off without a hitch otherwise. They'd done it often enough now that they had it down to a fine science.

"After you shot the radio," St Cloud said. Again, in a tone of disapproval.

"After I shot the radio," Keates clarified. That was standard procedure. Procedure that St Cloud himself had insisted on.

"Who was he talking to?"

"I don't know."

"You didn't ask him?"

Keates paused. "Not my job."

St Cloud studied him for a moment and then said, "Your job is what I say it is. I want to know who he was talking to."

"So, ask him," Keates said. He was pushing it, he knew, but he was in a bad mood, and he was getting tired of St Cloud's attitude.

St Cloud grunted. He kicked the chair. The man tied to it looked up blearily. He'd been crying, Keates thought, with some disgust that was aimed not at the prisoner, but at himself and his employer. He quickly tamped the feeling down. "Your name is Manny, I believe," St Cloud said. "Your brother was in charge of the pier camp."

"I- I- yeah. Where…" Manny began. St Cloud cut him off.

"Dead. As you will be, unless you answer my questions quickly and truthfully. Do you know the name Ariadne St Cloud?"

Keates sighed internally. That explained it. St Cloud had a mad-on for his sister. Having met her, if only briefly, Keates could understand it. And from what little St Cloud had let slip, he figured throwing her off a boat might have been a matter of survival.

"The Duchess?" Manny croaked, a puzzled expression on his face.

"The…" St Cloud trailed off and pinched the bridge of his nose. "Damn her." Keates had to fight not to laugh. Oh, he found it highly amusing that she insisted on calling herself a duchess. St Cloud cleared his throat and looked at Manny. "What do you know about her?"

"She- she brings us supplies," Manny said, clearly puzzled. "Helps people."

"Supplies…" St Cloud murmured. "What do you mean?"

"She brings everyone supplies. Trades for ammunition." Manny swallowed. "Is my brother really dead?"

"As disco," St Cloud said, absently. His gaze sharpened. "Was that who you were talking to, when Mr Keates found you?"

Manny hesitated. St Cloud glanced at Keates. Keates cracked his knuckles. Manny swallowed and said, "N- no. Someone else."

"Who?"

"I don't know. Some camp in the mountains. They said they could help."

St Cloud hissed softly. "The mountains – you mean the Adirondacks?" Something in the way he said it caught Keates's attention. Like he was familiar with the place in question.

"What does that mean? What's in the Adirondacks?" Keates asked in a low voice.

St Cloud glanced at him. "Nothing. An old story my father used to tell us when we were children. It's not important." He looked back at Manny, paused and said, "I think we're done here. Dispose of him."

"You want me to kill him?" Keates asked.

St Cloud was clearly too preoccupied with what he'd learned to acknowledge the question. Keates turned back to Manny, who was shaking in his chair. Keates's hand fell to his sidearm. He hesitated, and suddenly felt St Cloud's eyes on him. "Have someone else do it, if you're feeling squeamish," St Cloud said, offhandedly.

"No," Keates said. He looked down at Manny and drew his weapon. He could be this person. For now. "I'm sorry."

Panicked, Manny launched himself up and slammed his head into Keates's gut, knocking him down and sending his pistol clattering away. It was the second time the little man had surprised him. Still tied to the chair, Manny tried to hobble away like an injured turtle. He didn't get far, however.

St Cloud scooped up Keates's fallen weapon and fired once. Manny fell, gasping. St Cloud stepped out of the jacuzzi, still holding the pistol. "I'd get up if I were you, Mr Keates. He's going to turn in a moment."

Keates scrambled to his feet and out of the jacuzzi. Manny's gasps became liquid and then turned into a rattle. St Cloud watched the little man turn with interest. "Not everyone turns zombie, you know. I find it fascinating to watch. There seems to be no common factor. It's pure, random chance. A gamble. Appropriate, given where we stand."

Manny began to squirm and thrash. He bit at the broken tiles like an injured animal as his eyes clouded over into dull opacity. Bound as it was, the zombie wasn't going to make it out of the jacuzzi any time soon. Keates held out his hand, his eyes fixed on the writhing corpse. "Gimme my gun. I'll finish him."

"Don't waste the bullet. Take him to Brewer. The good doctor will make something useful out of him." St Cloud handed Keates the gun. "Do you remember Nucky Johnson's safehouse?"

Keates paused. "I think so, yeah. That was that cache we raided about a week into all this mess, wasn't it? The one hidden in that hotel?"

The first week into the zombie apocalypse, St Cloud had sent them running all over the city, hitting different places and taking everything that wasn't nailed down. A few of those places hadn't been on any map or blueprint that Keates had ever seen. But St Cloud had known about them somehow.

"A safehouse, created by Enoch L Johnson, one-time political boss of Atlantic City. He used to rent it out to organized crime figures. One of several such locations in the city. In the country. An invisible web of hidden redoubts, spread across this once great nation. Useful sorts of places, if you're lucky enough to find them."

"Yeah, I always wondered how you knew about it," Keates said.

"Old money has its privileges, Mr Keates. Go back far enough in any wealthy person's family history and you'll find more than a few criminals – and plenty of secrets." St Cloud looked at him. "My sister knows about them, too."

"You think that's where she's getting the food," Keates stated.

"Among other things." St Cloud was nervous; there was a subtle tension in his shoulders and the set of his jaw. Over the years, Keates had gotten good at reading body language. It was one of the tricks you picked up, working at a casino. Keates almost smiled, but kept his face expressionless.

"There's something I didn't get a chance to tell you earlier."

St Cloud frowned. "What is it?"

"We were ambushed on the route back from Playground Pier. Zombies got through the cordon." He'd been thinking about it ever since they'd gotten back. It was definitely sabotage, not just a random occurrence.

St Cloud gestured dismissively. "That has happened before. Hardly an ambush. More like an accident. Accidents happen."

Keates ran a calloused palm over his short-cropped hair. "It's not an accident if someone cuts through the fence. They must have done it while we were busy at the pier. Probably drove the zombies into our path." He wasn't certain about the latter, but it was the sort of thing St Cloud employed him to think about.

St Cloud took a deep breath. "You think it was my sister."

Keates rubbed his chin. He needed a shave, but he needed sleep more. He probably wasn't going to get either for a while. St Cloud kept billionaire hours, which meant Keates had to keep them as well. *For now,* he thought. "If it was her, it was probably just a test. Counting our guns, gauging our effectiveness. Making us waste resources." He paused, then added, "It might have been her the other times as well. And if she's running food to the other camps on top of that, you got to wonder why."

"Not out of the goodness of her heart, I know that much." St Cloud turned his attentions back to the zombie in the jacuzzi. "She's up to something, Mr Keates. I can feel it in my marrow. She's always up to something." He shook his head. "Why isn't she dead?" he murmured absently.

"Got me. You're the one who threw her off a boat." Keates regretted the words the moment they left his mouth. St Cloud didn't like being reminded of what had happened the last time he and his sister had spoken, just before the dead woke up. "No offense," he added. "You did what you had to do."

"Yes. I always do." St Cloud straightened. He looked at Keates. "I've had a look at the list of our new arrivals. I've marked the names for the arena."

Keates nodded. "How many?"

"Just a few."

Keates nodded again, feeling slightly sick. He didn't like

thinking about the arena or what happened to the people who got thrown in it. "I'll handle it," he said, softly.

"You always do, Mr Keates." St Cloud smiled. "That's why I keep you around."

CHAPTER FIFTEEN
Tunnels

It took Westlake the better part of an hour to remove the other screw, pry the access hatch loose, and descend into the corridor below. He carefully closed it behind him, not wanting to risk letting his fellow corpses get out. At least not until he had a good reason. Thankfully none of them paid him – or the opening – any mind. Which frightened him, and made him question how much human remained within him.

It took him longer than he liked to think about to get down the ladder. His joints had a tendency to seize up at inopportune moments. There was no pain, but more than once he'd come close to snapping his elbow or wrist. It was odd; he was simultaneously stronger and more fragile than he had been as a living man. There was a part of him that wanted to push himself past his limits, just to see if he could somehow walk on a shattered knee. He figured that if he didn't notice, he might just pull it off. It was his conscious mind that was getting in the way. The bit of him that remembered being alive.

But it was getting harder to remember what that had been like. Maybe he was just adapting to his new circumstances. He'd always been good at that. At least he thought he'd always been good at it. The truth was, he couldn't recall much of anything beyond the basics and more recent events. If his mind was a building, the lights on the top floors had gone off. He felt a faint sort of distress about that, but it was a dull ache rather than a sharp pain. Maybe a person wasn't meant to come through the other side of death intact.

The access corridor was dark. Even the emergency lights had failed. He kept one hand pressed to the wall as he walked and tried to remember how to get back to the loading dock. He didn't have a plan as such. At the moment, he just wanted to know more about the lay of the land, who was in charge, and what they intended. But first, he wanted to know where they'd stashed the people they'd taken from the pier. He'd seen the vans peel off and head towards the loading docks after the convoy had pulled in through the outer barricades. So that was where he intended to start.

The utility tunnels were a silent labyrinth. The only living things he saw were rats, and the only dead things he came across weren't the type that got up and moved around. At least not anymore. Just mummified carcasses, all but withered to nothing. He didn't disturb any of them. Just kept moving. He could hear sounds from above, but couldn't tell what any of them were. He paused only once, near a door that led down to the sewers. Something thumped against it from the other side when he put his hand flat on the door.

He waited, but the thump didn't repeat itself. "Yeah, you just keep waiting," he murmured, tapping the door with his fingers. He marked it in his mind, just in case. Going through the sewers didn't appeal to him, but beggars couldn't be choosers.

Fingers still pressed to the door, Westlake turned. It was all coming back to him now; they'd mapped these tunnels. He'd come down here with… who? Maybe Spinks, the small tech-guy from Reno. He couldn't recall who'd been on the crew that time. Westlake pushed away from the door and started moving again. It didn't matter, really. But remembering that might mean that his brain wasn't completely compromised.

It took him another hour to find the steps leading up to the loading dock. The door wasn't locked, but it was blocked by something heavy. Boxes, perhaps? He managed to get the door open a crack, and heard the murmuration of voices and the sound of a truck engine. They must've been backing out the trucks. He waited until the noise was at its loudest, and gave the door a strong shove. Crates skidded across the oily floor and he managed to squeeze through.

He spotted the pen immediately. It wasn't large, but there were around thirty people inside. Most were sitting; some stood or leaned against the chain-link fence and looked out at the few guards on duty, none of them on their feet. The guards were sitting near the doors, smoking and talking. Not very diligent. Then, maybe they didn't have to be.

The loading dock was crammed full of stuff – high shelves and stacks of pallets, most of them between him and the doors. The jury-rigged lights were focused on the front of the loading dock, away from him. Another stroke of luck. Maybe someone was watching over him. He thought briefly of Calavera and his skull-faced saint. If anyone was going to look out for a living dead man, it was probably Santa Muerte.

He didn't have much of a plan. Plans came after you cased the joint. Moving slowly and carefully, he took a roundabout path towards the pen where the survivors from the pier were being kept. As he did so, he saw Keates approaching the pen holding a clipboard, and flanked by several other guards. Keates stopped in front of the pen, he called out, "Right, all eyes on me, folks. When I call your name, step out of the pen. Try anything funny and we'll shoot you where you stand."

"What's going on?" someone called from inside the pen. A short, older man.

"None of your concern, unless your name is on the list."

There was a murmuring at this. Keates raised his hands for quiet. "Look, it seems harsh I know. But we got to think about the greater good here, folks." He paused, and from his expression Westlake thought the words gave him no pleasure. "It's a matter of survival. We need every edge we can get. Every warm body, every bullet, every can of expired food buys us another day to make this place into something great. Everyone has a part to play... even if that part ain't exactly fun."

While he spoke, the guards pulled the gate open. Keates started reciting names. One of them – Saul Blum – happened to belong to the older man who'd spoken. Ten people in all were selected. A mix of young and old, men and women. Their hands were zip tied by the guards and they were pushed towards the doors that led into the casino. No one protested, though there were some loud complaints from those left behind.

Westlake wondered where they were being taken. He strained to hear as Keates turned to one of his subordinates and said, "Go tell Brewer he needs to get some of his zombie freaks ready. St Cloud wants to celebrate."

Westlake's eyes narrowed. Brewer. That had been the name of the old guy who'd been with Keates earlier. The one who'd noticed him. Some sort of doctor – or mad scientist? What was going on here? Brewer had said something about being downstairs. What was downstairs? Sludgy memories stirred. Utility rooms. The laundry. So, what was happening in the laundry? And what did Keates mean by zombie freaks? Only one way to find out.

Westlake turned and crept back the way he'd come. He felt oddly satisfied. His mind had something to chew on, a problem to solve. Maybe that was all he needed to stay human for a bit longer.

He hauled the door shut behind him as quietly as he could and headed back down the corridor. Not quietly enough, as it turned out. The cattle prod took him in the chest as he rounded a turn. Everything locked up tight and he went down, jerking and spasming, unable to control his limbs. Two guards stood over him, both of them armed with cattle prods and catch poles. They tapped him with the prods again for good measure.

Zombies weren't fans of electricity. Westlake recalled that much from his time in the mountains. The Saranac Lake survivor camp had used an improvised electric fence to keep the zombies at bay – at least for a time.

For a moment, he was back there, feeling the wind, smelling the trees and the stink of burning meat. He heard a dog bark, and a woman's voice – Ramirez? No, someone younger. Moments from the past and present jangled in his head like shards of broken glass.

There was no pain, thankfully. Just annoyance with himself and the inability to get back on his feet. Obviously, they'd have someone patrolling the access corridors. It had been stupid to imagine otherwise.

"I told you I saw it," one of the guards said.

The other grunted and nudged Westlake with the toe of his boot. "Yeah, yeah. What I want to know is how the hell it got down here."

"Might be a sewer entrance open somewhere. Who cares? Get it looped and let's get it out of here." Westlake didn't struggle much as the noose from a catch pole looped over his head and tightened about his neck. Just like last time, he let them haul him up and shove him forward. "What do you think?" the first guard continued. "Throw him in the parking garage with the others?"

The other guard shook his head. "Nah, too much effort. Let's just take him to the arena. They can always use another walker. Even a vanilla one like this."

The arena, Westlake thought. What the hell was the arena? He pushed the thought aside and concentrated on putting one foot in front of the other. He made a few half-hearted lunges at his captors and made groans that sounded more pitiful than menacing, just to stay in character, but mostly he listened while they talked. They talked about the casino, and Keates. They talked about someone named St Cloud.

The name rang a bell in his head. Did he know this St Cloud? The answer came to him as they took him out of the tunnels and into the casino proper. The foreign investor. The one who'd financed the casino job. He'd found out the guy's name afterwards, wanting to know just in case the job came back on him somehow. He never imagined it would happen while he was one of the undead.

So, this St Cloud was in charge. That was interesting. He wasn't sure this information was useful, but it might be in the future. The march was slow going as well, and he had time to map out the route, which hadn't changed much since the last time. A few extra fire doors, but no substantial differences. Memories of his last visit percolated to the surface. Sketchy, still, but things were starting to settle back into place. The more he used his brain, the better it seemed to work. Like working the kinks out of a sore muscle.

He paid special attention to the armed guards who stood sentinel over the elevators and fire doors. St Cloud had plenty of security people. He'd spotted more than a dozen of them on the walk up from the tunnels. They roamed the halls in small teams of two or three, watching everything and everyone.

Besides the guards there were plenty of other people. None of them were armed. Only the guys and gals in black got to carry weapons. In other survivor camps, everyone carried a weapon. But that didn't seem to be the case here. Another fact filed away for future consideration.

Finally, he was brought to a room off the main drag of where the casino floor had been. The door had been reinforced and barred. One guard opened it, while the other shoved Westlake inside and hastily retrieved the catch pole. The door slammed and he was plunged into darkness. He smelled rotting meat and spoiled blood. For a moment, there was silence. Then he heard the scrape of metal on bone.

A moment later, something hissed next to his ear.

"Ah shit," Westlake said, out loud.

CHAPTER SIXTEEN
Friendly Skies

It had been harder than Ramirez remembered, getting a plane in the air.

Getting to the plane in the first place had been easy, and she wanted to knock on wood that the rest of this journey had just as much luck. Calavera's distraction had worked as they'd planned. All the noise and movement had drawn the attention of every zombie on the airfield. She and the others had managed to cut through the fence and slip across the parking lot to the hangars without so much as a walker stumbling into their path.

They'd found the right hangar quickly, with Sayers's help. It had been right where she'd sworn it would be. The plane had been sitting right there ready for takeoff, in Sal Bonaro's private hangar. There'd even been a fuel pump handy. It was like a gift from God or some other deity. Like some divine force had been trying to make up for the last few months of crappiness.

She'd run through the whole pre-flight check the way her

instructors had taught her. The plane – a Pilatus PC-12 – wasn't a model she'd flown before, but the basics were the same. Just like riding a bike, only this particular bike had a fifty-three-foot wingspan.

But once they'd gotten the hangar open, and the plane out onto the runway, she'd realized that the damn thing handled like a bus. And not a nice modern bus, but one of those old yellow clunkers that had been in service since the moon landings. She chose not to say anything about that to the others, however. Instead, she kept her attention on the instrument panel and her hands on the controls. And knocked on some wood for good measure.

Thankfully, Calavera had done a good job of keeping the zombies occupied while she worked out the particulars of the plane. Now they were finally in the air and heading in the right direction. "OK, folks," she said, over the intercom. "It'll take us about an hour to get to Atlantic City, depending on the weather. Just sit tight and we'll be back on the ground before you know it." She paused, then added, "The no smoking sign is on."

Ramirez sat back, trying to get comfortable in the narrow seat. She felt oddly nervous; anxious. She hadn't felt that way in a long time. Scared, yes. Worried, even. But never nervous. She peered at the instrument dial, tapping the fuel tank indicator.

"Is everything copacetic?" Ptolemy asked, as he clambered awkwardly into the seat beside her. She glanced at him.

"For the moment. How's Calavera?"

"Utterly mad, but otherwise in one piece." Ptolemy strapped himself in, his eyes on the windshield. "How high are we?"

"Closing in on fifteen thousand feet. Why?"

"I do not care for heights."

She did a double take. "What?"

"I am also scared of flying." She noticed that he was tightly gripping the armrests and sitting as far back as he could. "It is not as bumpy as I imagined it to be."

"Jesus, Ptolemy," she said, shaking her head. "Why did you even agree to this?"

"I thought I had made that clear. I wish to help these people." He paused. "I hope that they are still able to be helped."

Ramirez frowned. She'd thought that the zombies were the largest threat any group of humans could face. There were too many of them, and they were too relentless for any survivor group to do more than survive and subsist without attracting the wrong sort of attention. Unless they got lucky. But the gunshot they'd heard on the radio bothered her. "What do you think happened there, at the end?"

Ptolemy hesitated. "I have theorized on this possibility before – hidden enclaves, building strength, waiting for some opportunity to expand into their chosen territory. The zombies, bad as they are, are a finite threat. Eventually, they'll rot to pieces, or eat each other. At least, that is the logical trajectory based on decay rates. If one is patient, and pragmatic, one might be able to simply... wait it all out. If one has enough supplies. Enough ammunition. Enough skilled people to create and build and innovate."

"Like we're doing, you mean?"

"No," he said, firmly. "We are doing the opposite of waiting it out." He glanced out the window beside him, blanched and looked down at his hands. "What we are doing is a good thing. A necessary thing. We need items, but we also need knowledge. Abilities that only people have." He looked at her. "Why did you agree?"

Ramirez leaned over and tapped another dial. They were using more fuel than she'd anticipated. More than they ought to have been. Were they carrying too much weight? She finally registered Ptolemy's question and peered at him. "To what? This?"

"To what else would I be referring?"

Ramirez chuckled. "I was getting bored."

"Survival is boring?"

Ramirez nodded. "Before we found the Villa, it was one day at a time. Now we can think ahead. We've got breathing room. That means we've got time to think. Time to think means time to get bored." She glanced at him and saw the look on his face. "Probably not the reason you wanted to hear, is it?"

"I admit, I had not considered the issue of boredom." He turned his gaze forward, watching the clouds. "I rarely find myself without something to occupy my attentions." He paused and gave her a sly look. "Westlake mentioned Atlantic City once or twice when we'd first met him, as I recall. He found it to be a place where he was happy."

Ramirez tried to loosen a persistent kink in her shoulder. "I suppose he did." She didn't like the turn this conversation was taking.

"Does that have anything to do with your decision to go on our journey to Atlantic City?" Ptolmey asked.

The question came out of nowhere. Ramirez looked at him. "Westlake is dead."

"We have yet to find the body," he said. "And closure comes in many forms."

"That doesn't mean he's not dead. Dead people walk away all the time these days, or hadn't you noticed?" Ptolemy fell silent, and Ramirez shook her head. "It doesn't matter anyway. Wherever Westlake is, I doubt it's Atlantic City. He'd have had to drive, for one thing, and I've never heard of a zombie that could do that."

"Technically, it's possible," Kahwihta interjected. She leaned over the back of Ptolemy's seat. "Muscle memory can account for a lot. If a zombie can open a door, or work an elevator, it can probably get a car moving."

"Zombies can't drive," Ramirez said again, more firmly this time. She began to count things off with her fingers. "Zombies cannot drive. They cannot sing. They cannot operate heavy machinery. These things I know."

"I mean, we don't really know that," Kahwihta said, a slight smile on her face. "Frankly, we don't know anything other than that we've seen, and while there are definite patterns to their observable behavior…"

"Can we not have this discussion right now?" Ramirez asked, somewhat plaintively. The conversation had veered into the sort of territory she didn't like to think about. "I just had a vision of zombies flying planes and it's not something I want on my mind at the moment. It's hard enough to keep this thing in the air as it is." She peered at the dials again. Plenty of fuel left. But nonetheless something was wrong and had been since takeoff. It had taken them too long to grab altitude.

Ptolemy leaned forward as well. "What is it?"

Ramirez hesitated, then admitted, "I think we're carrying too much weight."

"How is that possible? We cleared the plane, didn't we?" Kahwihta turned back to the compartment where Calavera and Sayers sat. Calavera made to speak when there was an audible thump from the rear of the plane. They all fell silent.

"Sayers, you said the plane was clear," Ramirez called out. Sayers was half out of her seat, a knife in her hand. She glared at the rear of the plane as if it had personally offended her. Another thump, hard enough to make something rattle.

"There was no one on board, living or dead," Sayers said.

"Did you check the lavatory?" Ptolemy asked, fumbling with his seatbelt.

Ramirez heard Sayers curse under her breath. "There's a lavatory on this thing?" she demanded. "Where did they fit it?"

"In the back," Ramirez shouted. Another thump. Louder this time. "And don't get pissy with me. You're the one who knew about the plane."

"That doesn't mean that I know whether it has a bathroom or not." Sayers gestured to Attila in exasperation. "Why didn't the damn dog let us know?" Attila began to growl. "Oh, now he decides to be helpful," Sayers said, in frustration.

Kahwihta made her way into the compartment. "It's not his fault. He's never been on an airplane before." She sank down beside the dog. The thumping had increased as the volume of their argument had gone up. Ramirez took another look back.

"Will one of you please go handle that?" she asked, harshly.

Sayers looked at Calavera. The big man laughed. "If you like," he said, and squeezed towards the lavatory. The luchador barely fit in the compartment. He had to stoop just to make his way to the back. When he found the hatch to the lavatory he paused, one big hand pressed to it. Ramirez nodded and he made to open it.

There was a sudden bump of turbulence and, unprepared, he slammed back into the bulkhead. As Ramirez whirled to check on the situation, she saw the lavatory door unlatch and pop open, disgorging an overweight walker in a pilot's uniform, its face hidden amid a cloud of buzzing flies. The zombie fell against Calavera, teeth snapping for his throat. He bellowed and punched it away from him, sending it staggering along the aisle towards Sayers.

She didn't hesitate, but sprang forward, knife held low. The blade punched into the underside of the zombie's chin. Sayers, with a skill born of altogether too much practice, angled the knife so that it slid upwards and into the soggy meat of the dead man's brain. She winced as the corpse's weight sagged against her, and a black fluid filled with maggots spilled down her arm and onto the floor, eliciting a nauseated gulp from Kahwihta. "Someone get the hatch open," Sayers snarled.

"What?" Ramirez shouted. The flies had scattered through the compartment and she flicked one aside in annoyance.

Sayers glared at her. "You said it was too much weight, so I'm getting rid of it."

"It is physically impossible to open a boarding hatch mid-flight," Ptolemy spoke up. "Regardless of what cinema might have us believe it would require a strength greater even than Calavera can bring to bear. Especially at this altitude."

"Then what do you want me to do with it?" Sayers demanded, gesturing to the corpse.

Ramirez hesitated. Then, "Put it back where you found it."

"What?"

"Unless you want to share the compartment with it," Ramirez added. "Your choice."

Sayers growled something unintelligible and shoved the body back towards Calavera. He caught it easily and swung the dead weight around, booting it back into the lavatory. It took some doing, but he finally managed to push the door shut.

Ramirez was about to reply when another bout of turbulence gripped the plane. The sky had turned gray, like slate, and the clouds had taken on an ominous thickness. Ptolemy craned his neck. "Is that... New York City?"

Ramirez glanced out her window. She didn't like the way the sky was looking. She'd never flown through a storm before. "That it is. Ever been?"

"Once," he said, and she found that she was surprised.

Before Ramirez could reply, Kahwihta suddenly leaned between them. "What's that?" she said, in a hushed voice. "Look, there – over the city. What is that?"

Ramirez followed her gesture and looked down. She could make out the tops of buildings, rising like gravestones from the cloud cover. The extra weight had pulled them lower than she liked. To her eyes it appeared as if the clouds were moving – undulating, like a shroud caught in a breeze.

"What is that?" she asked softly, unconsciously echoing Kahwihta. A chill gripped her, as the answer came.

Birds. Hundreds of them, maybe thousands. A flock of enormous size, rising out of a dead city to greet the sole inhabitant of the skies. She met Kahwihta's terrified gaze. "Muscle memory," she whispered. "Walkers can walk and birds... birds can fly…"

"The noise," Ramirez said, to no one in particular. This was her fault. They hadn't seen infected birds in so long that she hadn't even thought to consider it. "I didn't think about the engine noise. What it might stir up."

Ptolemy looked at her, his eyes widening in sudden understanding. He sagged back in his seat. "Can we go any faster?"

"We can try. Go buckle in," she said, casting a quick look at Kahwihta. "All of you, strap in and hold tight. This ride is about to get very bumpy."

"What is it? What's going on?" Sayers asked.

Ramirez grimaced. "The skies just got a lot less friendly."

CHAPTER SEVENTEEN
Meeting

St Cloud wiped the back of his neck with a handkerchief. It was warm, and the air smelled of green, growing things. He took a sip of his drink and closed his eyes, trying to imagine it was something else. Recycled water had its merits, but taste wasn't one of them. Better than nothing, however.

He opened his eyes and looked around the gardens. Originally, they had served a dual purpose: both to supply the kitchens with fresh produce and a ready supply of common herbs, and to give his employees and customers a curated green space for relaxation. Now, they mostly serve as a place to supplement daily scavenging runs. It was all very basic, but enough to keep scurvy from the door, at least for the moment.

"The new seeds?" he asked the garden overseer, a thin, toned woman named Boudin. He could detect the faintest aroma of human waste beneath the green. Night soil was an integral part of his agricultural expansion plan. He watched a group of people trundling wheelbarrows to the elevators.

Survivors, impressed into service where they could do the most good. A pair of armed guards watched them work, alert for the slightest sign of dissent.

Boudin shrugged. "As far as I can tell, they're growing. I'm not a gardener though. I always had people to do that for me." Boudin had been a minor celebrity prior to the world's collapse; she'd hosted her own radio talk show apparently, though St Cloud had never had the misfortune to listen to it.

"You still do," St Cloud said, pointedly. She laughed, but it didn't reach her eyes. She'd been a guest at the casino when things had gone bad. One of around twenty high-profile and well-heeled individuals who now had to earn their keep with honest labor. Boudin was more amenable to the new status quo than some, but she still wasn't completely onboard. None of them were. Yet one more problem he was going to have to deal with.

His kingdom needed haves to oversee the have-nots. People with a vested interest in keeping the wheels from flying off his new society, if only to keep themselves from having to shovel shit. But if the current crop wasn't producing, maybe he needed to change things up. It might even improve morale among the lower orders if he tossed a few overseers into the arena to face Brewer's creations. From the covert looks that Boudin's people were throwing her way, he thought that there'd be more than a few people celebrating her demise. Then, much the same could be said of him.

"Word is, we got a good haul of supplies from the pier," Boudin said, avoiding eye contact with him. St Cloud smiled and took another sip.

"Yes. Canned, mostly. Some medicine. Not enough, of course."

"It's never enough," Boudin said, harshly. "Harold told me that there are more zombies clogging up the streets every day." Harold was Harold Dix, a former casino whale and professional poker player. He also had a military background. St Cloud had put him in charge of the scavenging teams. Dix was not happy about that. Few of them were happy about their roles in the new world, though they were smart enough not to say anything.

"Harold talks too much," St Cloud said. "Have you started expanding the gardens to the lobby as I requested?"

"Yes, but it's still not big enough. Especially with thirty more mouths to feed."

"Twenty," he corrected, idly.

"My point stands. An increased population means an increased demand."

"It also means a larger workforce," he said. "Which we also need. This place wasn't meant to be inhabited long term and by so many, even if the guestrooms on the lower floors have been converted into dormitories. It will take time and sweat to make it into something… lasting." He looked at her "If we are to do more than survive, we must have a redoubt. This is that redoubt."

"We could leave," she said, after a moment's hesitation. "Harold and I and some of the others were talking. We think maybe…" She faltered as she caught sight of his expression.

"What do you think? Tell me. I'm all ears."

She swallowed and looked away. "It's just… the city isn't getting safer, no matter how many zombies we shoot or how many fences we put up. They keep coming and soon there won't be anything left to scavenge. It'll just be us, in here, surrounded by them."

"Ah," St Cloud said, in a mild tone. He didn't like such talk. It was defeatist. Defeatism led to despair, and despair led to foolishness. "And what was the consensus you reached? What do you think we should do about that, eh?"

"Maybe we should leave. Go somewhere else. We have the-the trucks, the buses. We could move nearly everything…" She trailed off again.

"You know, I based our defenses on the descriptions of the Roman camps in Gaul," he said, idly. "Some difference, of course. Modern materials and city planning require different solutions."

He took a sip of his drink. "As we expand our perimeter, the defenses will expand as well. I am planning to establish frontier redoubts at the furthest extent of our territory. All self-sustaining, with a monthly rotation of personnel. We do not want anyone out in the bush for too long."

"Expand our…? But we don't have enough people for that!"

"Not yet. But there are a few more survivor camps left in the city. Perhaps a hundred, maybe one hundred and fifty people all told. Then, of course, we can go outside the city for resources." He eyed her and was disappointed to see her face go pale. "It was never my intention to stay here. There is a whole world out there."

She stared at him. "Someone… someone said that the new people made radio contact with another camp. In the mountains."

St Cloud tensed. "Was this someone Mr Keates?"

"One of the guards, I think," she said, quickly. Too quickly. "I'm not sure which one. They all look alike in those black uniforms." She licked her lips. "Is it true?"

"What if it is?"

"What does it mean for us?"

"Nothing." St Cloud poured the dregs of his drink onto the nearest patch of soil. "It means nothing." He looked at her. "And you would do well to remember that. All of you. You have the privilege of my trust. It'd be unfortunate for us all if I had to revoke that privilege – but mostly for you."

She fell silent and looked away again. He took a breath. "You'll be at the celebration later, of course. A new crop of gladiators will be testing their skills against Brewer's creations. I'm assured this new crop of zombies will be a bit more durable than the last. And there'll be a special surprise at the end." When she didn't reply, he frowned and said, "Attendance is, of course, mandatory."

She swallowed and nodded. "I'll be there."

"Good." He turned to go. There were other people to speak to, other problems to solve. Some days it seemed as if his work was never done. Either way, he was looking forward to tonight. He took the elevator down to the main floor of the casino to see how things were shaping up.

Accompanied by his guards, he made his way out onto a large open landing overlooking what had once been the casino floor. Only now, where there had once been slot machines and blackjack tables, there was only a stretch of sand and rock. It was, or had been, intentionally reminiscent of the main floorspace of the MGM Grand which he'd seen once on a trip to Las Vegas, but this was, if anything, larger.

The main floor was on an open plan, hovering above the lobby on the ground floor. Once, you'd been able to look down from one to the other, but he'd had it all walled off with plywood to better isolate it. The new walls extended down into the lobby, blocking off a portion of it. He had plans to use that area for gardens, but nothing had taken shape yet.

The stores and restaurants on the level above had been refurbished into improvised stadium seating, all of it angled to give a view of the sands below. The casino wasn't a casino anymore, but games of chance were still played. Only now, the wagers were matters of life and death. He was quite proud of himself for coming up with the idea. Books were too valuable as fuel or compost, and televisions didn't work. That left live entertainment.

He leaned against the rail and looked down at the sand and gravel where once there had been expensive carpet. He closed his eyes, remembering the way it had sounded before. A riot of noise, coming from everywhere at once. Beautiful.

The feeling didn't last. His chat with Boudin had unsettled him. Thing were clicking along well, but that meant they were also at their most precarious. Too many days of poor pickings by the scavenging teams, too many casualties, and it would all unravel. He needed something big to keep his subordinates in line.

Unbeckoned, Ariadne popped into his mind. His sister the smuggler. But where was she finding these supplies that she was doling out all willy-nilly? Some cache or bunker he had yet to uncover, obviously. Perhaps it had been a mistake to ignore her. To leave her free and running about the city. But at the time, he'd had better uses for the resources at hand than trying to find his errant twin.

She'd tried to take his casino from him once. Who was to say she wasn't planning to try again? Maybe that was what she was up to with this supply and trade nonsense. She was making alliances, making herself welcome. Something he'd never bothered with. There'd seemed no point to it, given his goal. There weren't enough survivors in the city to make a decent army, not really. Nothing equal to Keates and his people.

But what about outside the city?

He was still pondering the thought when a voice called out behind him, "Boss, you're looking good!" St Cloud turned. Herc Mondo strode towards him, dressed in slacker best. Another of his valued guests-turned-overseers, Mondo was, or had been, a former MMA fighter turned digital celebrity – a streamer or something, whose channel and podcast had made him the voice of a certain slice of humanity. Herc Mondo was clearly a pseudonym, but he never answered to anything else.

St Cloud allowed him his quirks because he was good at keeping the crowds entertained. Kept them invested and cheering instead of thinking about the cost of their entertainment. "Thank you, Mr Mondo. You look well yourself. Have you had a chance to check out your new gladiators yet?"

Mondo grinned. "The pier folks? I'm heading down there

now, as a matter of fact. Want to come with me, watch me explain the rules?"

"No, thank you. I trust you to make the limits of their situation plain to them. Brewer has promised some interesting zombies for tonight. Have you seen them?"

Mondo shook his head. "Nah, but I've heard them. Lots of rattling and snarling in the chute," he said, referring to the set of rooms that had been converted into holding pens for the zombies marked for the arena. "Whatever the doc has done to those deadheads, it ain't made them any friendlier, that's for sure."

"Well, friendly would defeat the purpose somewhat."

"Ain't that the truth," Mondo said, and laughed. He paused. "These new folks though, I don't think they're going to last any longer than the previous ones. They're starving, scared. I'll be surprised if any of them last longer than the first night."

St Cloud nodded. Every dead body left on the sands went either to feed the gardens or the zombies penned up in the parking garage. Some of them even joined the latter, depending on their condition. "Either way, the house wins, Mr Mondo." St Cloud smiled coolly, and knocked on the rail with his knuckles.

"The house always wins."

CHAPTER EIGHTEEN
Arena

Saul ran his hand through his thinning hair. He felt as if he'd been in worse spots, but since the world had ended it had all been worse spots. He wondered when he was going to get a break. Just five minutes without having to worry about something trying to eat him, or someone trying to kill him. Five minutes was all he wanted. He looked up. "Is that too much to ask?" he murmured. As ever, God answered with silence.

Sighing, he looked around. He guessed that the green room, as he'd begun to think of it, had once been the counting room for this floor of the casino. It had reinforced doors and insulated walls. The guards had brought them up from the loading dock and deposited them inside without so much as a how-do-you-do. At least they'd removed the zip ties.

There were seven other people in the room, beside himself, Amos and Ruth. He didn't know the others well. They'd been recent arrivals to the pier. Both Amos and Ruth looked worried. He figured they had a right to be. Whatever surprises were in store for them, he doubted they were going to be pleasant.

He nudged Ruth. "It'll be OK," he murmured. "Whatever this is, we'll make it." She swallowed and nodded but didn't say anything. She was visibly stressed; so was Amos.

"Don't lie to the kids, Rabbi," a heavyset woman wearing combat fatigues said. She slouched against the wall, hands in the pocket of her field jacket. "Ain't nothing OK about this here shit."

Saul looked at her. "I agree, Miss... Carter, wasn't it?" As with the others, he didn't know much about Carter besides her name. She'd been with a National Guard unit at some point. What had happened to it, and why she was alone, were questions she had never volunteered answers for.

"Corporal," Carter corrected. "Or I was." She straightened. "I figure they picked us to make an example out of. Plain and simple."

"Yeah, what do you know that we don't?" one of the others asked – a biker with a shaved head and a face full of unpleasant tattoos. Saul thought his name was Leroy, though he'd steered clear of the other man as much as possible. The end of the world made for strange bedfellows but, given what he'd chosen to ink on his flesh, he didn't think either he or Leroy would get anything out of a conversation.

"I know we ain't useful. The kids have no skills to speak of, unless you want to raise a barn. The rabbi's old and you're trash. Me and Donovan are unneeded authority figures – seems they have their own hierarchy here, and we're probably surplus to requirements." She gestured to a balding, middle-aged man in the remains of a filthy highway patrol uniform, who grimaced but said nothing. Donovan was another latecomer to the pier; his car had broken down somewhere along the boardwalk, and the others with him hadn't survived the subsequent race to safety.

Continuing, Carter indicated an older man with a prosthetic foot. "Wachowski there is disabled – no offense, Wachowski. Perkins was a CPA, and it's not like those are in demand nowadays. Myra was a fortune-teller on the boardwalk, but since she didn't foresee any of this, she probably wasn't a very good one." A round man in a parka and dress pants made to protest, but fell silent as the woman beside him, dressed in what might have been considered boho chic before the dead had risen, shook her head. "And Gus over there, well, he's busy talking to the people in his head."

Saul glanced at the last of their little group. Gus was young, the same age as Amos, but there the similarity ended. He was skinny and unshaven, with a tendency to isolate himself and stare blankly into space. He'd barely interacted with anyone at the pier after his arrival. Traumatized, Saul suspected. It happened to a lot of people.

Gus paid them no mind. Saul felt a lurch of pity for the young man. He didn't belong here. None of them did – save perhaps Leroy. Carter's smile was sour as she went on. "What I'm saying is, for whatever reason, we didn't make the cut. So now, they're going to make an example of us."

Leroy snorted. "You, maybe. I got skills."

"That's good to hear, man. Because you're sure going to need them." The voice belonged to a short man dressed like a wrestling promoter in a violet jacket with fringe and matching suit, who stepped into the room. The newcomer was accompanied by a young woman with a sensible ponytail, dressed in a tracksuit and carrying a clipboard. They were flanked by a pair of guards, dressed as always in anonymous black.

"Welcome, ladies and gentlemen, to the arena," the man in the violet jacket said. "My name's Herc Mondo, and I'll be your humble host on this, whatchamacallit, auspicious day." The man began to hand roll a cigarette as he spoke. "First, let me congratulate you for being assigned the easiest job in Elysium. I should mention that there is a therapist on staff – wave, Phyllis – just in case you'd like to, y'know, discuss some lingering issues before or after tonight's bout." He nodded to his companion, who waved cheerfully. He finished rolling his cigarette and popped it between his lips. Phyllis stepped forward with a lighter and he was soon puffing away.

"Bout?" Saul asked.

Herc gave him a grin. "Like I said, man, this is the arena. And you guys are tonight's main event. Ain't that exciting?" He made a show of looking them over. "Yeah, I got to say, I got a good feeling about you guys. I think you've got what it takes to go the distance."

Saul stared at him. "Arena? What arena? What are you talking about?"

"Dig it, man. Elysium ain't just about survival, kids. We got the laughs, too. Entertainment for them what live upstairs. The bosses, you know?"

Saul glanced at the others, and then back at Herc. "Bosses? You mean St Cloud."

Mondo nodded. "Oh yeah, the Duke of A.C. himself. But not just him. He's got a whole court, brother. Everybody from that guy who was rich and famous to that other guy who was just rich, to poor old streaming stars like myself. The whole top floor of this place is for the uppermost of the crust, man. Including yours truly."

Leroy snapped his fingers. "I knew I recognized you. You were an MMA fighter, right? Then you had that show..."

"Always good to meet a fan," Mondo said, smiling.

"Man, you got your ass beat *a lot*," Leroy continued, smiling nastily. "It's no wonder you had to find a new gig."

Mondo's smile faded. "Yeah, well, we all got new gigs nowadays." He blew smoke into the air. "Regardless, they like to see some blood when they come downstairs."

"Our blood," Carter said. She took a step towards Mondo, but his guards moved to intercept her. Batons telescoped out and she hesitated. Mondo tapped his cigarette ash onto the floor and nodded, still smiling.

"Your blood, other people's blood, it all stains the sands red. But maybe it doesn't have to. Maybe you survive. You survive, maybe you walk out of there in one piece." He looked around. "Here's the deal. Once you go in, you're in for the duration. Zombies come into the arena and you fight them. You beat them, you get let out. Simple, right?"

"Let out as in freed?" Saul asked, doubtfully. The thought wasn't as pleasant as it might otherwise have been. Something told him that the good people of Elysium wouldn't be returning any of their possessions or supplies.

Mondo chuckled. "Oh no, my man. You get brought back here. You get to rest and recover. And then you get to do i t all over again tomorrow. Like I said, easiest job in the place."

"So why don't you do it?" Carter said.

"Someone's got to keep score," Mondo said, eyeing her warily. "We all got jobs to do, sister. This is mine. Yours is to go crack zombie skulls for the entertainment of the masses. They watch you fight and bleed, because they don't have to anymore. Lets them blow off steam and keeps them chill. You don't like it, take it up with the universe."

Leroy spoke up. "We going out there barehanded or what?"

Mondo nodded. "Glad you asked. If you'll direct your attentions thisaway…" He gestured as the door opened again and several people came in, wheeling trolleys full of weapons. Leroy and Carter immediately took a step towards the trolleys, but again the guards intercepted them. They'd obviously attended these proceedings before.

Mondo went over to one of the trolleys. "We've got a selection of the finest and most lethal weapons human ingenuity can provide. You got your machetes, your baseball bats, your hockey sticks – even a cricket bat, for your international types. And if you're looking for something less basic, well, we got you covered there, friends."

He picked up a baseball bat studded with nails. "Here's a fan favorite. We call it the brain basher." He set the weapon down and reached for a length of chain with either end connected to a chunk of cinder block. "This one requires a bit more skill, but it's another super addition to the arsenal. Give it a swing and try it out, if you like."

Mondo set that aside and patted a battered chainsaw

atop another trolley. "Another audience-approved entry. Everybody loves a chainsaw, especially when you don't have to worry about scrounging gas."

"Is that a weed whacker?" Saul asked, pointing to an awkwardly shaped trimmer at the end of the table. Mondo grinned and nodded.

"Good eye. That one's my favorite, I got to say. I removed the safety plate and replaced the blades myself. It'll puree a walker in seconds." He hesitated. "Or it'll jam up, but if that happens you can still hit'em with it."

"How about guns?" Carter asked. "You know, something with a bit of range?"

"No guns, but if you want range we have a nice selection of spears, made from a variety of gardening implements," Mondo said. "I encourage you to take two weapons, just in case. Once the walkers start swarming, you're going to be glad for a backup."

"Swarming?" Amos asked, doubtfully.

Mondo nodded. "Hoo-boy, yeah. We start you off with a handful, and then let a few more out to play every time the buzzer sounds." He paused. "A bit of advice: you'll want to watch out for the weird ones."

"Weird ones?" Ruth asked, looking at her brother.

"You'll see. Anyway, when the first buzzer sounds, that's your cue to skedaddle out into the arena, you dig?" He pulled an old-fashioned pocket watch out of his coat and made a show of checking it. "You got maybe twenty minutes before you have to go out, so use them wisely."

"What if we decide we don't want to go out?" Carter asked, pugnaciously.

Mondo pointed his cigarette at her. "Then we toss you out anyway. But we shoot you in the stomach first." His tone had lost all its previous jocularity.

"Living or dead, you belong to the arena. And you'd best not forget it."

CHAPTER NINETEEN
Zombie Brawl

Westlake pressed himself against the wall as the things that smelled of rotten meat and rusted metal paced and jostled one another in the crowded space. He couldn't tell what they were, other than dead. And big, for walkers. But not the kind of dead and big he was used to. These weren't normal walkers, but something else.

Thankfully, they seemed to share the rest of the zombies' lack of interest in him. At least, after they'd shoved him around and sliced him up a bit. He wasn't missing anything important, but he did feel a bit like he'd tripped and fallen into a Cuisinart.

He didn't know how long he stood there, out of the way, listening to the scrape of metal and the querulous grunts of his fellow captives. An hour at least. Maybe two. It was getting harder to judge the passage of time with any accuracy. His mind wandered if he didn't concentrate, and there was no way of telling how much time had passed when he finally snapped back to lucidity.

He tried to stay focused by thinking of a way out. He made a slow circuit of the small room, shuffling along, staying out of the way of his fellow captives. They stank in a way that was nasty even to him. Walkers smelled sweet in comparison. The guards had referred to him as a vanilla zombie and he didn't figure they were referring to how he might taste.

He pushed the thought aside and concentrated on the room. The store, rather. That was what it had been. He found a counter and a second door that probably led to a stock room. But everything else had been ripped out to make room for the small crowd of zombies that now occupied it. Another holding pen, then. The guards had mentioned an arena.

He suddenly recalled passing through a few survivor camps, back when he'd been alive. In one of them, the survivors had dug a pit and dropped two walkers in it. Every few days, they'd throw in a stray dog as well, and watch the walkers tear at each other in an effort to get to the animal. They'd placed bets on the outcome. Maybe it was the same here, only this wasn't two tattered walkers in a dirt pit.

He'd made his second slow circuit of the room when a red light suddenly flashed overhead, illuminating everything. For the first time, he saw his fellow captives – and froze. Not in fear, just in a sort of dull surprise. They didn't look like any zombies he'd ever seen before, something for which he was grateful. There were six of them; their ravaged flesh somehow scaly. More, they were covered in scrap metal.

Some had crude blades or bludgeons for hands, while the heads of others were completely enclosed in makeshift helmets. Others had been gutted, their chests and abdomens replaced by riveted plates, studded with shards of metal, wood and glass. A few crawled about on all fours, their spines and heads twisted and bent in exoskeletal harnesses that forced them to move like animals. At least one had had its mouth replaced by a set of ill-fitting steel jaws that resembled a beartrap.

The light began to flash and the zombies became agitated. Music started to blare and the doors at the far end of the room popped open. The zombies raced out in a clanking, clashing stampede. Westlake followed, but not too quickly. A rush of noise met him as he stepped out through the doors and into what he realized must be the arena.

The arena lighting reminded him of a disco. A mix of golden oldies and more modern hits – or modern before the music industry had gone the way of everything else. An announcer was standing on a raised section of seating, shouting a play-by-play through a bullhorn.

From where he stood, the stretch of sand and gravel seemed impossibly vast. Maybe it was just the noise. The stands above him were almost full – sixty, maybe seventy people and all of them seemed to be yelling at the top of their lungs. More than that, he could almost hear their heartbeats; the pulse of their blood; the industrial thrum of their brains.

He could almost see it, like a roadmap superimposed over them. The hum and pulse called to him, and the smell – God, the smell! He couldn't remember real food, but he somehow knew this would taste better.

He turned as the sound of a chainsaw close by tugged

at him. The metal zombies were loping towards a knot of activity a short distance away. Walkers – normal ones – were attempting to swarm a small group of survivors. The latter were armed with a variety of improvised weapons, including the chainsaw and what looked like a weed whacker. He started moving towards the confrontation without thinking.

As he approached, a survivor took a zombie's head off with a swing of his spiked bat. The body lurched past him, hands flailing, before it finally toppled over, to the cheers of the crowd. Westlake saw that the survivor, a young man, was bleeding from several scratches on his arms and face. He imagined taking a bite out of his neck. Of ripping away a mouthful of meat and chewing and chewing *and chewing…*

He thrust the thought down. Stamped on it. Padlocked it. The metal-zombies had reached the fight and were smashing and slashing at the walkers in their eagerness to get to living prey. Above him, in the stands, people were on their feet, leaning over to get a better view. That only riled the metal-zombies up more. Some of them were attacking each other, bludgeoning or hacking ineffectively at their armored fellows. But the rest were laser focused on the survivors.

An old man with a prosthetic foot was the first to die as a metal-zombie slammed into him and grappled him, piercing him through with the spikes and shards on its chest. He was dead even as it started to feed. Westlake circled the creature and saw that the old man had dropped a baseball bat studded with nails.

He snatched it up and turned to see a biker-type covered

in tattoos catch a zombie in the back with a blow from a weed whacker. The zombie fell onto its face and the biker pinned it down with his foot while he trimmed its hedges. The zombie twitched and gurgled as he chopped it apart, filling the air with the flaky remnants of golden body paint.

The biker spotted Westlake, and his eyes widened. Before he could say anything, however, one of the metal-zombies removed his head with an awkward, flailing slash of its blade arm. It hadn't even been looking at him while it did it, too focused on pursuing one of the other survivors.

Westlake stepped back as the biker's head bounced past his feet. The crowd roared in what might have been pleasure. Westlake cursed under his breath. It was mayhem.

A metal-zombie lurched past him, slamming its bludgeon fists together as it pursued a young woman and an older man. "Rabbi, look out," she cried, as the thing reared up over them, fists raised. The older man, holding what looked like a hockey stick with a knife attached to the end, thrust his weapon at the zombie. The knife end skidded across the metal-zombie's reinforced hide. It gave a guttural roar as it brought its fists down on the ground, knocking them both sprawling. It turned, focused on the young woman.

"Ruth – run!" the older man shouted, as the metal-zombie raised its fists over her. Westlake, behind it, slammed his bat into the small of its back. There was no metal there, just scaly skin. The metal-zombie staggered and whirled, nearly clobbering him with a fist. Westlake ducked and hit it again, across the face this time. The metal-zombie stumbled and he hit it a third time, breaking the bat across its skull. The crowd screamed.

It shook its head, as if trying to clear it. As it did so, Westlake stabbed the jagged end of the broken bat into the side of its skull. He rode it to the ground, stabbing it again and again, until it finally ceased twitching.

As he rose, he caught a flicker of steel out of the corner of his eye, and felt something grate against his ribs. A knife; someone had stabbed him. He turned and saw the young woman backing away. He looked down and saw a clasp knife jutting from his side. He plucked it out and stared at it, at the tarry muck that coated the blade. His blood, gone sour now. He looked at her. "That was uncalled for," he rasped.

"What…?" she began, staring at him in horrified wonder. Westlake shook his head.

"No time. Get moving. Help your friends." He indicated the knife. "Oh, and I'm borrowing this." He turned away from her, towards another of the metal-zombies. The other survivors were falling back, grouping up now that they didn't have so many walkers pressing them. The metal-zombies stalked after them. Only three were left. Good odds, but not the best. Maybe he could even them.

He took a step towards them, but he was interrupted by one of the few remaining walkers, this one in glasses and a sports jacket. It staggered towards him, or maybe it was just trying to get past him. Either way, he didn't hesitate. He stabbed it through the broken lens of its eyeglasses, and the zombie folded up like a discarded box.

He heard a grunt and turned. One of the metal-zombies prowled awkwardly towards him on all fours, the hinges of the steel struts on its limbs squeaking. It had evidently decided he was either prey or a rival. It scrambled towards him with startling speed, dragging a tail made from several lengths of bike chain.

Acting on instinct, he let the knife snap forward, out of his hand. It struck the zombie in the head, cracking bone. It reared back, clawing at the knife embedded in its skull. While it was distracted, he circled it and leapt onto its back. Before it could throw him off, he caught hold of either side of its head, hauling backwards with as much strength as his dead muscles could muster. The zombie reared, grabbing vainly for him.

Westlake kept pulling, ignoring the sensation that warned him his own muscles were at their utmost. Then, with a sound like a melon being cut in two, the zombie's head came apart in a splatter of gore. Westlake fell to the ground and his opponent collapsed almost on top of him. He clambered to his feet, feeling gingerly at his arms and shoulders. Nothing seemed torn or dislocated; rather, everything was working, at least. A buzzer sounded, and a set of doors opened along the nearest wall.

Expecting more zombies, he went for the knife. But instead, guards in black riot gear thundered into the arena. The remaining metal-zombies stiffened and he smelled the acrid tang of electricity, but saw no cattle prods. Smoke billowed from the head of one of the zombies as it collapsed in a twitching heap. The few remaining walkers did so as well, thrashing and clutching at their skulls as if in pain.

In moments, Westlake was the only dead man on his feet. But not for long. Several of the guards advanced on him, catch poles and batons at the ready. He considered playing dumb walker again, but realized the jig was up. He tossed the knife aside and raised his hands.

"No need for violence," he croaked. "I'll go quietly."

CHAPTER TWENTY
Flock

Kahwihta watched as the flock rose up out of the ruins of New York City. They were far enough away for the moment that she couldn't make out individual birds, just a dark mass boiling upwards. It spread as it rose until the city skyline was all but blotted out by the sheer number of feathered shapes.

Animals were not as susceptible to turning zombie as humans were. It took more time and special circumstances. The most common cause was the regular ingestion of zombie flesh. Eat a zombie, become a zombie. Scavengers were prone to this; she'd seen it in rats, birds, dogs, bears – even a house cat, once. That had been a bad one. Attila had nearly lost an ear. She reached down and scratched the dog on the snout.

"They're still coming," Ramirez muttered. "How many of them can there be?"

"There was supposed to be one pigeon per person in New York City, before things went wrong," Kahwihta said, absently. "So, around eighteen million, give or take."

Ramirez grimaced. "Oh, that makes me feel better. Thank you for that."

"Could be worse," Kahwihta said. "Could be rats." She leaned over the back of Ptolemy's seat. "Can we go any faster?"

"Not without using up a lot of fuel. And even then, I don't figure it'll be fast enough." Ramirez tapped a gauge. Kahwihta wasn't certain what that accomplished, but it seemed to make Ramirez feel better. Maybe it was akin to sympathetic magic. Tap the gauge enough, and maybe it'll change the reading. Ramirez cleared her throat. "Between the extra weight and the headwinds, we can't get enough altitude."

"Altitude doesn't matter," Kahwihta said. "Nor does speed, really. If those birds are dead, they'll keep going until they fall apart." She bit her knuckle, trying to think. She was supposed to be the zombologist, after all. "The noise of the engines is drawing them after us. So long as we're in the air, we're a target. They'll keep after us until they catch up."

"How dangerous can a few pigeons be?" Sayers asked from the compartment. She and Calavera were standing near the hatch. From Sayers's expression, she felt as useless as Kahwihta did. It was hard to tell how Calavera felt, what with the mask, but the way he kept flexing his hands said he wasn't happy.

"If they get sucked into the engines, very," Ptolemy said. "How close are we to Atlantic City? Do we have time to reach the airfield before they catch up?"

Ramirez frowned. "Maybe. I might have to put down before then, though. Especially if we keep pushing it this way. Faster we go, the more fuel we burn."

"What about the plan?" Sayers asked.

"A plan is only as good as its first meeting with the enemy," Calavera said. He went back to the rear of the compartment and sat down. Sayers looked at him.

"What are you doing?"

"Resting. For when I am needed. Which is what you should be doing." Calavera gestured to the seat nearest him. "Ramirez will do what she can, but our fate is now in the hands of Santa Muerte. We must be ready for her call."

"Good idea," Ramirez said. "I could do with a bit less crowding up here, thanks." She glanced at Kahwihta. "That means you too. Take the dog with you. And buckle your seatbelt, please."

"I don't think a seatbelt is going to help," Kahwihta said. The birds were still rising. Not as one, as she'd first thought, but in clumps – flocks within flocks. Zombies – human ones – did something similar. She pulled a battered Moleskine travel notebook from her coat pocket. She'd filled up almost a dozen notebooks of varying sizes since the end of the world. Notes, sketches, theories. She wasn't sure how useful any of it was, but it kept her mind busy, and that was a good enough reason to do it.

Ramirez shook her head. "Humor me."

Kahwihta saluted. "Sure thing, Boss."

"Don't call me Boss!"

Kahwihta laughed and made her way to a seat. It felt good to prod Ramirez in such a way, falling back on old nicknames from when they'd first met a long time ago at a resort town. As she strapped herself in, she took a look out the nearest window. The birds were a lot closer now, and the city far behind. Like regular zombies, the closer they got to prey, the quicker they moved. They were shedding pieces of themselves as well, leaving a cloud of particles in their wake. She imagined she could hear the thunderous flutter of their arrival.

That was interesting. They were also definitely hunting by sight and sound rather than by scent. Something to remember for the next time they decided to use a plane. If there was a next time. She started making notes.

Rather than taking a seat, Sayers went to the small galley area at the back of the compartment. "What are you doing?" Kahwihta asked.

"Looking for something to drink." Sayers found a bottle of something Kahwihta thought was wine and gave it a shake. "Oh, that's a good vintage."

Kahwihta stared at her. "You know about wine?"

Sayers popped the cork and sniffed. "You don't?"

Before Kahwihta could reply, a dull thump echoed through the compartment. Then another, and another. Attila began to growl. Kahwihta looked at the window. What might once have been a pigeon struck it hard enough to spiderweb the outer layer of glass. The remains of the bird slid away, caught by the wind. More thumps, like gunshots. She heard Ramirez curse. "Hold on, everyone! They caught up with us quicker than I thought. I'm going to try and punch through them – gah!"

There was a boom, a flash of light, and the plane bucked sideways, making Kahwihta glad she'd buckled herself in. She grabbed Attila as he shot to his feet, whining, eyes wide. Sayers wasn't so lucky. She bounced off the galley door and fell back, cursing. Calavera reached out to steady her. "What was that?"

"We've lost an engine," Ptolemy called out, looking back at them from the cockpit. "I suggest you take your seats and hold on."

Sayers fell into a seat, cradling her head. "I don't think we're going to make the airfield," she snarled, as she hurriedly buckled herself in.

The next few minutes were chaotic ones. The plane seemed to spin and roll. Bird strikes continued. *Thump-thump-thump-thump*. Kahwihta heard Ramirez cursing as she struggled to keep the plane in the air. She felt a chill draft and turned. A crow, its ribcage split and maggots wriggling in its fur, pecked at the window, losing pieces of itself to the slipstream even as it worked.

She watched in sickened fascination as it carefully pried away at the broken outer glass and started to go to work on the inner, losing a wing and most of its feathers in the process. It was resisting the wind through sheer cussedness. Determined. Insistent. Persistent. Like all zombies. The dead had nothing but patience.

Her world shrank to the crow and the window. Entranced, she put her hand to the glass, and felt the *tap-tap* reverberation. What was left of the bird grew frantic, frenzied. Down by her feet, Attila's growling increased. The plane shuddered. Ramirez shouted something that Kahwihta couldn't make out over the sound of the plane going down. All she could do was watch the crow do its damnedest to reach her eyes.

A lick of flame from the damaged engine caressed the

crow, setting its few remaining greasy feathers alight. Kahwihta shrank back into her seat. The burning bird gave no sign that it had even noticed the fire that slowly consumed it.

The plane jolted. The crow vanished. Kahwihta felt her stomach hurtle upwards into her mouth. G-forces pressed her painfully back into her seat. The compartment shook wildly, and it was all she could do not to vomit. A scream backed up in her throat. The next few moments stretched into an eternity of sound and fury. Then–

Impact.

Everything blinked out, just for a moment. At least she thought it was just a moment until Kahwihta found herself on the floor of the compartment. Everything hurt. She looked around. Smoke filled the interior. She coughed. Her eyes blurred with tears. She couldn't breathe. Her chest felt as if something heavy were pressing down on her. She heard Attila whimper and felt the rough rasp of his tongue on her cheek. "I'm OK," she wheezed. "I'm all right. Let me up." She flailed, found an armrest, and pulled herself into a sitting position. She blinked, trying to orient herself.

The compartment looked as if it had been crushed in a giant fist. There were sparks in the air, and she could detect the tang of spilt fuel. The smoke was too thick to see much past her own nose. Attila pressed himself against her, whining urgently. "Yeah, I know," she murmured. "We have to get out of here. But where's the hatch?"

As if in answer, there was a crunch from nearby. She heard a grunt and another crunch. Then a third, and with a definite creak of metal as something gave way, a shaft of grainy light pierced the smoke. She saw a vague outline she thought was Calavera wrench the rest of the hatch free of its busted hinges and hurl it aside.

The big man paused, and for a moment, as the smoke whirled about him, she thought she saw something – someone – behind him. A woman, maybe. But thin, oh so thin, and white – too white, bone white. The woman had one impossibly thin – fleshless? – hand on Calavera's shoulder, as if urging him on. Or perhaps restraining him. It was impossible to tell. The woman was gone, and Calavera was stretching a hand towards her. "Kahwihta, come – hurry!"

She lurched towards him, the world spinning. He caught her hand and pulled her to him, before tossing her out. Attila followed with a bark. Calavera ducked back inside, and she could hear him shouting.

She looked around. They'd crashed on an oceanfront boardwalk, tearing up the wood and the street alike. Abandoned cars littered their path, and busted storefronts surrounded them. She could smell the ocean, taste the salt on the air. She took a shaky breath. "I guess we made it," she coughed.

"You OK, kid?" Sayers asked, roughly. She stood nearby, atop the twisted wreck of a car. She had her bow in her hand, an arrow nocked and ready. Blood stained the side of her face and matted her hair.

"I'm in one piece, I think," Kahwihta said, hauling herself to her feet. "You?"

"My head hurts." Sayers squinted. "We made a lot of noise coming down."

Kahwihta understood why Sayers wasn't actively pulling the rest of them from the compartment. She was defending them from attack. Kahwihta followed her gaze and saw forms stumbling through the smoke that marked their trail. A lot of them, in fact. She'd lost her gear in the crash, but she still had her icepick. She fumbled it out but it seemed a paltry defense at best. Still, something was better than nothing. "Oh, that is definitely sub-optimal."

"You sound like Calvin," Sayers said, peering down the shaft of the arrow. She loosed it, flinched, and shook her head. "Dizzy."

"Concussion?" Kahwihta looked up at her. "You're bleeding."

"I don't have time to bleed."

Kahwihta grinned. "Love that movie."

Sayers blinked. "Movie?" She reached for another arrow but was distracted as Calavera returned, carrying both Ramirez and Ptolemy over his broad shoulders. "What happened – Calvin?" She forgot what she'd been doing and scrambled down off of the car as Calavera laid his burdens on the ground. Both Ramirez and Ptolemy looked the worse for wear; they were bloody and covered in glass and broken metal.

Kahwihta took Ramirez's pulse. It was thready, but there. Ptolemy was the same. He groaned as she checked him, and tried to sit up. "What … ?" he mumbled.

Sayers knelt beside him. "Calvin, look at me. How many fingers am I holding up?" She held up two fingers. Ptolemy blinked in apparent confusion. Sayers frowned and looked at Kahwihta. "How's Ramirez?"

"Unconscious," Kahwihta said, lightly slapping the downed woman on the cheeks. "We need to wake her up. There's no telling how long she's been out."

"A minute, maybe less," Calavera said, looming over them. His clothes were ripped and bloody. There was glass in his bare flesh, but he didn't seem unduly concerned. "She got Ptolemy out of his seat before she passed out. Tough woman."

"That's good," Kahwihta said. She looked at the others. "I took some general first aid courses, but I'm not a doctor. I think we've got to wake her up."

"Is that strictly safe?" Calavera asked, doubtfully.

"Absolutely not, but if she stays out of it for too long, she might not wake up." Kahwihta turned. The sound of that all too familiar moaning was getting louder. The smoke was thinning, and she could see the approaching walkers clearly. They'd probably been drawn from all over the city by the sound of the crash. Like the birds, they would keep coming until they reached critical mass.

"We can't go anywhere with her out of it," Sayers said, rising to her feet. "Calvin's in no shape to run either."

"I could carry them," Calavera said.

Kahwihta looked at him. "Both of them? While running from zombies?" She shook her head. "You're strong, but not that strong. We need them on their feet."

Calavera nodded. "Fine. Do what you can. Sayers and I will buy you time." With that, he stripped off the remnants of his shirt and wrapped the rags about his forearms. He looked at Sayers. "Cover me."

Then, with a roar, he charged to meet the oncoming horde.

CHAPTER TWENTY-ONE
Interruption

"Yes, there's a good boy," Brewer said, holding up the scrap of meat. Pierogi danced on his hind legs, ragged jaws open and gave a thin, wet whine. Brewer tossed the meat into the animal's waiting mouth. "Nummy-num. Eat it up, there's my cheerful boy." He still wasn't sure how the dead animal's digestion processes worked, but Pierogi never seemed to suffer unduly from a belly full of food.

The little dog had been his constant companion since Myrtle Beach. He'd been living in a retirement community there, before the world had come to an end. Playing golf every other day. Rotting his mind with all the delights on offer from modern television. Heaven, for a certain simple sort of soul. Pierogi had been a gift from his daughter for Father's Day or his birthday, he forgot which. It didn't matter.

When his neighbors had smashed through his door, looking to feast on his insides, he'd dispatched them, packed up Pierogi, and taken to the road. His first thought, of course, had been for his daughter and her family: his son-in-law, his granddaughters. He'd gone to them, but he'd arrived too late.

Brewer swallowed and took a steadying breath. As always, that served well enough to banish the memories before they overwhelmed him entirely. He'd always been good at compartmentalizing his emotions. Pierogi was all he had left now.

He scratched the dog behind the ears and then absently wiped his hands on his trousers. Pierogi, like all zombies, was subject to consistent, if somewhat slowed, rates of decay. Eventually, his beloved Pekingese would be nothing more than a sack of wet carrion. He'd considered numerous possible solutions, including a course of formaldehyde or other preservatives. But he intended to test his theories on more disposable subjects before subjecting poor Pierogi to any further experimentation.

He tossed Pierogi another scrap of meat and spun his office chair back to face the whiteboard that occupied the far wall. A list of needed supplies to make the receivers was taking shape there, but some items on the list would be for his own use. St Cloud's people couldn't tell the difference, and he saw no reason to make it obvious.

He leaned forward and added formaldehyde to the list, as well as methanol and glutaraldehyde. With those, he could mix up an embalming fluid that might serve to preserve Pierogi as well as his other test subjects. Not that he didn't have other uses for it as well.

A large part of his time was spent preserving zombies for use in the arena. No one wanted to see a common rotter bashed to pieces. They wanted a challenge, such as walkers in good condition, ready to put up a bit of a fight. He did what he could to set broken bones, stiffen collapsed torsos and otherwise put some pep in their shuffling steps.

Sometimes he even outfitted them with weapons to spice things up a bit. Claws, fangs – a tail, once. All easily assembled from scrap metal and plastic. Taxidermy had been a hobby of his for many years, and the old skills were coming in handy. But that wasn't why St Cloud kept him around. It wasn't even for his anti-zombie measures. No, St Cloud had bigger plans. Grandiose ones, in Brewer's opinion, but he kept that to himself.

An influx of supplies would allow him to make another two dozen receivers, depending on the quality of the materials, both mechanical and otherwise. Of those, he estimated that roughly a third would burn out on first use, the way Pierogi's had. He glanced down at the dog and frowned. Pierogi was now on his fifth implant, the others having either malfunctioned or simply not worked to begin with.

It was a tricky thing. An ad hoc concept, cobbled together from old notes and designs. There was no guarantee it would work for any real length of time. But it would serve well enough to keep St Cloud happy, at least for now. Brewer calculated that he had another four weeks before the other man skewed his courage to the sticking place and started asking outright for a zombie army, and then demanding it.

He turned his chair to face El Gigante's cage. The hulking zombie crouched in its web of chains as silently as ever, seemingly dead to the world. Its docility was another of his innovations. A steady diet of a cerebrospinal fluid cocktail, drawn from other zombies, and delivered via a jury-rigged insulin pump to the base of its brain stem.

He wasn't sure why soured spinal fluid had a medicating effect on the creature, but then he wasn't a biologist. Just an engineer. All he knew for certain was that El Gigante required injections every half hour, save on those occasions where it had fed well in the arena. Then it entered a torpor-like state for at least twelve hours.

Brewer rose from his chair and went to his instrument table, where he selected a steel industrial syringe and a plastic milk jug. Pierogi followed him, snuffling at his heels. He gave the needle a flick and went to the pens, where his current crop of test subjects waited. Since he was thinking about it, he might as well collect more.

Normally, he would have had assistance for the extraction procedure, but he'd let his assistants go to the arena for the night's show. In truth, they weren't very helpful. They mostly just brought him food or got in the way or cowered in fear when having to administer El Gigante's injections. But St Cloud insisted that many hands made for swift work. Brewer had tried to explain that swift work wasn't necessarily good work, but he wasn't sure it had penetrated. He'd chosen not to argue the point further.

It wasn't as if he needed the help in any event. Extracting the cerebrospinal fluid had much the same effect as injecting it, but since they apparently had no capacity to produce it, or at least not in the amount needed for a functioning system, the effects were permanent: a loss of mobility, of function and of awareness. It reduced them to little more than ambulatory organ farms. The three from the current crop paid him little attention as he let himself into the pen and began the extraction procedure.

Soon enough, the jug was full. But as he turned to go, one of the walkers gave a sudden grunt and lurched towards him. Brewer stepped back, out of immediate reach. "Little bit of fight left in you, eh, my friend?" The zombie replied with a guttural growl and shuffled after him. Brewer set the jug down carefully – no reason to waste it, after all – and readied the syringe. When the walker had drawn close enough, he stepped forward lightly and thrust the syringe between its eyes with all the grace of a trained fencer. The steel needle punched through the rotted bone and into the brain.

The walker stumbled, and he swung it around, slamming it against the wall of the pen. It gurgled and flailed weakly at him, trying to grab the syringe. There was no strength in its grip, no ferocity. Just a stubborn persistence. It glared at him with eyes that were at once empty and determined. He twisted the syringe, forcing it deeper. The walker's struggles faded, and it slumped in his grasp, the undead light in its eyes fading. He jerked the syringe free and let the body fall.

He stared down at it, wondering if its attack had been as mindless as he'd first assumed. He'd made copious notes since the dead had risen, filled reams of foolscap with idle speculation. Half of it contradicted the other half. Some zombies moved fast, some slow. Some swelled into musclebound monstrosities, others withered to nothing. Some people turned when bitten, some didn't.

The one constant he'd found was zombies, whatever their pedigree, were simple creatures. All but impossible to train.

Complex thought processes were burnt away by the fires of resurrection, leaving them little more than animals. Less than, in some cases. Even the most simpleminded predators displayed an instinct for survival, an instinct that zombies largely lacked. Or so he'd thought.

He nudged the fallen one with his foot. It was well and truly deceased now. Had it attacked out of hunger – or a desire to punish its tormenter? He assumed the former, but if it were the latter, why now? Why not the first time he'd made an extraction, or the second? Was it because he was alone? If so, that implied a level of calculation he had not previously observed. He paused, as he realized that wasn't strictly true.

"I heard it laugh," he murmured, looking down at Pierogi. The dog was sniffing the fallen zombie and tugging on its tattered flesh. He'd heard a zombie laugh – or something close to it. A sound, in reaction to something Keates had done. Keates had heard it as well, and correctly identified it for what it was. Brewer had convinced him otherwise, but only because he himself had not quite believed it.

Brewer retrieved the jug of fluid, locked up, and left the pen. A zombie that laughed. Could it be? If they were smarter than he'd thought, that implied that they could, perhaps, be trained after all, and possibly without the use of increasingly rare components. He set the jug down on a bench and fell into his chair, turning the matter over in his mind. Pierogi leapt clumsily onto his lap and grumbled. Absently, he reached for a scrap of meat from a nearby tray and began to feed the dog.

A zombie laughing. The thought seemed unbelievable,

and yet he had heard it. The more he thought about it, the more certain he became. One of the zombies in the pen had been acting strangely, as if trying to avoid being noticed. He'd spotted it only because he was used to observing zombie herds and could identify when one was doing something out of the ordinary.

The door banged open and Pierogi stiffened, barking gutturally. Brewer looked up as several guards dragged a struggling walker into the lab. And a familiar walker at that. He deposited Pierogi on the floor and stood. "What is this? What's going on? When you didn't come to collect El Gigante, I assumed you'd canceled the bout."

"A sample for you, Doctor," St Cloud said, following his guards into the lab. He fiddled with his cufflinks as he spoke. "I had to end tonight's bout early. Ruined the final surprise for the crowd, but it appears we had a ringer in the mix."

"What do you mean?"

"Our friend here is not what he seems." St Cloud indicated the walker. "He dispatched two of your freaks."

"Zombies often fight," Brewer began, studying the walker more closely. It was, or had been, a man in his early forties. Tall, well-built. Clearly dead, suffering a number of recent minor injuries to his corpus, as well as an older one to his abdomen. More interesting was the look in its – his – eyes. There was a definite gleam of calculation there. Of an awareness that not even El Gigante possessed. He felt his pulse quicken. *I heard it laugh,* he thought triumphantly.

St Cloud shook his head. "Not with weapons they pick up off the ground. Not in defense of living people."

Brewer paused, considering this. The thought was a

startling one; unprecedented. "He protected someone. Why?"

"I was hoping you could tell me." St Cloud frowned, staring at the zombie as if it had personally offended him. "I want to know what this thing is and where it came from. And I want to know as soon as possible. The guards say it spoke. Take it apart if you have to. I'll leave two guards on the door, in case you should require assistance." With that, St Cloud turned and left.

At Brewer's direction the guards deposited the walker on an observation table and strapped it down. Then they too departed, leaving Brewer and his new sample alone in the lab. "You can speak now, if you like," Brewer said, shining a penlight into the dead man's eyes. "There's no one to hear but you and I."

"Guess the cat's out of the bag," the zombie croaked.

Brewer nodded absently as he studied the dead man's eyes, his veins, the condition of his epidermis. He was in better condition than most walkers. Brewer felt a cold thrill as he traced the wounds in the dead man's body with his eyes. A zombie that could talk. A year ago, such a discovery would have made him famous. It still might, come to that. "That it is. You were doing so well, too. Sneaking in with the others. Hiding in plain sight. How did this happen to you?"

"Bad luck, I guess."

"Mm. Well, sorry to say it's not going to improve anytime soon." Brewer put the penlight down and reached for a battery-operated bone saw. He almost hated to do it, but he had to know why. And the only way to learn what made the dead man's brains different was to cut them out and examine them up close. He caught the zombie by the chin and twisted his head to the side as much as the head restraint would allow. "I shall start with the brain, I think. Safe bet there's something going on in there." He tapped the button, activating the bone saw. He lowered it towards the zombie's head.

"Hold still, please."

CHAPTER TWENTY-TWO
Unforeseen

"Just there – you see the smoke?" Keates said, handing St Cloud the binoculars. St Cloud peered in the direction Keates indicated. They stood on the balcony of his penthouse, looking out towards the ocean.

"I see it. What am I looking at?"

"It appears to be a plane crash."

St Cloud stiffened and turned to his subordinate. "Explain."

"Apparently, a small plane went down near or on the boardwalk about a half-hour ago." Keates had met him coming up from Tartarus and told him that there'd been an emergency. He'd been expecting another break in the fences, or the zombies in the parking garage getting out. This was, somehow, worse than either of those things.

St Cloud stood for a moment, digesting the information. "A plane. That doesn't make any sense, unless ..." He handed Keates the binoculars. "This has been an odd day."

"They've all been odd days since the world ended," Keates said.

St Cloud nodded absently, eyes still on the distant column of smoke. "I need you to take a team and get out there. Find it, and quick. Before Ariadne does. I want to know who was on it and where they came from, do you understand?"

Keates nodded. "I can do that."

"I should hope so. If you can't, don't bother coming back."

Keates nodded wordlessly and hurried out. St Cloud gnawed lightly at his thumbnail, thinking, not really seeing. A plane crash – yet another unforeseen occurrence. It couldn't be a coincidence. There was a pattern, it just hadn't come into focus yet. Something was happening out there, and every instinct he had told him his sister was behind it.

As children, she'd often played pranks on him. Jumping out of closets and pushing him into traffic. Maybe that was what she was up to. Maybe this was another prank, only this time she wouldn't settle for seeing him cry and wet himself. This time, she'd kill him.

Perhaps it was only fair. He'd tried to kill her, after all. More than once, in fact. When he'd realized that she'd survived their last meeting, he'd expected her to come roaring in after him, guns blazing. That was how she thought, how she'd always thought. He was careful, she was impetuous. He was the investor, she was the spender. She never did anything quietly, preferring to make as much of a racket as possible. That was why he found her silence disturbing, especially after she'd made a point of letting him know that she'd survived.

He recalled the grisly nature of that notice and frowned. She'd hung a walker with a cardboard sign pinned to its chest from a window across from the casino. Immediately after finding it, he'd sent Keates back to the marina with a team and orders to capture her. It had been a foolish assumption – obviously, she wasn't going to be there. Neither was her yacht.

He'd come to the conclusion that she was changing berths on a daily basis, moving from one marina to the next. He'd given up looking for her, even trying to outmaneuver and capture her, and had tried to ignore her instead. He knew now that had definitely been a mistake. It hadn't worked when they were children, and it wasn't working now.

But what would she be doing with a plane?

He turned away from the ocean and went back inside, where he stood in the center of his penthouse and looked around without seeing any of it, his hands clasped behind his back. Everything he'd worked for was in danger so long as Ariadne roamed free. And now, at last, she appeared to be making her move. The more he thought about it, the more certain he became that it had something to do with the Adirondacks. As he'd told Keates, his sister knew the stories as well as he did.

There were a few other survivor camps left in the city limits, none of them populated by more than a stubborn handful of people. But there were other camps, outside Atlantic City. Ones in Ventnor City and Egg Harbor. They were larger than most, better organized – for a given value of that term. He'd intercepted their radio messages often enough to know that they were aware of the Elysium, but only in the vaguest sense. Could Ariadne have paid them visits? If she was using the yacht, it was entirely possible.

A spike of pain brought him back to himself. His fingers

had been so tightly interlaced that he'd accidentally dislocated one. He gritted his teeth and popped it back into place, barely a grunt of discomfort escaping him.

She scared him more than any zombie. He was not too proud to admit it. Fear was often the source of action. A scared man had two choices: freeze or act. Too often when dealing with Ariadne, he'd frozen. The one time he hadn't, he'd thrown her off her boat. A bit extreme, but warranted. He expected that there were very few people who knew Ariadne and hadn't wanted to kill her at one time or another.

But that night aboard her yacht had been different. They'd argued. Not the familiar back and forth he'd come to know and hate, but something raw and wild. A lifetime of acrimony, spilling onto the deck. She'd convinced the board of St Cloud Enterprises – *his board* – to sell the casino out from under him, and after he'd gone to so much trouble getting control of it in the first place. He'd been so preoccupied making the Elysium profitable that he hadn't noticed.

That alone hadn't made him angry, not really. Such dirty tricks were to be expected. No, what had driven him to the edge, and then over, was her revelation that it was her company purchasing the casino. Not on paper, of course. A shell company. But it was hers, nonetheless. Once again, she was taking something that belonged to him, just because she could. The smile on her face. The look of triumph.

It had been more than he could bear. He'd gone after her. It was just the two of them on the boat, by long-standing arrangement. She wasn't the one scared of her sibling, after all. Why should she be? She hadn't run. She didn't even try to defend herself, not until it was too late. For once in his life, he'd surprised her.

The triumph he'd felt had been short-lived. He'd come off the boat and almost been eaten by a very old woman; a shocking experience. He'd beaten her down with a fire extinguisher and hurried to his car. By that time, the news had told him what he needed to know. The world had changed, and his perspective with it.

It was as if throwing Ariadne off the boat had freed him from his previous limitations. He had seen instantly what was needed, what would be necessary in the days to come if anyone was to survive. He would have to do what his ancestors had done in the dark, bloody days of the Norman conquests. His fiefdom would need fortifying, his people a leader.

He'd done his best, but it wasn't enough. The dead were ever at the gates. He thought about the disruption in the arena. Things had been going so well until that disruption. He'd shaken hands with his guests. Men and women in suits and dresses; high rollers and whales. The formerly well-off and well-to-do, trying to pretend that they still were important in this strange new world. He'd smiled politely, accepting their effusive, if calculated, praise. His kingdom's aristocracy knew enough to be grateful.

But gratitude was a tricky thing. If you weren't careful, it soured into resentment. He wasn't naïve enough to believe that the survivors he put to work were happy about it. It didn't matter that he was protecting them from the undead hordes overrunning the city, or ensuring the survival of humanity itself. No, they just didn't like being made to shovel shit.

The arena allowed them to vent their spleens in an acceptable manner. They could watch some poor fool get eaten by walkers and cheer, safe in the knowledge it wasn't them. It also served as a reminder that it could be them, if they complained loud enough or made moves against him. But today's interruption had changed things.

A zombie that killed other zombies, that seemed self-aware, that could talk, if the guards were to be believed. The thought unsettled him. Where had it come from? One of the guards had informed him that they'd caught it prowling the utility tunnels under the casino. They'd assumed it had slipped in through one of the sewer entrances. But those had all been closed up and welded shut on his orders. He grunted and ran a hand through his hair, wondering if he ought to order Keates to double the patrols... if they had the bodies to complete such as order.

More, he wondered if the creature was a coincidence or part of some larger scheme. An intelligent zombie, one that could follow orders – what might a clever person do with that sort of thing? He could think of more than a few things, and he bet Ariadne could too. Had she somehow sent the creature to infiltrate the casino? Had she guessed why he was gathering so many zombies in one place?

Playground Pier had only been a field test, and a successful one. A hundred walkers was nothing compared to what he had planned for Egg Harbor and Ventnor City. He closed his eyes, imagining it. Walkers pouring out of trailers, towards the camps of his enemies. An army of the dead, dispatched at his discretion. And should anyone be foolish enough to attack Elysium, they'd find themselves swamped by a horde while he and his loyal followers waited things out safely in the casino.

He frowned. If only he could use the dead against Ariadne as easily as he had the pier. Even she couldn't survive a horde of zombies. But unless he could find her, unless she came out into the open, there was no point in even dreaming about such a thing. And impetuous as she was, he couldn't imagine Ariadne doing something that foolish.

St Cloud opened his eyes and sighed. The plane. The plane was the answer, he thought. It had to be. It was one too many coincidences. Whoever was on that plane held the answers to all his problems. Once he had them, he'd question them and find out where they'd come from. And if they had come from a certain site in the Adirondacks, well – that just opened up new avenues of possibility.

If that were the case, perhaps Boudin and the others might get their wish. Much as it pained him, if Atlantic City had nothing left to offer, then the only pragmatic option was to seek out new lands to conquer.

St Cloud smiled and sighed again, this time in satisfaction as he considered new possibilities. Indeed, why stop with the Adirondacks? As he'd told Keates, there were many such places. With enough resources, enough people, a forward-thinking person such as himself could acquire everything they might need to rebuild the country in their own image. He looked around the penthouse.

"Someone has to do it. Why not me?" he murmured.

CHAPTER TWENTY-THREE
Cavalry

Calavera caught a walker by the jaw, and with a twitch of his wrist tore the bone loose. Jaw in hand, he laid about him until it snapped and splintered in his grip. He tossed it aside and stooped, snatching up a loose tire. Spinning in a tight circle, he sent the tire hurtling into the packed ranks of the dead. Some fell, but not all.

Smoke stung his eyes and filled the street. Most of the zombies were an indistinct mass, lost in the smoke and the dust of the plane's landing. But even if he couldn't make all of them out, he could certainly hear them. The dead sang a song that was recognizable whatever language you spoke: a bone-deep hymn of hunger and longing.

He'd chosen a spot some distance from the plane, where several abandoned cars had converged on a rusted bulwark. The dead had to come around or over it to get to him, and he was making enough noise to attract the bulk of their attentions. But some were still moving towards the plane. He reached over, tore a dangling bumper free of a car and hefted it. It would make a better tool than a jawbone.

"Any luck?" he called out, glancing over his shoulder back towards the plane.

"She's still out," Kahwihta replied, from where she crouched beside Ramirez and Ptolemy. Beside her, Attila began to bark at the zombies as they shuffled closer. Sayers, perched on the wing above the others, sent an arrow humming into a walker, knocking it flat. She drew and loosed again, and a second walker joined the first.

"We need more time," she shouted, as she reached for another arrow.

"Understood." He rolled his shoulders, preparing his muscles for what was to come, and bounced lightly on his feet. Around him, broken storefronts watched the battle, unimpressed. He swung the bumper against a car, as hard as possible. "Hey," he bellowed, as loudly as he could manage. "Over here! Come and get me!"

As he'd hoped, more zombies pressed forward over the bodies of their fallen compatriots, heading in his direction. They staggered through the curtain of smoke like drunks on day four of a five-day bender. Between the weather, the birds and the sea, most of them had been reduced to withered caricatures of the people they had been. Gender and age were consumed by entropy, with only the remnants of clothing to identify them. Almost all individuality was lost.

That, most of all, was what saddened him about the dead. It was as if some remorseless force had stamped the humanity out of them. They were nothing more than machines, now. Automatons of meat, driven by hunger.

He saw the members of what must have once been a high school marching band, their towering hats and epaulets no longer a brilliant white but a filthy yellow. A street performer in a speedo and a cowboy hat, broken guitar bumping against gnawed pectorals. Car wash attendants and casino croupiers stumbling alongside beachcombers and tourists.

Perhaps most disturbingly of all was the immense, yellow cartoon chicken – a mascot, maybe part of the marching band or for a restaurant. The costume, padded as it was, had apparently provided little protection for its unfortunate wearer from the teeth and fingernails of the dead. They stumbled along, bumping into other zombies, cars and lampposts.

The dead were converging on the plane from all directions. Too many to count. The smell was unbearable. In the mountains, it was diffused by the raw odors of nature, but here, the seaside air seemed to enhance the stink rather than mute it. Gulls and crows swooped overhead, crying out raucously before descending on a zombie and tearing at it. The zombies ignored these parasites, their attentions fixed on the plane.

So taken was he by this sight that he almost missed the scrape of flesh on a car hood. He spun, dropping his makeshift weapon, and caught a lunging runner by the wrists. The momentum of its charge drove him back against the side of a car, and he grunted in annoyance as it snapped at him. An instant later an arrowhead sprouted between its eyes. It went limp and he slung it aside.

"Watch your back," Sayers called, from the wing of the plane. She was already readying another arrow as he waved his thanks. A tough woman, Sayers. She was hurt, but still game. Still fighting. The hand of Santa Muerte was on her shoulder, guiding her as she released a second arrow. The saint was with them all, Calavera knew. If she wasn't, they wouldn't have survived the plane crash. Their escape was nothing short of miraculous. But even a saint could only do so much.

The air reeked of fuel and, from what little he knew, one errant spark could set it alight. They needed to get away from here and quickly. He stooped to retrieve the bumper as more walkers closed in. As he did so, he felt a faint tremor and, acting on instinct, hurled himself aside even as the brute slammed into the bulwark and flipped one of the cars completely over. The shadow of it passed over Calavera, and then the car came down with a tooth-rattling crunch, crushing several of the slower walkers.

Calavera looked up. The brute was clad in the split remnants of a wetsuit, and a thick mane of blonde hair hid much of its distorted features. The brute gave a wheezing roar and lifted its heavy fists over him. Calavera shot to his feet, the bumper extended before him like a spear. He drove it into the brute's spongy flesh, but with no apparent effect. The brute slammed a fist down on the bumper, snapping it in two. Calavera staggered back and the brute swept its arms out, as if to embrace him.

He ducked under its groping reach and sprang for the shard of bumper still jutting from its chest. He caught the blood-slick metal and wrenched it free. The brute clawed for him, groaning hungrily. He heard Santa Muerte's whisper in his ear and laughed. A single, quick thrust was all he needed to drive the shard of metal up through the brute's chin and into its brain. It gave a gaseous sigh and its weight settled on top

of him. He threw it off with a titanic heave, but had no time
to celebrate. While he'd been dealing with the brute, much of
the rest of the horde had kept moving towards the plane.

He turned to try and head them off, but a snatch of
sound – a song, perhaps – caught his attention and he
turned back. Santa Muerte stood at the far end of the street,
her robes billowing in the sea breeze. In her black gaze was
an infinity of peace and calm.

Calavera met her gaze, and felt, as always, a longing to join
her in that far realm where the dead knew neither hunger
nor pain. He snapped from his reverie and drove an elbow
into a walker's head, slamming it into a car. He caught it by
the scalp and the back of its shirt and spun, launching it like
a javelin into its nearest fellows.

A kick took another in its exposed pelvis, dropping it
writhing to the ground. He stamped on its neck and kicked
its head away. There were still too many between him and
the plane. He could hear the *pop-pop-pop* of a handgun, and
the *hum-crack* of Sayers' bow, but the wind had shifted and
the smoke was wrapping everything in an oily shroud.

Head down, he charged. Zombies surrounded him, biting
and clawing. Teeth scraped against his wrapped forearms.
He caught a zombie by the shoulders and headbutted it. He
tore the arm from another and whirled it about him, trying
to drive them back. He sought out the saint's gaze, hoping
that she might have some wisdom for him.

She was still where he'd seen her last, still watching.
Waiting, but for what? "Is it to be today?" he whispered. A
walker came for him, and he dispatched it without thinking,
his body reacting on instinct. "Are my labors at an end?"

She shook her head, and he felt a sudden pulse of sadness. One day soon, perhaps, that privilege would be his. But not today, he knew. Today was for the living, and for fighting. She gestured and the smoke around her thinned.

Calavera blinked. It was no longer Santa Muerte he was looking at, but instead a tall, dark-skinned muscular woman, dressed in black, and holding what appeared to be a Thompson submachine gun. She grinned, raised the weapon and fired, gunning down several zombies.

As if this had been a signal, more gunfire erupted from nearby storefronts and windows. Dozens of zombies were scythed apart by the sudden salvo. What followed was a succession of concentrated volleys. The newcomers retreated as the horde turned its attentions to them and away from the plane.

Calavera saw the strategy immediately, for it was one the Saranac Lake survivors had used on several occasions. Each salvo served to break up the horde a little more, to reduce its effectiveness by drawing the zombies in all different directions at once. Hordes were terrifying, in the abstract. Enough zombies could overwhelm even the strongest defenses. But individually, or in small groups, walkers were less trouble.

As the horde unraveled, the woman in black advanced, alongside several others; all of them dressed in dark clothing and wearing knapsacks and bandanas over their mouths and noses. They kept up a steady rate of fire as they advanced, chopping through the middle of the mass of zombies, as if they had ammunition to spare.

The big chicken was the last to fall. A shotgun blast

knocked the walker sprawling, and the butt of an assault rifle crumpled the cartoon beak and the rotting face inside. The woman with the Thompson stepped over the twitching mascot, her weapon braced against her hip. The rest of the horde had largely dispersed, drawn down side streets and into storefronts. "I know what you're thinking," she said, as if reading his thoughts. "But they'll be back. They always come back. We don't have much time."

"Thank you for your timely assistance," he said.

She circled Calavera. "Well, you are a big one, aren't you?" The slight trace of an accent in her voice marked her as being from somewhere else, but he couldn't tell where.

"I am–" he began.

"I didn't ask. Where did you get a plane?" she continued, in a tone of mild curiosity. "I think I would have heard if someone in this city had a plane. That's the sort of gossip that gets around." She turned and looked at Sayers, still standing on the wing. The former park ranger had an arrow nocked and ready. "I wouldn't, if you know what's good for you."

Calavera saw that her companions had their weapons aimed at him and Sayers. He felt a chill. Something told him this wasn't strictly a rescue. "Sayers," he said, in warning. Unsurprisingly, Sayers ignored him.

"You put your weapons down first," she said, through gritted teeth.

The woman laughed. "Oh, that's funny. Best joke I've heard in months." She gestured. "Put the bow down, or my people will put you down."

"Do as she says," Calavera said. "If they wanted us dead, they could have simply left us to the zombies."

"Smart and big," the woman said, looking at him. "I was mostly curious as to how a plane wound up on my boardwalk." She glanced at where Kahwihta crouched protectively over Ramirez and Ptolemy. "Looks like you got some hurt people here. Bet you'd like a place to rest up and get your bearings."

"We would." Calavera straightened and crossed his arms.

The woman looked up at him. "It'll cost you. As I said, this is my boardwalk. Everything you see – mine. So, what are you going to give me, in return for my hospitality?"

Calavera glanced at Kahwihta, and then said, "What do you want?"

The woman laughed. "My favorite question. Information will do for now. Later – who knows?" She gestured and her people slung their weapons and moved forward. "The name's St Cloud, by the way. Ariadne St Cloud." She smiled and Calavera was reminded, somewhat unsettlingly, of a tiger's grin.

"But most people just call me Duchess," she added.

CHAPTER TWENTY-FOUR
Survivors

Panting, Saul practically fell inside as the door opened. Within, the two guards from earlier waited for the survivors of the bout, along with Mondo. Carter helped Saul to his feet as Amos and the others stumbled back in as well. All of them were covered in blood, most of it belonging to the zombies but some of it their own. Saul felt sick, hoping none of the zombie blood had seeped into any unknown cuts or wounds, turning him into humanity's worst fear.

The fight had been confusing and chaotic from the outset. The walkers had practically been on them as they stepped into the arena, and any thought of maintaining group coherency had crumbled the moment the first zombie lurched into view. They'd become separated; isolated. Gus had been one of the first to go. He'd almost seemed to welcome it. He'd just… walked into the thick of the walkers, his gaze turned inwards. Donovan and Wachowski had tried to get to him, but there'd been too many and he'd been too far away.

The rest of them had been holding their own, if barely, until the metal-zombies had been released. Wachowski had died then, Saul thought. And Leroy too, probably, though he hadn't seen what had happened to the biker. They'd managed to down two of the beasts, somehow. Armored though they were, they weren't invincible. The chainsaw had done for one, though the tool had split its chain in the process. Amos and a sledgehammer had worked for the other, though the young man had nearly lost his life in the process.

Amos was pale, his arm wrapped around his bloody midsection as Ruth helped him to sit down. The metal-zombie had cut him open even as he'd pulped its armored skull. "My brother needs medical attention," Ruth said, looking at Mondo, as the guards swiftly disarmed the group.

"Myra's hurt too," Perkins cried, helping the woman stumble to a bench near the wall. She was limping, her face taut with pain. Donovan nursed an injured arm, and Carter had cuts and bruises on her face. Saul himself felt as if his heart were about to explode in his chest. But he forced himself to go to Amos.

"Myra will live. Amos might not. Not unless we can see to this wound." Saul looked at Mondo. "I need a first aid kit. Some bandages. Anything."

"Yeah, yeah, we'll get to that. First, who's left?" Mondo asked, raising a clipboard. "Seven of you? All right, all right, all right. I knew I had a good feeling about you guys. Sound off, who bought it – guy with the unfortunate tats, one-legged dude and … the weird one? Is that right?" He peered at them, his cigarette bobbing on his lip as he spoke. "No big loss there, am I right?"

Carter hit him and Mondo went ass over kettle, his clipboard flying. One of the guards caught her high in the back with a baton, knocking her to her hands and knees. The guard made to strike her again, but Donovan tackled him into the wall. They wrestled for a moment until the second guard got her sidearm out. Then Donovan was forced to step back, hands up. The first guard clambered to his feet and hit Donovan in the stomach, knocking him to the ground beside Carter before drawing his own weapon.

"Nope! Nope! Holster them," Mondo spluttered, rolling to his feet, his nose purpling. "The boss wants them in one piece for tomorrow's show. You shoot them, it's all our asses." He dabbed at his nose with his sleeve and sniffed. "Besides, way I hear it, the boss has something special planned. Shooting them would probably be a mercy." He grinned nastily at them as the guards stepped back, holstering their weapons. "Speaking of which, first things first – anyone get bit?"

Saul looked at the others. "Getting bitten doesn't mean one will turn," he began, hesitantly. Mondo shook his head.

"It just increases the likelihood, old dude. But I bet you knew that. So, fess up, who got bit? Anyone?" His gaze went to Donovan. "What's wrong with your arm, buddy?" He gestured to one of the guards. "Check him."

The guard hauled Donovan to his feet and twisted his arm up in a painful manner. Donovan winced. "Clean. Just a scratch," the guard said, shoving Donovan against the wall. The second guard moved towards Myra.

"Show him your leg, babe," Mondo said. "Don't worry, just standard procedure."

Myra reluctantly hiked up her skirt. "I think I just twisted it," she said. The guard stooped, then glanced at Mondo and shook her head.

Mondo sighed. "How bad?"

"Already going black," the guard said, rising to her feet.

"Shit. Sorry babe." Mondo snapped his fingers. "Do it. Make it quick."

Before Saul or any of the others could react, the guard shot Myra in the head. The sound was loud in the enclosed space of the room, and Saul stared in shock at the crimson crescent that decorated the wall. Perkins leapt up with a cry and stumbled back. Myra bent forward on the bench, smoke rising from her head. Mondo clucked his tongue.

"Man, I hate when this happens. Unfair, you know. But rules are rules. We'll take her with us, dump her outside. Let the gardeners come get her." He caught Saul's eye and smiled. "Waste not, want not, my man. Mulch for the gardens." He spun a finger. "Circle of life, just like the song." He paused and frowned. "You want to talk to Phyllis? She's better at this sort of thing than me."

Saul hit him. It was childish. Foolish. But down Mondo went again, with a squawk and a yelp. Saul raised his hands immediately and stepped back as the second guard helped Mondo to his feet. "Jesus," Mondo spluttered. "I was trying to be nice." He touched his nose and winced. "I think it's broken."

"Good," Carter said.

"Up yours," Mondo replied, glaring at her. He turned away. "Just for that you can stay in here for the night with your pal there." He indicated Amos. "If you're lucky, I'll send someone to shoot him when he turns." He departed, still probing his nose gingerly. The guards followed a moment later, carrying Myra's body.

When they'd gone, Carter turned to Saul. "I'm surprised, Rabbi. I didn't know you had it in you."

Saul frowned and rubbed his hands together. They were starting to ache again. Not a day went by that God didn't remind him that his body was falling apart. "Yes, well, it seemed to be the thing to do." His eyes strayed again to the blood spatter on the wall. Perkins was sitting on the floor, crying softly. Donovan went to him, as Carter turned to Amos.

"I don't think they're going to bring back a first aid kit," she said, as Saul joined her. Amos looked awful, shivering and only half-conscious. Ruth whispered to him, keeping him awake, or trying to, at least. From the looks of him, Amos wasn't going to last long.

"We need to staunch the bleeding," he said. Carter nodded and stripped off her jacket. Saul began to tear it into strips with some difficulty until Donovan handed him a knife. He looked at the former highway patrolman, startled. Donovan shrugged.

"I stowed it, just in case we got out. They didn't think to search us."

"Clever," Saul said. The knife made his task easier, and soon they had enough makeshift bandages to wrap about Amos's midsection. The jacket wasn't clean, but neither were Amos's wounds. In fact, Saul was privately surprised that Amos hadn't turned yet. But he said none of this. Instead, when they'd finished, he left Amos in Ruth's care and conferred with the others. He pitched his voice low. "I fear Amos won't last the night."

"He's a tough kid," Donovan said, glancing at the siblings. "He might surprise us."

Carter grunted. "He might. But it might be kinder if he didn't. You heard that asshole – they've got something special planned for us. I don't know about you, but I didn't like the sound of that." She looked around the room, as if searching for a way to escape.

"Wonder why they ended things early?" Perkins murmured. He still looked shaken by what had happened to Myra. "They'd just released those… those… whatever they were on us and then – *pfft*. That was it."

"It was the other zombie," Ruth called out, from the couch. Saul froze, wondering how much she'd heard. He turned.

"Which one?" He paused. "The walker, you mean?" There'd been a walker. It had seemed more aggressive than the others and focused on the metal-zombies. That happened sometimes, he knew. Some zombies just plain didn't like other zombies.

"It wasn't a walker," Ruth said, stroking Amos's head. "At least not like any walker I've ever seen. It talked. To me. When I stabbed it." She looked at them, her expression daring them to disbelieve her.

"A talking zombie?" Carter scoffed.

"Why not?" Saul said. "There are big ones, fast ones and now ones covered in metal – why not a talking one?" He shook his head. He didn't doubt that Ruth had heard what she heard. The young woman wasn't given to stories. "What did it do, after you stabbed it?"

Ruth frowned. "It killed that other metal-zombie. I think it was trying to help us." She looked down at Amos, her expression unreadable. "Why would a zombie help us?"

"God works in mysterious ways," Saul murmured.

"I don't think God was in the office today," Donovan said, bluntly. "Did you hear that crowd? They wanted those zombies to tear us apart."

"They were cheering, actually cheering for us to die." Perkins rubbed his arms nervously. "I don't understand. What did we ever do to them?"

"It's relief, not animosity," Carter said, glumly. "I saw some of that overseas. They're happy to cheer because it means it's not them."

"Maybe," Saul said. "But then, the guards might have had something to do with it." The others looked at him blankly. He shrugged. "I saw them. Standing around the top. Guards. A dozen of them, all armed. Not facing the arena, like you'd expect. No, they were watching the audience." He paused and sighed. "I would bet it is the same throughout this paradise of St Cloud's – guards on every floor, eyes on you wherever you go. If you don't work hard enough, or cheer loud enough, or say thank you quickly enough, well... into the arena you go." He looked at the others. "This place isn't a community. It's as much a zombie as those that just tried to kill us. Like them, it'll eventually fall apart at the seams."

Carter grunted. "Yeah, but the question is, how much damage is it going to do before then?" She sat down in a chair near the door, a solemn look on her face. The others did the same. The adrenaline of the fight had faded, and they were all tired. Saul felt as if he could sleep for a week. Instead, he went to sit beside Ruth and Amos.

Saul settled himself back against the lower half of the couch, wincing slightly as he did so. He wasn't built for sitting on floors, but it did no good to complain. There were others in worse straits. Amos, for one. He sat silently for a time, his mind working over the problem at hand. His eyes were fixed on the door, but he wasn't actually seeing it. Instead, he was seeing beyond it, to the casino, and the city. Beyond that even, to the wider world.

"Planning our escape?" Ruth asked quietly. Saul's smile was tepid and brief.

"Not as such. More thinking about whether it's worth it."

She frowned. "What do you mean?"

"This is the largest survivor camp I've heard of. Do you know of another that's bigger?"

"I haven't heard about many, but… yes, I agree with you."

Saul nodded. "Most are small. Maybe a dozen people, at most. Not enough resources to go around. I passed through a few in the days before I got to the pier. Enclaves hiding in parking garages, shops and convenience stores. But here – sixty, seventy, easy. Infrastructure, resources. Safety." Their group had not had much time to become close. McCuskey's abrasiveness hadn't helped. And, well, it didn't pay to get too close to people these days. Monday's friend was Tuesday's zombie.

"We're all survivors, but we cannot exist in Gehinnom in perpetuity. We need rest. Ease of mind and spirit, if not body. Else we will break. That is what this place provides, like it or not. If only we could harness its potential, instead of creating a new kind of hell on Earth, it might be able to do some good for mankind."

Ruth grimaced. "They hurt my brother."

Saul looked at her and nodded. "*Tch*. They did. Forget what I said. An old man's maunderings. I am only thinking of what could be, not what is." He held out his hand, and she took it. "We are like family. *Mishpocheh*, you know? The blood of the covenant is thicker, yadda yadda, as Lenny Bruce said." He patted her hand. "I'll get you out of this, Ruth. You and Amos both."

He released her and sat back with his eyes closed and his hands interlaced. He had to think of the future, but in a different way than he had before. Amos and Ruth were family, and they had suffered. It seemed only fair that their tormentors suffered in turn. "God of retribution, Lord, God of retribution – appear…" he murmured, praying for the first time in a long time. Not for salvation or safety.

But for vengeance.

CHAPTER TWENTY-FIVE
Necrology 101

"Doc – can I call you Doc? – let's be reasonable here," Westlake said, squirming away from the bone saw. "Cutting open the head of the only talking zombie you've ever seen is bit like killing the goose that laid the golden egg, isn't it?"

Brewer turned off the bone saw and paused. "Knowledge requires sacrifice," he said. He started up the bone saw again. "I thought I asked you to hold still."

Westlake tried his restraints, but he had no leverage. Brewer had made sure that no amount of thrashing would snap the straps. "How about a compromise?"

Brewer turned off the bone saw again. "What sort of compromise?"

"Start with my arm. Answer some of my questions, and I'll answer yours. Everybody gets what they want. Knowledge is power and all that. Sound good?"

Brewer sat back in his chair. Then, deliberately, he set the bone saw aside on the nearby cart. "You're right, of course. I was getting a bit ahead of myself." He chuckled. "Pun not intended."

"Hilarious." Westlake sagged and relaxed, but not much. "First things first. I'm Westlake. You go first. Ask your question and I'll do my best to answer."

"Do you feel anything?" Brewer asked, drawing a tray of instruments on the cart towards himself. He selected a scalpel and took hold of Westlake's forearm. "Hold still."

"Physically or emotionally?" Westlake asked, as the other man began to slice open his arm from wrist to elbow.

"Either?"

"Respectively no, and maybe."

Brewer paused and looked at him. "What does maybe mean?"

Westlake smiled. "My turn, Doc."

"Fine. Ask." Brewer bent back to his task.

"Why don't you tell me about St Cloud? About this place."

Brewer paused. "A broad question. But I'll allow it." He set his scalpel aside and picked up a pair of forceps. "St Cloud is insane. Not in a horror movie sort of way, but in a quieter way. He thinks this place will be the nucleus of a new Roman empire, with him as Caesar. To that end, he has taken on the Roman philosophy of expansion via conquest."

"By which you mean he's kidnapping other survivors and forcibly relocating them."

Brewer smiled. "Not always. Sometimes they see the benefits of joining him. But when they don't, he endeavors to convince them by any means necessary."

"He sends zombies after them, in other words."

"A recent innovation, but yes."

Westlake filed that away. "The drones at the pier were your work."

"Is that a question?"

"No. But it's your turn regardless."

Brewer chuckled. "How much do you remember about your death?"

"I'm not dead, yet."

"I beg to differ, Mr Westlake. You are very dead." Brewer probed inside Westlake's forearm. Westlake could feel it, but there was no pain. Just a vague sense of something moving around. "How much do you remember?"

"Bits and pieces. I was in a vehicle. I hit a tree."

"Is that all?"

"I might have been bitten a few times," Westlake said.

"Interesting. Bites are rarely a cause for such transformations as yours. The wound can easily turn septic, leading to death which greatly increases the chances of an untimely resurrection, but a bite in and of itself is not the cause."

"Then what is?"

Brewer paused. "Is that a question?"

Westlake smiled. "Think of it as a request for clarification."

Brewer chuckled. "Then prepare to be disappointed. I'm an engineer, not a biologist. All of my discoveries have been happy accidents. I do know that no one has thus far displayed an immunity to whatever is causing the dead to rise. Animals are somewhat more resistant, of course. But even they can succumb, in time." He put down his forceps, leaned down, and held up a small zombie dog.

"Pierogi here is a prime example. He tried to protect me from a zombie, ended up swallowing a bit of it. A few days later… he turned. I couldn't bear to put him down, of course. It wasn't his fault, after all."

"Yeah, I get it," Westlake said, though he very much didn't. Pierogi stared at him.

Brewer smiled. "I even saw a shark with it once. In Myrtle Beach. At an aquarium. Some zombies had toppled into the tank somehow, and the shark had done what came naturally. Poor beast was left to bump its snout ceaselessly against the walls of its habitat, having devoured every other living thing in easy reach." He put the zombie dog down. "Another innocent victim of man's hubris."

"I wouldn't exactly call a shark innocent," Westlake said.

Brewer chuckled. "A smile only a mother could love, you might say." He used the forceps to probe at Westlake's tendons.

Westlake grunted as something in his arm twanged. "Something like that. Careful there, Doc. I'd like to keep use of the arm, for a little while at least."

"Never fear, my friend. I don't intend to do any permanent damage. At least not immediately." He sat back. "Your tendons, your muscles, they're not showing any signs of decay. Tell me, have you eaten anything, lately?"

"No."

"But you desire to do so, don't you?"

"My turn, Doc," Westlake said, quickly. "The convoy I was in got attacked by zombies, despite what looked like some decent defenses. Keates looked nervous about it. Makes me think that's not an everyday occurrence."

"Is that a question or an observation?" Brewer asked.

"Why did he look nervous?"

Brewer was silent for a moment. Then, "It's not as if they take me into their confidence, you understand."

"But I bet you hear stuff, don't you?"

Brewer's expression became sly. "On occasion. And to answer your question, it's not the first time it's happened. Someone is testing Elysium's defenses. St Cloud's sister, would be my guess."

His words drew shards of memory to the surface of Westlake's mind. A woman's face, a cool voice. Something about money. A price. "Ariadne," he said, softly.

Brewer sat back. "You know her?"

"I might." Westlake closed his eyes, trying to encourage more memories to stir. He saw himself in a restaurant, sharing a drink with the woman. She wanted him to do something – but what? Tell her something, maybe. About the heist? He didn't know. It was like trying to grab sand. No matter how tightly he gripped it, the memory slid out from between his fingers.

Brewer eyed him speculatively. "Interesting. Apparently, she's causing our Mr St Cloud no end of difficulty. I suspect she will be his next target. If he can find her, that is."

"That is interesting," Westlake said. More bits and pieces broke the sludgy surface of his thoughts. He remembered something about a boat. Wouldn't that be the safest place during a zombie apocalypse? It wasn't like zombies could swim all that well. Or maybe they could? Memories of the water – a dog? – hijacked his train of thought for a moment. He twitched his head to clear it. "Your turn, Doc."

"Where did you come from?"

"Where do any of us come from?" Westlake replied. "A stork dropped me off."

Brewer sighed and reached for the bone saw. Westlake

flinched. "Fine. The last I remember I was in the mountains. Upstate."

"And you came here? Why?"

"Search me. My turn. Are you happy here, Doc?"

"What an odd question."

"Going to answer it?"

Brewer paused. "Not especially, no. I am not satisfied with my current employment. Not that it matters, of course. Having given me the benefit of his protection, I doubt St Cloud will just let me leave. In fact, I suspect that once I have fulfilled his objective of a zombie army – however laughable that concept might seem – he will do away with me."

"And why would he do that?"

A low, bone-rattling growl interrupted Brewer before he could reply. Westlake's eyes widened and Brewer smirked as he set his tools aside. "If you'll excuse me for one moment, El Gigante needs me. Perhaps you'd like a better look."

Brewer reached forward and undid the restraint holding Westlake's head in place. Westlake craned his neck and saw that the monstrous zombie at the far end of the room was stirring in its cage. It thrashed slowly side-to-side, like a drunk waking up from a nightmare.

El Gigante tried to rise, but the chains kept it from doing so. Its eyes widened, and Westlake was reminded of a lion realizing that the cage door had been left unlocked. It growled again, gnashing malformed jaws as it began to test the strength of its chains. Westlake didn't like to think about what it might do if it got loose.

Brewer stood and walked to the monster, stepping into the cage and drawing a syringe from his coat pocket. He jabbed it into the base of the monster's skull without hesitation, and a shudder ran through the thing. The noise it was making ceased moments later. It looked almost asleep. "Damn and blast," Brewer muttered, as he probed at El Gigante's bowed head with his fingers. They came away black, and he held a small, squarish computer chip up to the light. "The chip's burnt out. That's the fifth one this week."

"Chip?" Westlake asked.

Brewer left the cage, locking it behind him. "Another minor achievement of mine. Think of it as an invisible fence for zombies. Tap a button, a signal flies to a receiver and the zombie gets a little jolt right through its medulla oblongata. Stops them cold, when it works."

"What's the point in that?" Westlake asked, interested now, despite himself. Brewer was clearly brilliant, if off his rocker. He wondered what Kahwihta would make of the old man's theories. Or what Brewer might make of hers.

"It's about control, Mr Westlake. It's proof that zombies can be guided – tamed. Trained, even." Brewer stooped and scratched his dog. "Like Pierogi here. Why, with the right hardware, you could even remotely pilot one, or two, or ten."

"Meat drones," Westlake said, and laughed hoarsely.

Brewer nodded. "If you like. Think about it. Why risk human lives when a zombie can bludgeon another zombie easily enough? Or search for food and medicine. Enter dangerous areas. The possibilities are virtually endless." He looked at Westlake. "That's why you interest me. How have you retained your intelligence, and how might we replicate that?"

"I wouldn't wish this on anybody," Westlake said, softly.

"I can't feel pain. But I can feel everything else. I can feel myself coming apart at the seams. I don't know how much longer I've got, Doc. How long can a body last like this?"

"I'm more concerned about your mind," Brewer said. "Eventually your brain will start to degrade, if it hasn't already. What will you be then? Will you retain any traces of your intelligence, your cunning?" He paused. "And what might happen if we fed some of your cerebrospinal fluid to your fellow walkers, or even El Gigante here? Would they regain some use of their minds, or are they too far gone for such measures to apply?"

"What the hell does spinal fluid have to do with anything?" Westlake asked.

"Some of them seem to crave it. In small doses, it invigorates them. Larger doses make them docile; almost comatose. And, as they lose it, they become... well, you must have seen them, the ones that just seem to stagger about with no particular malice? Oh, they'll attack if you get too close, but they won't chase you." He lifted up a strange mechanism, resembling an insulin pump, that was attached to the back of El Gigante's neck. "That's how I keep our large friend here so calm."

"You're keeping him doped on zombie juice? That's pretty twisted, Doc."

Brewer chuckled. "Oh, it's not a permanent solution by any means. I'm having to increase the dosage regularly. Either he's building resistance to it, or he needs a fresher supply." He frowned. "I don't know which, and without proper testing I won't find out before he stops responding to it entirely. At which point, we'll have to put him down." He patted the somnolent creature's cheek in a paternal fashion. "Poor fellow. It's not his fault."

Westlake grunted. "If what you say is true, if he gets loose, you're going to have a problem. I've seen one of them in action before. The results aren't pretty."

"I suspect that will only please Mr St Cloud."

"What will please me, Dr Brewer?" St Cloud asked, as he pushed the doors open. "Some good news, I hope. Something I can use." He crossed the lab and looked down at Westlake. "Have you found out what this… creature is?"

"I got a name," Westlake said. St Cloud blinked and stepped back.

"So, it does talk. The guards were right."

"He does, yes," Brewer said. "Quite a bit. He's been asking questions."

"Has he?" St Cloud picked up a scalpel and traced the line of Westlake's cheek. "Have you? About what, exactly?"

"This and that," Westlake said. "I'm a curious guy."

"You're a dead guy, is what you are. A walking, talking dead man. Where did you come from, dead man?" St Cloud asked. He pressed down on the scalpel, and Westlake felt the skin of his cheek part.

"I can pretend that hurt, if it'll make you feel better," he said.

St Cloud grunted and tossed the scalpel back onto the tray. "That's not necessary, thank you. Your evaluation, Doctor?"

Brewer picked up his dog and scratched it behind one decaying ear. "He's not a walker, though I expect he passes for one quite well. He's lucid; articulate. Cunning, even, given that he snuck in here." He paused and smiled. "He hasn't said why, but… well."

"Well, what?" St Cloud asked.

"Yeah Doc, well, what?" Westlake added.

"He knows – or claims to know – your sister."

St Cloud hissed softly and looked back down at Westlake. "I knew it. She sent you, didn't she? She dug you up somewhere and sent you to spy on me. Clever witch."

Westlake raised his head to reply, but Brewer took the opportunity to jam a syringe into the base of his skull. He jerked in his straps, as something cold crept through him. Brewer had played him. His brain really was stuck in neutral. He slumped, his world spinning, his limbs twitching. No pain, but something else – a sort of bubbling euphoria. His sight hummed and dimmed. It was as if he were sinking into a pool of black water.

He heard St Cloud talking. "Cut him open. Find out what he knows."

"I have a better use for him, if you're willing to listen to a suggestion," Brewer said. "Something much more… entertaining."

St Cloud was silent for a moment. Then, "Oh, that would be something to see, wouldn't it?" He laughed softly. "Yes, that is a good idea, Dr Brewer." Westlake felt St Cloud lean over him, but couldn't convince his eyes to focus.

"A very good idea indeed."

CHAPTER TWENTY-SIX
At Sea

Ramirez snapped awake with an undignified snort. She sat up, immediately regretting the too-quick movement. She grunted and clutched at her ribs. Someone had bandaged her midsection, and done a decent job of it. Her ribs weren't broken, she thought, but definitely cracked. Still sitting up, she looked around.

She was in a ship's cabin. She knew she was on a ship because she could smell the water and feel the motion of the boat. It reminded her of an old girlfriend in Florida, and altogether too much time spent on a houseboat parked in a rundown marina. The cabin was well-appointed. Luxurious, even. Big bed, bookshelves and a closet full of clothes. Expensive clothes, she thought.

She looked down at herself. For the first time, she noticed that someone had taken the opportunity to remove her trousers and her coat. Examining herself, she noticed more bandages, on her hands and wrists.

Dimly, she recalled cutting herself as she dragged Ptolemy

out of the forward compartment of the plane. It didn't hurt, and she wondered if the fogginess in her head was due to some form of painkiller. She looked around.

A sound cut through her reverie, and she looked up to see a seagull perched in an open porthole, staring at her with a red-rimmed eye. It squalled at her and she snatched up a pillow and hurled it. The gull vanished in a flurry of loose feathers and indignant squawking.

"Bad luck to kill a seagull, you know," a woman's voice said from the doorway. There was a faint accent to the words, but Ramirez couldn't place it.

"What if it's already dead?" she asked, hoping to hide her confusion. She tried to stand up and the room spun for a moment. She clutched her head, trying to stop the spinning. Her visitor dragged a chair across the floor to the bedside.

"Different sort of problem, that. Though I expect you know all about it, given the way your plane looked when it skidded across my boardwalk. Mashed pigeons everywhere." The woman smiled. Ramirez eyed her warily, noting the possessive in reference to the boardwalk. She wasn't sure what was going on, but she decided to play it cool until she knew more.

"Sorry about that. Didn't have much choice."

"No, so your friends said." The woman turned the chair backwards and leaned over it. She was slim and dressed in black. Her outfit was stylish but practical. The sort of thing a celebrity on an outdoor reality show might have worn, back when there was television. Her face was familiar; maybe Ramirez *had* seen her on television.

"Where are my friends, exactly?" she asked carefully.

These days it was hard to tell the difference between rescue and capture.

"The brig."

Ramirez tensed. The woman laughed. "Kidding. We don't have a brig. They're on the main deck, enjoying the finest peanut butter and jelly sandwiches in Atlantic City." She grinned and peered at Ramirez. "Want one?"

Ramirez nodded slowly, still not sure how to process the situation she'd found herself in. "Sure. But first, maybe tell me who you are?"

The woman straightened. "My apologies. I'm so used to people knowing who I am. Ariadne St Cloud. Welcome to my yacht."

Ramirez blinked, dredging her memory for the name. "Didn't you once set fire to some celebrity's pool house?"

"I was provoked," Ariadne said primly. She smiled and leaned close. "I'm told you were a federal agent. How interesting."

"And who told you that?"

"The young woman with the dog."

"Kahwihta," Ramirez said, with a flush of relief. "Did they – was anyone…?"

Ariadne sat back. "They're all alive. Banged up, but alive. I probably should have led with that. Sorry. I don't have much experience with unconscious people. Or rather, people who were unconscious." She stood. "I expect you'd like to get dressed. Your clothes are over there." She paused and gave Ramirez a lingering look. "Or you can take something out of the closet, if you prefer. We look to be the same size, and I have more than I need."

Ramirez nodded her thanks. "My sidearm?"

"I'll hold onto that for the moment. Just a precaution. You understand, I trust."

"I do."

"Good. I'll leave you to it, then." Ariadne left the cabin, closing the door behind her. Ramirez gathered her strength and stood. The floor pitched and shivered beneath her feet, and she had to catch herself on the bedpost. She went to the porthole where the gull had been perched and looked out. They were anchored maybe a mile from shore. In other words, close enough to land to reach it without too much difficulty, but far enough away that wandering zombies probably weren't much of a problem – unless they were floaters. Instinctively, she scanned the water, but saw nothing.

Mulling over her situation, she got dressed and headed for the door. Ariadne was waiting in the small corridor outside. Past her host, Ramirez could see the door to another cabin situated beneath the prow. Ariadne straightened as Ramirez joined her, gave her a once-over then indicated a set of narrow circular steps positioned just outside the door. "Your friends are up here."

Ramirez followed her host up the steps. From what she'd seen out the window and her own quick estimation, the yacht was around ninety-five feet long. Impressive, but not ostentatious. The steps led up to the aft outdoor portion of the main deck. A set of glass doors led into the enclosed central sitting area.

Upon entering, Ramirez saw the familiar faces of her companions, who were seated on a set of comfortable couches. Relief nearly overwhelmed her. Also in the room were a man and a woman, both armed. They stood a professional distance from Calavera and the others, and had positioned themselves so as not to get in one another's line of fire.

"Hey, Boss," Kahwihta called out, waving. "We got sandwiches." Attila barked in greeting and trotted up, tail wagging.

"So I see," Ramirez said, scratching the dog between the ears, grateful that even the mutt had made it out seemingly unscathed. She looked at the others. "Is everyone all right?"

"Bruised, but in one piece," Ptolemy said. His head was bandaged, and Sayers sat protectively by his side. Calavera sat perched on the back of the couch, a tiny plate held in his big hands. He'd rolled the bottom of his mask up so he could nibble at a sandwich.

"It was a close thing," he said. He glanced at Ariadne. "If Miss St Cloud had not shown up, we might well have been overrun."

"Well, I couldn't have that, could I?" Ariadne said, as she looked at the woman on guard duty. "Carrie, be a dear and fetch some coffee."

"Coffee?" Ramirez said, suddenly feeling the need to sit as the room began to spin again. They'd run out of coffee two weeks after claiming the Villa. The first few days without had been the worst, and just the thought of it made her head hurt – but in a good way.

Ariadne slumped back on the opposite couch, one leg thrown over the armrest. "Luckily, the old tub was fully stocked when things kicked off. And since we were still at the marina, we had our pick of my neighbors' ships to plunder as the need arose. Anything else we need we can get by trade."

"Trade?" Ptolemy asked, sitting forward. "You have established a barter network among the local camps?"

Ariadne nodded. "Some of them, at any rate. I make trading runs when I can to the survivor camps near the boardwalk and the waterfront. None of them are very big. The largest has maybe half a dozen people, based out of a bar near the state marina." She paused. "I do what I can for them, when I can."

"And is that why they call you the Duchess?" Kahwihta asked, feeding the last bit of her sandwich to Attila. Ariadne made her fingers into pistols and mimed firing.

"Among other things," she said. She pushed herself up on one elbow as the woman returned, bringing a tray with a coffee carafe and cups.

"What does that mean exactly?" Ramirez asked.

"First, let me ask you a question. Why did you all come here?" Ariadne asked, as she poured Ramirez a cup of coffee and then one for herself. Ramirez took it gratefully, but paused before answering. She was beginning to wonder that herself. So far all they'd done was nearly get themselves killed and for what? She looked at the others and Ptolemy nodded.

"We made contact with a group of survivors here. They wanted help." Ramirez paused, wondering if she should elaborate, then added, "We were planning to evacuate them, if possible. Get them out of the city and to safety."

Ariadne frowned. "That plane of yours wasn't big enough for that."

Ramirez blew on her coffee to cool it then took a sip. It

was the real thing, and she closed her eyes for a moment, enjoying the sensation. "We can find a bigger one at the airport. Maybe. If we're lucky."

Ariadne whistled softly. "You're lucky, in a way. The airport is – well, you can probably imagine. We think, maybe, there are survivors holed up there, but we've had no contact with them. It's been on my to do list for ages, but you know how it is. I suspect Rupert has been eyeing it as well." She tilted her head. "Where were you planning to evacuate everyone to, exactly?"

Ramirez tensed, wondering who Rupert was. She decided to play things close to the vest. Ariadne might have saved them, but that didn't make her a friend. "The mountains," she said, vaguely.

Ariadne nodded, seemingly accepting this at face value. "I've never been one for roughing it. I like my comforts." She scratched her chin. "Still, I suppose I can see the appeal. Fewer zombies, for one thing."

"Sometimes. What about the plane? What'd you do with it?"

Ariadne guffawed. "Left it, what do you think? There wasn't much useful on it, except some stale snacks. Nothing we could make use of anyway. It's not like we had the equipment to move it."

"So, as far as you know, it's still sitting there?"

Ariadne nodded. "I suppose so." She knocked back her coffee and asked, "These survivors who contacted you, were they holed up in Playground Pier, by chance?"

Ramirez hesitated, immediately wary. "Yes. You know them?"

Ariadne frowned and set her cup down. "I did. In fact, I think I heard the same radio message you did. We were running a supply of canned food to one of the camps on the other side of the marina when we caught the tail end of it. We tried to reach them but by the time we got there, it was over."

"What was over?" Ramirez asked, setting down her own cup. "We know they were attacked. What exactly happened?"

"My brother is what happened. Rupert St Cloud."

"Your…" Ramirez stared at their host. "Your brother?"

Ariadne smiled, grimly. "Unfortunately." She leaned forward, a serious look on her face. "We arrived too late to do more than watch them load the last of their ill-gotten gains up onto those trucks of his and vamoose." She glanced at her people. "As good as we are, I'm not entirely certain what we could have done to help."

"But you were willing to try," Ptolemy said.

Ariadne shrugged and sat back. "As I said, we arrived too late."

Ramirez frowned. "What happened to them after that?"

"He took them. Dragged them all off to his little castle in the city – a casino called the Elysium. Just like he's taken everyone else he could get his hands on."

"Everyone…?" Ramirez asked. "How many camps has he done this to?"

"More than I care to think about," Ariadne said. "And knowing Rupert, he isn't going to stop at the pier. In fact, that's what I was hoping to talk to you lot about."

Ramirez suddenly realized what was coming next. She could practically read the hope and desperation on the other woman's face. Her heart sank and her headache was back, but it wasn't as pleasant as before. She looked at the others and Sayers spoke up for the first time. "Good job, Ramirez. You landed us in the middle of a goddamn warzone."

"Bingo-bango, give the scary lady a prize," Ariadne said. She shook her head. "Rupert and I have always had something of a… competitive relationship, I admit. But the end of the world has brought out the worst in my brother. I've decided to shut him down once and for all." She leaned forward.

"But to do that, I'm going to need some help."

CHAPTER TWENTY-SEVEN
The Duchess of Atlantic City

Ariadne stood at the back of the aft lounge, looking out over the water. The moonlight played across the surface, turning the wide, empty black into a field of silver.

Once, she'd found looking at the water to be relaxing. That had been before her brother had chucked her over the side of her own boat. Now she simply found any sort of mental relaxation frustrating. But she forced herself to do it anyway. It was how she reminded herself of the danger Rupert posed. It was how she steeled herself for what she had to do.

Inside, Ramirez and the other newcomers discussed their options. She'd left them to it, under the watchful eyes of Eloise and Coop, her bodyguards. She had half a dozen people altogether, counting those two. The others were busy with the task the plane crash had interrupted – namely talking to the other camps in the city, telling them what had happened to the pier. She hadn't been entirely convinced it would matter, but the new arrivals changed things. It meant that there were options other than hide, run, or be enslaved.

Maybe that would be enough to convince these newcomers to do what needed doing.

Something splashed in the water below. She took a peek. Pallid heads bobbed in the water, empty eyes staring up as hands flailed uselessly at the hull of the yacht. "Floaters," she muttered, skin crawling. It was the sound of the engine. It drew them up sometimes. Occasionally, when there was nothing better to do, she and her people went fishing for them, if only to cut down on their seemingly endless numbers.

The floaters were only really dangerous if a boat stalled or rested at anchor for too long. But sometimes...

She sniffed, catching a whiff of spoiled meat and salt water. "Ah. Bugger." Something wet slapped against the deck and she turned, going for her sidearm as she did so. She pulled the weapon and fired. The shot caught the floater in its mushy skull. The bloated zombie pitched backwards over the side, striking the water with a splash. But there was more where that one came from. It didn't help that she'd added to the noise.

Mostly the floaters weren't much trouble, but sometimes you stirred up a shoal of them – a veritable reef of putrefying flesh and jellied muscle, floating just beneath the surface. They were all over the coast; a Sargasso of corpses, drifting with the tides.

Another floater came over the rail, this one all sloppy limbs and oozing face. It was followed by two more. She shot the first and whistled sharply. Her bodyguards came running, accompanied by the newcomers. Eloise and Coop knew the drill and took up firing positions on either side of the deck. They had to be ruthless with ammo conservation. Every shot might as well be a dinner bell.

The newcomers didn't seem bothered by their lack of hardware. The big one in the mask – Calavera – gave a yell and pounded towards one of the floaters. At the last second, he leapt into the air and drove his elbow into the zombie's skull, puncturing the rotted mass like a balloon. He had the floater up and over the side a moment later.

The dog handled the next zombie, yanking it off its feet and dragging it backwards with practiced ease. Kahwihta stomped on the zombie's head until it was a gooey stain on the deck. Then she quickly and efficiently crouched to clean out her pet's mouth with her sleeve. She glanced at Ariadne. "I should have guessed there'd be floaters here as well. Saranac Lake's full of them."

Ariadne paused. Saranac Lake. Suddenly several things slotted into place. "The Villa," she said, smacking her forehead. Kahwihta and the other newcomers froze and looked at her. Ariadne held up a hand to forestall any questions and turned to Eloise. "Get the boat moving. We're attracting too much of the local wildlife. Aim us towards the nearest marina. The others should be getting back soon anyway."

"Getting back from where?" Ramirez asked, as Eloise hurried to obey. "And how do you know about the Villa?" She was tense, on edge. Ariadne put on her best smile.

"I've never been there, obviously. Not our sort, as Mumsy always said. But when you're rich and you're, well, involved in a certain sort of business, you hear things. Stories. I never imagined that such places truly existed, or that they even survived. That does certainly put a new spin on things."

"I knew your name sounded familiar," Ramirez said. "It took me a bit to think of why. I blame the plane crash. You and your brother were both persons of interest in a dozen cases. Art theft, mostly. Forgery. Rare books."

Ariadne laughed. "Art is – was – the easiest way to launder money. Your average oligarch wouldn't know a Picasso from a Renoir, but a pretty painting is a tangible asset regardless." The yacht's engine started up and they began to move. The marina wasn't far, thankfully. Fuel was getting harder to come by. She leaned against the rail. "Of course, none of that matters now. Who has time to paint a masterpiece these days – or steal one, for that matter?"

Ramirez snorted. "I suppose the perk of living on a yacht is that a quick getaway is always on offer."

Ariadne chuckled, her eyes on the slowly approaching shore. "But it does make it hard to mount rescue attempts. Big as my lovely girl is, she's not large enough to house many more people than what we've got."

"Speaking of which, the pier."

Ariadne looked at her. "The pier. We both want the same thing. To help them."

"Sounded like you might have warned them, if you suspected something was going to happen," the woman called Sayers said.

Ariadne hesitated. "I tried to, but I made a mistake." She didn't like admitting it, but there was nothing for it. She needed their trust, and their help. Sometimes the best way to do that was to tell a story. The truth, of course… the truth was always a story. She paused and looked back at the city. "Like I said earlier, my brother and I had our problems.

But I was willing to put aside my misgivings and see if he could do what he was trying to do. He had the resources, the people. If he could keep people safe, keep them fed… who was I to upend that?"

Ramirez and the others looked at one another, and Ariadne knew that they'd likely had similar conversations themselves. Cold calculations were the order of things these days. Weighing the practical against the perilous. Sometimes, you just needed a bastard to hold things together. She gripped the rail. "He tried to kill me, you know," she said, staring down at the water. "It was a spur of the moment thing – I don't think he meant it. But he tried and he failed. I thought about taking him down. I really did."

For the first few weeks, she'd had her share of nightmares about drowning. About dead hands dragging her down and down, into the darkness. But nightmares paled in comparison to reality, and she'd gotten over it. Or told herself she had. "So why didn't you?" Ramirez asked, startling her.

"As I said, I thought he was trying to help people. So, I decided to do the same. Only it turned out that I was wrong. He wasn't trying to help people at all, or at least not in the way I'd assumed. He's created a fiefdom of his own, kidnapping other survivors to be a part of it and making them do what he tells them to."

"He's playing warlord," Ramirez said.

Ariadne nodded without looking at her. "I never thought he had it in him, to be honest. Just goes to show that you never really know what someone is capable of." She turned to face them, her elbows resting on the rail. "It was the hordes that convinced me. If you get enough zombies going in the right direction, you can accomplish a lot. Draw a horde here or there, surround a building, cut off a street. He's found a way to use them to his advantage. That's what happened to the survivors at the pier. He used the zombies' natural biology for his own gains." She paused and glanced back towards shore. As ever, the dead stood on the boardwalk, on the beach, staring out to sea.

Ramirez and the others followed her gaze. "Are those…?" Ramirez began.

"Boats aren't really safe," Kahwihta said, absently. "It's just a different kind of dangerous. A different sort of vulnerable." She paused. "They're gathering at the water's edge, the same way they do back at the Villa."

Ariadne nodded. "Every time the engine turns over, more of them show up." She looked at Ramirez. "Every time we move, they follow." She hesitated. "My brother is smart. He doesn't have the people to play Genghis Khan, but he does have zombies. Lots and lots of zombies. The thing is you can't control them. Not really. Every time he unleashes his pets or uses noise to direct them where he wants them to go, it's like setting off an avalanche. It stirs up the rest of them and makes things more dangerous for all of us. Soon, there won't be anywhere in the city free of them."

"What about the other camps?" Ramirez began.

Ariadne looked at her. "Eight or nine within the city limits, last I checked. All small. Barely forty people between them. They're scraping by. They're not sitting on any substantial resources and they don't have enough guns to worry Rupert. The pier might have…" She trailed off. She'd spent weeks trying to talk McCuskey around to offering sanctuary to the other groups. But he hadn't been a charitable sort. She shook her head. "It doesn't matter now, I suppose. Like as not, he's planning to scoop them up during his inevitable expansion plans."

Ramirez frowned. "And spread this so-called fiefdom into a kingdom."

Ariadne nodded. "From the looks of things, he's gearing up for something; probably planning to take down the larger camps outside the city. Or to try, at least. And if he fails, it might be worse than if he succeeded."

"Why?" Kahwihta asked, looking at the others. "Wouldn't that be a good thing?"

"Win or lose, the collateral damage would be immense," Ptolemy said. "Not even counting the number of new zombies that might potentially be added to whatever horde he unleashed as part of his attack. And it sounds like living under his rule would not make for personal prosperity."

"That's why I was planning to try and talk to the leaders of the remaining survivor camps in the city – before your arrival interrupted me, that is. Rupert has to be stopped. We at least have to try, otherwise there are going to be a lot more dead people wandering around the city in the immediate future, and a transformed Atlantic City ruled by one man using the undead as his army." Ariadne took a deep breath. "And that's why I need your help."

As she'd hoped, Ramirez got her meaning immediately. "You think we can convince them to listen to you." She paused. "But that won't be enough, will it? There simply aren't enough people among the survivor groups."

Ariadne sighed. "No. Not with Rupert holed up in his casino."

"Even if we could get in," Sayers pointed out. "If I were him, I'd have that place as tight as Fort Knox."

Ariadne smiled thinly. "Getting inside isn't the problem. It's what happens after that. He's got at least twenty armed professionals in that building – a small army, in other words. They'd cut us to pieces as soon as they knew we were there."

"What if they weren't there?" Ramirez asked. "Some of them, at least."

Ariadne frowned. "What do you mean?"

"What if we could get your brother out of the building?"

"You mean lure him out?"

Ramirez nodded, clearly thinking about something. "We'd need bait, though. Something he wants. Something he couldn't resist."

Ariadne laughed softly. "Oh, well that's easy. He wants me."

Ramirez looked at her. "So how do we let him know that you're available?"

Ariadne glanced back towards the boardwalk and the zombies prowling there. They'd been drawn by the noise of the plane crash as much as anything else. They weren't going anywhere anytime soon. A slow smile spread across her face. It was one of the things she did best – using Rupert's own skills against him.

"Leave that to me."

CHAPTER TWENTY-EIGHT
Salvage

The runner sprinted through the field of wreckage, trailing its intestines like a cape. Its tongue flapped through the hole in its cheek, and its feet were little more than stumps of raw meat. It wore some sort of uniform, a casino worker, maybe a dealer or a security guard. Keates couldn't tell and didn't much care.

It burst through the loose cordon of trucks they'd set up around the plane, moving too swiftly for the perimeter guards to get a shot in. Runners were always tricky. They used walkers to get close and then started sprinting towards you before you knew it.

Keates waited until he could smell it, drew his sidearm and fired. The runner's momentum kept it moving for a few more feet before it pitched forward and slammed face-first into the scorched surface of the boardwalk.

He lifted a fist, signaling the others. "Eyes open, boys. More where that came from." Always more, he wanted to add, but didn't. Always more. He'd stopped counting zombie kills the second week of the apocalypse. There was no victory there, no sense of triumph. There were always more. Kill one, two more would show up. Kill ten, soon there'd be a hundred at your door. As an afterthought, knowing what kind of count mattered more, he added, "And for the love of all that's holy, keep count of your shots. You start to get low, switch to something more labor intensive." He patted the baton hanging from his belt for emphasis, and turned back to the plane.

Or what was left of it, rather. It had been picked over already, but there was still some fuel to be siphoned, and he'd put his people to work. It had taken them most of the night to find it, and the entire morning to cut through the horde that had congregated around it. He reckoned St Cloud was probably fuming by now, but there was nothing for it. Zombies didn't give a shit about your schedule.

He clambered inside the plane, trying to ignore the reek of spilled fuel. "Sitrep, Dubois. Tell me something good." Dubois had been a mechanic. He'd never worked on planes, but he knew enough to be able to tell what had been taken and what was just smashed up. Or so he claimed.

Dubois squeezed himself out of the mess of the pilot's compartment. He was a short man, shaped like a bowling ball on steroids. No black uniform for him; just a stained set of coveralls beneath his tactical gear, and an Arizona Cardinals baseball cap. "It's a mess in there. I'm surprised anyone survived, frankly. Everything that ain't been smashed has been jimmied out and taken."

"Shit. The radio?"

Dubois shook his head. "Smashed. Looks like they mostly

took wires and gauges. Spare parts would be my guess." He lifted the brim of his cap and scratched his head. "Or maybe just to keep us from having it."

"Yeah, that sounds like them." Keates cursed again and awkwardly made his way back out into the open air. The chatter of gunfire echoed across the boardwalk. He had a dozen people thinning out the walkers that came to investigate. But more were coming, drawn by the noise or maybe the stink of burnt flesh. "Osborn, report," he called out.

"We're at a thirty-count, sir," Osborn shouted. She stood on the back of a truck, a smoking AR-15 in her hands. "I give it ten minutes before we're swamped."

"Then we go in five," Keates said. Empty-handed to boot. Not a pleasant thought. St Cloud was going to be angry. Angrier, perhaps, than he had been when Keates had called in to report what he'd found earlier. The plane had left parts of itself all along the boardwalk. They'd collected what they could. St Cloud thought Brewer might be able to make something of it. Keates had his doubts, but he'd kept them to himself.

In and of itself, his employer's anger wasn't particularly worrying. It wasn't like St Cloud could afford to feed him to the arena, after all. The thought sent a flicker of unhappiness through him. He didn't like the arena, or what it did to people – not just the ones St Cloud had tossed in. It wasn't guilt he felt, not exactly. He'd left that behind the minute the dead had risen and he'd been forced to put more than one of his own friends down. Maybe even before that. No, it wasn't guilt, but rather regret. Regret that he hadn't taken a stand when St Cloud proposed it, and now it was too late. After this long, it seemed easier to let it happen, but that didn't stop the regret.

The familiar popping of a flare interrupted his train of thought, and he looked up. The bristly splash of light cut across the sky. Dubois peeked out of the plane. "Was that what I think it was?" he asked. His arms were full of wiring and mechanical parts.

Keates nodded slowly. "A flare. A goddamn flare. I guess the Duchess didn't get to the plane's survivors after all." He paused, thinking it through. Whoever they were, they were bound to know something, either about Ariadne – because who else would've invited a plane full of outsiders into the city? – or about the whereabouts of another plane. You didn't fly into a place like this without having a plan to fly out, after all. And it wasn't like the undead took leisurely vacations.

Of course, the question was, who'd they fire off the flare for? He pushed the thought aside. He could ask them when he found them. "Right. I'll take McWhirter, Stoye and Stewart. Everyone else, Osborn is in charge. Finish scrapping this thing and head back."

Osborn frowned. "Sir, are you sure we should divide our forces?"

"Whoever set off that flare might be in trouble," Keates said. And if they weren't yet, they soon would be – once St Cloud got hold of them. Osborn frowned but nodded. She was good at following orders. Even ones she thought were stupid.

He and the others took one of the trucks. It had started life as a delivery truck, and after an application of elbow grease and scrap metal, it had been turned into the perfect vehicle for a supply run. They'd attached a snowplow to the front, to act as an improvised cowcatcher – or zombie catcher, as it were. Stoye was driving; it had been his truck originally, so it seemed only fair. Keates stood in the back with McWhirter as they navigated through the streets.

The sound of their engine drew the dead out of the surrounding structures, and zombies stumbled in their wake. Walkers were no immediate threat to a vehicle in motion, but there were more than walkers abroad. Keates looked up.

The flare pulsed overhead, already fading against the growing dusk. Once, nighttime in Atlantic City had been as bright as day. Now it was as dark as a tomb. The only sounds to be heard were the groans of the dead and the yowl of coyotes and dogs. Despite what St Cloud thought, the city was dead. There was no bringing it back, no turning it into a new utopia. It'd take them years to reclaim it and by then, there might not be anyone left outside.

But Keates kept his opinions to himself. At least for now. Until he could be sure that he had the loyalty of Osborn and the others. Until he was certain that St Cloud's grand experiment wasn't going to work. A working plane changed things. With a plane, there was no reason to stay here in zombie-central. Maybe that was what Ariadne was up to. Maybe she'd decided to let her brother have the city and find somewhere more congenial to start over. Maybe even one of those hidden places St Cloud liked to hint about.

The truck lurched, brakes squealing unpleasantly. Keates

nearly fell on his ass. He lurched forward and hammered on the roof of the cab. "What the hell are you playing at?" he demanded. "Why'd we stop?"

"Roadblock," Stoye called out.

Keates looked up and, sure enough, Stoye was right. Someone had pushed several cars across the street. That wasn't good. Maybe Osborn had been right. He grunted and climbed down out of the truck. "Eyes open, people. McWhirter, with me."

"We going to try and push them out of the way?" McWhirter asked, following him. He was a big man, with a heavy beard spilling out from under his riot helmet.

"No. We're just going to take a look-see for the moment. Keep your head on a swivel, though. I don't want those walkers sneaking up on us."

McWhirter nodded and trotted towards the rear of the truck, his weapon at the ready. It would take the walkers some time to catch up with them, but there was no sense in taking the chance that a runner wouldn't show up. He waved at Stoye and Stewart, motioning for them to stay put. He checked the cars but stopped when he came to the middle one. Someone had written something on the inside of the cracked windshield.

Frowning, he wrenched open the door and slid into the driver's seat. "BEHIND YOU" was written on the glass in what he thought might have been lipstick. He tensed – and something cold and metallic was pressed to the base of his skull. He heard the distinctive click of a revolver being cocked.

"Hi, Harold" whispered a familiar voice. "How's tricks?"

"Ariadne," Keates said, not moving.

"That's Miss St Cloud to you. I can't believe you fell for that. You must be slipping." Ariadne St Cloud leaned over his shoulder, studying the truck. "How clever. I should get one of those."

"You can have this one, if you want." The others hadn't noticed his predicament. Too busy watching for zombies. They weren't used to people being the enemy.

She giggled and patted the back of his head. "No thanks. Not yet, at least."

"Then what do you want?" Keates grated. He glanced up at the rearview mirror and saw a flash of her grin. "Because I don't think you did all this just to chat."

"Smart boy. But then, that's why Rupert hired you. Heck, I bet most of his recent success is down to you, isn't it?" She chuckled. "He's not much of a people person, my brother."

"No argument here," Keates said. "What do you want?"

"To talk."

"With me?" Keates asked, somewhat bemused.

"No, Harry."

"Your brother," he said, mind racing. What was she up to? No way to tell. Best to keep her talking until he could alert one of the others without provoking her. "Why?"

"Things have changed," she said. "The balance of power in the city has shifted. I've been talking to the other camps, and they agree with me."

"The other camps? So?"

"That's forty people who are now of a mind that my brother needs to go. And not just them. So, being a dutiful sister, I want to give him a chance to surrender with some dignity intact. You have a satellite phone on you? Never mind, I know you do." She reached over him, found the satellite phone and took it. "I'll just borrow this, shall I? I promise I'll give it back."

He grimaced. "Is that your plan?"

"It is now."

Keates swallowed. "And the plane's passengers?"

"None of your concern." Ariadne leaned close again. "I want you to tell him something for me, Harry. Let him know that I want to speak with him. In person."

"Where?"

"Where else? Playground Pier."

"It's probably full of zombies by now," he protested.

"That sounds like a you problem. If he agrees, tell him to call me." She tapped him on the back of the head with the satellite phone. "I'll be there this evening. Sunset. If he decides not to show up, I'll consider it a declaration of war." She paused. "Now, get out and go back to your truck. From the sound of it, there are walkers on the way and neither of us wants to be here when they arrive."

CHAPTER TWENTY-NINE
New Acquaintances

Saul sat on the couch and held Amos's hand. The young man was getting worse. He was feverish and barely conscious. Muttering constantly. Arguing with someone. His father, from the sound of it. Saul tightened his grip on the young man's hand, trying to will life into him. But he knew it wasn't to be. Amos would be dead soon. Or worse.

Ruth sat beside him, Amos's head in her lap. She hadn't spoken at all since the previous night, save to whisper in Amos's ear. He was dying and she knew it. Saul wished the angel of death would hurry and collect the young man; but then, that particular angel was probably quite busy these days.

Carter and the others were asleep, or pretending to be. There was only so much moaning one could take, he supposed. But when the door opened, they all jolted awake. Saul was the first on his feet. "We need a first aid kit, medicine," he began, but the guards weren't listening. Instead, without a word, they dragged a zombie into the room, deposited it on the floor and backed out, locking the door behind them.

"Jesus," Carter said, clambering to her feet. "Bad enough they left the kid to die, but now they're just dumping zombies in here with us?" She wrenched her chair into the air and raised it over her head as the walker rolled over with a rusty grunt.

The chair came down – and stopped, as the walker caught it in mid-swing. The walker shoved itself upright and snatched the chair away from Carter. But it didn't hurl it away or drop it. Instead, it righted the chair, set it down, and collapsed into it with a grunt.

"I'm gonna bite the next person who tries to hit me with something," the zombie said, in a guttural voice. It looked around the room as if seeing it for the first time. "Well. This is awkward. Forget what I just said. Heat of the moment."

"It's… talking," Donovan began. "Ruth, is this the one that spoke to you in the arena?"

Ruth looked up briefly. "The one who helped us," she said softly.

"Hey," said the zombie to Ruth and pointed to his midsection. "You're the one that stabbed me."

"You took my knife," Ruth answered.

"Zombies shouldn't talk," Perkins said, pressing himself against the wall. "Zombies shouldn't talk!" He sounded on the verge of panic, as if everything he knew about the world was collapsing.

"This one apparently can," Saul said, softly, trying to calm things down before someone did something they'd regret. The walker acted like an actual human instead of a ravenous monster. A snarky, grumpy human but a human, nevertheless. The zombie glanced at him, and then past him, at Amos. Its nostrils flared, and its jaws parted.

"He dying?" he asked.

"My brother isn't dying," Ruth said, looking back down to her brother.

"Well, yes and no." The zombie's gaze flicked to her, and then to Saul. "Kid's turning." The zombie tapped its nose. "I can smell it on him. Like milk going sour. One of you should probably do something about that."

"He wasn't bitten, though," Ruth said.

Carter frowned. "No, but he was cut up by something leaking zombie-juice all over itself. There's no telling what was smeared on that blade." She glared at the newcomer. "Which doesn't explain how he knows that. What the hell are you? Another one of those freak zombies? Were you actually trying to help us in the arena?"

"I'm a prisoner, just like you and–"

"You ain't like us," Donovan growled. His hands were balled into fists. "Are you pretending to be human for entertainment? Are there cameras in here? How long before you turn ravenous and attack us?"

The zombie leaned forward. "No, no, and no. Calm down, OK?"

"Let's not overreact. This zombie helped us. Remember what Ruth told us," Saul said, gently, before turning to the walker. "What is your name, if you don't mind me asking?"

The zombie looked at him. "Finally, somebody with manners. Westlake."

Saul nodded, uncertain but inclined to press on. He

waved Carter and Donovan back. "My name is Saul. Rabbi Saul Blum. We would like to speak with you, Westlake and thank you for helping us earlier."

Westlake inclined its – his – head. "Sounds good to me. But we don't have much time. Like I said, the kid there is turning."

"Rabbi, are you sure about this?" Perkins hissed, seemingly calmer now, catching Saul by the arm. "How can a zombie be… so aware like this? It might be a trick or something, like Donovan said." He looked nervously at Westlake, clearly disturbed by the dead man's presence.

"It's not," Westlake croaked. "They threw me in here because they want a special show tonight. And, to test how strong my will power is, I bet." Westlake said.

Carter snorted. "Let me guess, you're supposed to fight us in here. This whole thing is a set up. Pretending to save us only to turn us all."

"No. I'm supposed to fight something a lot nastier than you, lady. And bigger." Westlake grunted again and ran a hand over the back of his head, as if in pain or bothered by something. He was still looking at Amos. Was there hunger in that gaze, Saul wondered. If so, it wasn't just hunger. There was something that might have been pity as well. "Not that I'm particularly looking forward to that."

There was a sudden groan, and Ruth cried out as Amos began to convulse. Saul turned back to check on him. The young man was wide-eyed, staring at nothing. Sweat beaded on his pasty skin, and the crude bandages they'd wrapped about his midsection were leaking – not blood, but something tarry and foul. "Oh God," Saul murmured.

Amos shuddered and looked at his sister. He seemed about to speak, but no words came. Instead, he slumped back, eyes staring upwards blindly. Saul quickly caught Ruth by the shoulders and pulled her up off the couch. If Westlake was right...

The dead man sat up with a rattling exhalation. The newborn zombie turned, made to rise. There was a crack of splitting wood and Westlake lunged forward, holding a broken chair leg like a spear. Ruth cried out and turned away as Westlake slammed the weapon into Amos's skull with impressive force. He twisted the leg and Amos went still; truly dead at last.

"My brother, my brother," Ruth moaned, her face pressed to Saul's chest. He hugged her tightly and met Westlake's gaze.

"I told you," the dead man said, hoarsely. After a moment's hesitation he said, "I'm sorry."

Saul nodded and led Ruth away from the couch as Carter draped what was left of her jacket over Amos's face. Westlake followed them. "How long have you been like this?" Saul asked, softly, in an effort to think of something – anything – else. Westlake shrugged.

"Long enough to know it's not much better than the alternative."

"I'll take your word for it. Does it – does it hurt?"

Westlake considered the question. Finally, he said, "I don't feel much of anything anymore. Has its benefits, I guess."

Looking him up and down, Saul nodded, even as his stomach threatened to revolt. "I suppose it would at that." He helped Ruth sit down in one of the remaining chairs. He frowned. "God's mercy, perhaps. Your mind is working, but your body is clearly dead. Decomposing." He refrained from mentioning the smell.

"Rotting on the bone," Westlake said, and tried to smile. His face was mostly there, but the muscles weren't working right and part of his cheek was open, revealing a shadowed semi-curve of jaw and teeth. "Wonder what'll happen when the last of me is gone?" He flexed his hand, and Saul watched the exposed muscles there pull and twitch. He felt a ripple of nausea pass through him and turned away.

"Perhaps you will be free."

"What's that supposed to mean?" Westlake asked.

"Purgatory. Do you know this term? It refers to the final purification of a soul – an intermediate state, occurring after death but before a soul's final journey into the afterlife. We of the Hebrew faith have a similar concept, actually. So do many faiths. Perhaps that is what you are undergoing… a purification of sorts. A refining process, stripping you of all earthly impurity."

Westlake stared at him for a moment. Then he shrugged. "Probably going to take a while, if that's the case."

"I didn't say it would be easy," Saul said.

Westlake made a sound that might have been a chuckle. "No, I don't suppose you did. So, how did this work last time?"

"What, the arena?"

"Yeah. What was the procedure? You all had killer machines. Like, weed whackers on steroids." Westlake started to prowl about the room. Carter and the others watched him warily, but Saul followed him. He sensed Westlake was a good man, or at least his present circumstances appeared to have turned him into a good man. "Do they give you weapons? Or do you have some stashed in here?"

"They brought them to us before we were sent out. I imagine they will do the same this time. Why?"

"Because we might be able to use that to our advantage. They'll cover me, obviously, but that means they won't be paying as much attention to the rest of you."

"What are you saying?" Carter asked.

"I'm saying if we're quick and lucky, we could grab the weapons, overpower the guards, and get past them. Out of this room, and into the casino."

"What good does that do us?"

"You want to escape, don't you?" Westlake said, looking at her. He indicated Amos's body. "Otherwise, you're going to end up like the kid there. Or worse."

Carter made as if to protest, but Saul waved her to silence. "And you'd help us to escape, Mr Westlake?"

"If I can. It was fun being helpful earlier." Westlake's attempted grin was self-deprecating.

"Might I ask why?"

Westlake's tone became serious. "Call it purification," he said.

"And where would we go, in the event we were successful? As a whole, Atlantic City is no longer safe for us."

"Away from here," Westlake said.

"A bit more detail wouldn't go amiss," Saul said.

Westlake ran a hand over his crumbling scalp. "I might know of a place. A safe haven. Protected. Well supplied. Everything you might want."

Carter studied him suspiciously. "Sounds good. So why

are you here rather than there?" She gestured as if to indicate his whole state of being.

Westlake hesitated. "Complications," he said, finally. "But the place is real. I can get us there. All we have to do is get to the utility tunnels."

"The what now?" Saul asked.

"There are tunnels under this place that stretch from the parking garage to different points under the casino. But the ones under the parking garage connect to the street. The sewers specifically." Westlake tapped the floor with his foot. "I expect that no one thinks much about the sewers since the water stopped working. St Cloud has people patrolling it, but from what I've seen, I don't think they're very serious about it."

Saul rubbed his chin and looked at the others. "Well, that changes things. A way out, and a place to go. Now the only question is, how do we find the others?"

Westlake paused. "The others?"

"The rest of our people. Surely you don't expect us to leave them here?"

Westlake stared at him for a moment, and Saul began to wonder if that was exactly what the dead man had assumed. "Yeah, no. Obviously not."

Saul looked at the others. "Last we saw of them, they were penned up in the loading dock. That might have changed by now."

"We can get them out easy," Westlake said. "I know where that's at. We just need weapons and an opportunity."

"And if that opportunity never presents itself?" Saul asked.

The dead man attempted another smile. "Well then, we'll just have to make our own."

CHAPTER THIRTY
Alliance

The marina was silent save for the creaking of abandoned vessels still moored and waiting for crews that would never come. Gulls circled above, squawking. "So many of them," Ptolemy murmured, watching the flock twist and undulate like a single, serpentine organism. The birds, to all appearances, were still alive. He sat on a box near the boarding ramp for Ariadne's yacht, his shotgun across his knees.

"Apparently they come every day," Kahwihta said as she sat down beside him. Attila, as always, was right beside her. "Instinct, I suppose. I wonder if they miss us."

"I doubt it," Ptolemy said, scanning the marina for any sign of movement. He didn't like being so exposed, but it was necessary. They were waiting for reinforcements, or so Ariadne claimed. Ptolemy didn't know what to make of her. He didn't trust her, but that was only common sense. She might have saved them, but she'd done so for her own reasons. Not that they weren't good ones.

Regardless, she'd spent most of the night and the morning talking to her people via the radio. The yacht's communications set-up was second-to-none, far better than his hodgepodge array at the Villa, which mostly only got the occasional numbers station.

There was something comforting about a synthesized voice reciting a string of numbers relating to a secret, a government, a plan, whatever – that no longer existed or had any purpose. But it kept going, kept spilling numbers into the air.

Sometimes, Ptolemy wondered if he was doing the same thing. Just an automaton, going through the motions. Following its last set of programming. He knew better, of course. He was no machine. Machines didn't bang their heads and get a splitting migraine from a plane crash. Machines didn't get frustrated.

"Seen anything yet?" Kahwihta asked, setting her hunting rifle down by her leg. Ariadne had returned their weapons last night.

"Nothing save birds."

"Sayers?" she asked.

He indicated the street opposite with his chin. "Securing the perimeter, as she put it." They'd been anchored at the marina most of the morning, waiting to see if anyone responded to Ariadne's message.

"Want me to spell you?"

"Thank you, but I am content. I am still not good for much else." He indicated his head. He'd gotten banged up in the crash and was still seeing double. A concussion, perhaps.

Kahwihta nodded but settled in beside him. "Ariadne seemed pleased when she got back." She idly stroked Attila's head as she spoke, her eyes on the water. "And her crew seemed to think the other camps would hear her out." Ariadne's people had returned over the course of the night, looking exhausted. "You think this brother of hers will fall for it?"

"I do not know. I hope so. I hope this all goes according to plan." He paused. "Perhaps I am becoming an optimist in my old age."

Kahwihta grinned. "Maybe we all are."

He chuckled softly. "Maybe." A groan drifted on the breeze and he stiffened. Kahwihta raised her rifle and peered through the scope. She lowered the weapon.

"Walker. Trapped in a car over there."

"It might draw others," Ptolemy said, doubtfully.

Kahwihta shook her head and set her rifle aside. "It can't see us. No eyes. Birds must have gotten to it." As she spoke, several gulls peeled off from the flock above and drifted down towards the car she'd indicated. Squawks and screeches drowned out the zombie's groaning. "I've been thinking about them – the dead – a lot lately," she said. "Trying to work out how they know where we are, wherever we try to hide. I finally realized that they know where we are because they're us."

Ptolemy looked at her silently.

She went on. "They don't really think anymore, at least not in any way that we understand, but something is going on in there. Muscle memory, maybe. They go where we go because we can't leave the old places behind. We entomb ourselves in the past; old ways of living, old ways of doing things. Is it any wonder we have the dead on our doorstep?"

"Or maybe it's because they go where the food is. Simple as," Sayers said, as she stepped out into the open, appearing as if from nowhere.

Kahwihta jumped, startled. Even Attila looked surprised. "Jesus Christ, we need to get you a bell," the young woman said.

Sayers smirked. "You two need to learn the value of quiet. I heard you chatting all the way up the street, even with the birds." She indicated the birds overhead. "A word of advice: sound carries a lot farther than you might imagine in cities."

"We will keep that in mind. Did you see anything?"

"Zombies, zombies, and more zombies." Sayers frowned and looked down at him. "I think we should get out of here while the getting is good."

"There's a surprise," Kahwihta said. "What's the problem?"

"What isn't the problem?" Sayers looked at her. "I thought this was a dumb idea when it was just a rescue mission. Now Ramirez wants us to get involved in a war."

"It is still a rescue mission," Ptolemy pointed out.

"Problems like this don't go away," Kahwihta added. "We can either deal with it now, or later. I'd rather deal with it here and now rather than later on our doorstep." She looked up at Sayers. "If even half of what Ariadne said about this guy is true, he's not going to stop with the city. She even knew about the Villa. What if he succeeds here, and turns his eyes on our sanctuary?"

"Listen to yourself," Sayers said. She gestured towards the nearest building. "This city is full of reanimated corpses.

It is zombie-central. I don't care how rich this guy was, he's not taking the city back. He's spitting into the wind. We all are."

"Then why are you here?" Ptolemy asked, softly.

Sayers didn't reply. Her eyes were on the street. She drew an arrow, nocked it, and loosed it all in one motion. The arrow hissed up and across the street, embedding itself in a traffic sign. "That's far enough," she called out.

Silence. Then a man stepped out from behind a car, hands raised. He wore a filthy raincoat and a pair of Bermuda shorts. He had a gasmask on as well, and a cowboy hat. A semi-automatic rifle hung across his chest from a strap. "We were invited," he called out.

Ptolemy stood and waved them forward. There were fifteen of them in all. Men and women, young and old. But they all had that certain look, that hard edge and tension twitch that only people who went out into the nightmare on a daily basis had. Cowboy hat was the spokesman but not the leader, Ptolemy thought.

"Not exactly Delta Force, is it?" Sayers murmured, as the group approached.

"We take what we can get," Ramirez said, as she stepped off the boarding ramp, one hand resting on her sidearm. "Afternoon," she called out. The group stopped.

"Where's the Duchess?" a short woman, dressed in a red hoodie and wearing a bandolier holding a truly impressive array of cutlery, replied.

"Right here, Imogene," Ariadne called down from the deck. She had a satellite phone in her hand. "Fifteen of you? That's more than I expected."

"There were twenty of us when we started," Imogene replied, pointing at Ariadne. "So this better be worth it."

Ptolemy and the others followed the newcomers up the ramp and onto the yacht. There were no pleasantries, no small talk. Ariadne got right to business. "Playground Pier is gone," she said, flatly. "Elysium is on the move, and any one of you could be next."

The survivors looked at one another. Imogene spoke up first. "You wouldn't have sent your people to convince us to come if you didn't have a plan. So, let's hear it." The others nodded and murmured in agreement. Ptolemy studied them with a survivalist's eye. They were thin, malnourished, and suffering from vitamin deficiency. The city was killing them by inches. If the zombies didn't get them first, they'd starve to death. Atlantic City was on its last legs.

"A small group," Ariadne was saying. She'd unrolled a map on the lounge table. "Ten, maybe a dozen people. No more than that. The entrance is here, at the junction, in the back room of a clothing store." She tapped a point on the map. Ptolemy wasn't familiar enough with Atlantic City to say where it was, but it seemed unsettlingly far from the water.

"So how do you know about it?" the survivor in the cowboy hat asked.

"I had access to the casino's blueprints, prior to – well, all of this. And I kept them in mind, just in case I needed to get in – or out – quickly."

"Just in case your crazy brother tried to kill you, you mean?" Imogene said. "Why didn't you warn us about this? You've been bringing us food for almost a year, Duchess. Why not drop a warning or two to go with it?"

Ariadne raised her hands, as if in surrender. "I made a mistake. I thought – I hoped – my brother might do some good. I thought he might be the answer to my – to *our* – prayers. But I was wrong. And if we don't stop him, I fear none of us will see another year."

There was a minor outburst at this, but they soon quieted down. Ariadne was good at calming them down, Ptolemy noted. She was authoritative without being domineering. She reminded him of Ramirez in a way. Ramirez leaned over the map, studying it. "If you're right about the tunnels, then we can access the parking garage as well as the loading docks. That gets us inside without having to deal with the Elysium's defenses."

Imogene frowned. "But to get there whoever goes will have to cross through several heavily-infested areas. At night. No easy task."

"We could use a car," Calavera said, speaking up for the first time. He traced a street with a blunt finger. "It's a relatively straight shot from the boardwalk, provided there are no obstacles."

"Do you see one handy?" another of the survivors countered. "You might be able to get one of the ones cluttering up the boardwalk moving – if the gasoline hasn't gone bad, if its engine hasn't dropped out, if the battery isn't dead. But by the time you find one that works, you'll have lost most of the night. If, of course, the zombies don't get you on account of all the noise you'll be making."

"I don't make noise," Sayers said. The survivors looked at her and then back at the map. Ptolemy felt a peculiar flutter of pride at that. If there was one thing Elizabeth Sayers was good at, it was being the most intimidating person in any room she happened to be in. "And we don't need a car. We just need to get ashore someplace quiet and clear of corpses, then we head inland. If we keep the noise down, we can probably make it to where we need to go by dusk." She looked at Calavera. "Between me and him, we can probably take care of whatever gets in our way. I'm more worried about the sewers. No telling what it's like down there."

"You won't have to go far, thankfully," Ariadne said.

"And once we're inside?" Imogene asked.

"We lock it down," Ramirez said. "Ariadne is going to lure her brother out, and hopefully most of his security people with him. If we can get in, we can keep him out. He'll have to negotiate with us then, whether he likes it or not."

"So, who are you then, or any of you?" Imogene asked, glancing at Calavera. "New crew members, Duchess?"

Ptolemy decided it was his turn. "We are from outside the city. Upstate. We arrived here last night on a plane." That got them talking. He cleared his throat. "Regrettably, it crashed. But we know where to get another, and we have a place to go. A place that would welcome all of you, if you were willing to make the trip."

"You mean if we're willing to help," Imogene said.

Ptolemy paused and then shook his head. "No. We will take anyone who wants to go, regardless. We are here to help. But that includes the Playground Pier survivors. So, we are going to go get them, with or without you. If we survive, we will happily fly you out of here." He paused again. "Granted, the odds of our survival, let alone our success, are greater with your aid than without."

There was a moment of silence as Imogene and the others digested this. Finally, she said, "We need a minute to discuss this."

Ariadne gestured to the aft lounge. "Make yourselves at home."

Ptolemy watched the newcomers huddle and took a deep breath. He hoped he hadn't come on too strong. The lounge wobbled slightly, though whether due to the sea or his concussion, he couldn't say. Ptolemy made to sit down but didn't quite make it and was forced to steady himself on the back of the couch. Ramirez looked at him. "You OK?" she murmured. He nodded.

"Still a bit out of sorts, I fear. You?"

"Hurting, but kicking." She frowned slightly. "You might want to sit this one out. Stay here, out of the line of fire."

"Actually, I was thinking I might accompany Ariadne." Ptolemy looked at their host. "If she will allow me, of course."

Ariadne frowned, hearing her name. "Why would you want to do that?"

"Because for all that your meeting is a distraction, some good might come of it," Ptolemy said. The idea of the situation before them devolving into a bloodbath wasn't a pleasant one. If it was possible to avoid largescale carnage, he intended to do so. "Especially if we can convince your brother that his position is not tenable. That compromise might be the only way we all walk away in one piece."

Ariadne hesitated, and then nodded. "If you wish. But I warn you, Rupert has never been a big fan of compromise." Before Ptolemy could answer, the satellite phone made a noise. "Speak of the devil," Ariadne said, and snatched it up. She looked at them, took a breath, and answered.

"Hello, brother. So glad you called."

CHAPTER THIRTY-ONE
Celebrations

St Cloud looked down at the arena, hands clasped behind his back. He could hear the zombies groaning in their rooms, waiting to be unleashed. "It's ready then?" he asked, turning to look at Brewer and Mondo. Brewer nodded. He had his vile pet in his arms, and he shifted the creature about as he pulled something that looked like a garage door remote out of his pocket.

"One tap of this, and El Gigante will wake up. A second tap, and he will shut down." He paused. "Or catch on fire." Brewer didn't seem overly worried about the latter, so St Cloud chose to interpret that as a joke.

"Be hot stuff either way," Mondo interjected. He had a bandage over his swollen nose, but seemed otherwise physically unhurt by his rough treatment at the hands of the pier survivors. His pride on the other hand had suffered quite a blow. "The crowd will love it, Boss. This will be the biggest thing to hit Atlantic City since, well, the apocalypse."

"I hope so. I want them entertained and preoccupied

for the entirety of the evening. And I want no problems."
He looked at Brewer meaningfully. "That means, Doctor
Brewer, you will be attending. Just in case our star attraction
gets unruly."

"I'll call it a field test, shall I?" Brewer said, somewhat
sourly. He paused. "And what about the living walker?"

"What about him?"

"What if he survives?"

St Cloud gestured dismissively. "Feel free to collect
whatever is left of him and do what you like with it. I have no
interest in it." He pointed at Mondo. "Remember – I want
everyone focused on tonight's bout. Send in every one of
Brewer's remaining freaks, and every walker left in the arena
pens. Everyone must attend, except those on guard duty."

"Speaking of which, I need to talk to you," Boudin said as
she joined them. She glanced at Brewer and Mondo. "Alone,
preferably."

"Of course. I think we're done here anyway. Gentlemen,
I leave tonight's festivities in your capable hands." St Cloud
turned away, dismissing them with a gesture. He motioned
for Boudin to follow as he started for the elevator, his guards
following at a discrete distance. "We'll need to walk and
talk, I'm afraid. I have an errand to run."

"That is what I wanted to talk to you about. You're
stripping the casino of half the security force. Do you think
that's wise?"

He glanced at her. "Obviously. Otherwise, I wouldn't be
doing it. What are you worried about? We'll be back before
tonight's festivities are over. By the time the hoi polloi
notice that there are fewer guards, it'll be too late for them

to attempt any foolishness. And if they do attempt it, my people have orders to shoot to kill."

"I thought we needed every warm body we could get," Boudin said.

"I've learned there are more where they came from. And if it happens, it will only be to our benefit. Object lessons such as that are worth their relative cost. Besides, you're armed, aren't you?" He indicated the revolver holstered on her hip. She looked at it, her expression one of distaste. Boudin, like many of his chosen people, preferred to let others do her fighting for her. It was one of the reasons he'd chosen them to be in charge. "They're not. Nor are they as durable as the average walker. Being in charge comes with certain risks."

"Still, are you sure this is wise?" Boudin frowned. "After the interruption last night… and by the way, what *was* that about? We are all very curious."

"I'm sure you are," St Cloud said, looking down his nose at her. He hadn't mentioned the plane to any of them, nor would he. No sense muddying the waters or giving them ideas about leaving Atlantic City on some nonexistent flight. "But I'm afraid that must remain a state secret for now. For the good of Elysium, you understand."

"Of course," Boudin said, bowing her head. She was afraid, but not as afraid as she had been. Could they sense his anxiety? His worry? No. They weren't that observant. They were fishing, and Boudin was the lure. That was why she was speaking for the group. Plausible deniability. He felt a flicker of disappointment.

They didn't love him. He wasn't foolish enough to think that. But he had expected at least a few years' grace before they started looking for his weaknesses. He stopped, turned, and studied her. She grew uncomfortable, and he caught her glancing at his guards. "Tell the others not to worry. Tonight will go off without a hitch, and tomorrow will be a new day for all of us." He leaned close to her, smiling. "Tomorrow, it all begins."

Boudin didn't look reassured, but she voiced no further concerns, and he left her standing there. The elevator ride down to the parking garage was quiet, allowing him to think. He was worried, of course. Ariadne was cunning. Her offer to meet him, to discuss an alliance, could well be a trick. In fact, he was almost certain it was. She wasn't the forgiving sort; neither was he. She obviously intended to draw him into an ambush. Well, turnabout was fair play.

In the parking garage, the zombie corral was empty for the first time in months. Keates was overseeing the loading of the horde. They'd backed the trailers up to the garage entrance and were funneling the dead into them. The zombies were making quite a racket, and it was aggravating the ones outside the fences. Despite all his precautions, zombies inevitably managed to get through the outer barricades.

He heard a *fwoosh* and peered at the gates. The trucks that would lead his convoy were already parked there, and the improvised flamethrowers mounted on them were stretching tongues of fire toward the knots of nearby walkers.

He frowned at the waste and intended to make note of it to Keates, as the latter joined him. But Keates beat him to it. "We have to clear the gates, otherwise they'll just pour in around us. Must be a hundred of them out there."

St Cloud waved it aside with a sigh, calculating the costs of the expedition and comparing them to the potential return. "There are a lot of them out this morning," he said.

"Too many," Keates said, chewing on a cigar. "Some of the fences are down again."

"Convenient timing."

"Not really."

"I didn't mean for us," St Cloud said. Another annoyance to be laid at Ariadne's feet. He'd long guessed that the repeated failings of his defensive stratagems were largely due to her efforts. "She's forcing us to waste fuel and ammunition."

"Maybe we shouldn't go," Keates said. "Let her come to us if she wants to talk so bad. Going to the pier is a bad idea."

St Cloud didn't look at him. "She's not going to come to us. If we don't go, she'll slip away again – only this time, she won't be content to hide. That plane was a signal, Mr Keates. I don't know what she's up to, but I intend to put a stop to it tonight."

He watched as a guard was forced to shoot a burning runner as it tried to climb the fence. He made a note to finish setting up their own arsenal. They needed to be able to produce ammunition and quickly, given how the number of zombies in the streets seemed to double with every passing day. "Ariadne is dangerous. But she's kept herself out of my way until now. That means she has either the resources or a plan or both."

"All the more reason we should let her make the first move," Keates said. The improvised fencing they'd erected to either side of the trucks was holding, but barely. There were simply too many walkers and not enough places for them to go. Keates watched them warily as he continued. "Let her try and come at us head-on. We can take it. We've got supplies, ammunition and manpower. What does she have?"

"That's just it, Mr Keates. We don't know. All we know is that she has had a year to lay the groundwork for whatever scheme she's concocted. That she brought someone in from outside to help her. And that she had a goddamned zombie on her payroll."

Keates paused. "A- a what?"

"A zombie, Mr Keates. You saw it. In the arena. She turned a zombie into a spy." St Cloud poked Keates in the forehead. "Do you understand now? Do you see? All this time, while I have been attempting to rebuild society, my sister has been planning to snatch it all away from under my nose. The same way she tried to do with the casino. Now she is finally making her move, and we must be ready. Somehow, she has managed to outdo us in developing zombies as a usable weapon."

"Then why did she say that she wanted to negotiate?" Keates asked, frowning.

St Cloud chewed on his thumbnail, listening to the groaning of the zombies and the hiss of the flamethrowers. "Whatever the answer is, it came with that plane. Are you certain you found nothing on it?"

"Some blood stains, and a corpse stuffed into the toilet. Nothing else. She completely stripped it before we got there." Keates paused. "If we do this, we're going to draw every corpse in this part of the city down on us. The horde always draws more of them and this time we might not be able to contain it. Setting it loose, just for Ariadne..."

St Cloud rounded on him, forcing the other man back a step. "Just? There is no 'just' when it comes to my sister. She will be expecting a trap, but not something like this."

He hammered a fist against the nearest trailer, causing the walkers inside to groan and claw at the metal. "I intend to finish what I started that night on the yacht. She has been a thorn in my side for too long and that ends tonight. No more looking over my shoulder. No more worrying about when she's going to make her move. No more of her tampering with Elysium. Tonight, I become an only child." St Cloud realized he was shouting.

Keates frowned and looked around. St Cloud followed his gaze and saw that they were being watched by the security personnel. He turned away and pitched his voice low. "This is going to happen tonight, Mr Keates. You can stay here, if you like. But I am going. Now, are you coming with me?"

Keates swallowed and looked away. "Yeah. Yeah, I'm coming."

"Good. Now let's get the rest of these trailers loaded." He smiled thinly. "My mistake was in trying to drown her in water." He smacked the trailer again.

"I should have been using the dead."

CHAPTER THIRTY-TWO
Infiltration

Finding the place had been the easy bit. There was no way they could miss it, given the state of the street and the number of zombies that clustered at the edge of the ruptured pavement. Sayers ducked back down behind the abandoned car and looked at Ramirez and the others scattered among the other cars.

They were fifteen strong, with Imogene and several of her fellow survivors, plus three of Ariadne's people, including Coop. A small army by post-apocalyptic standards. They'd had to fight some, so the extra guns had come in handy. But mostly, they'd avoided the zombies that clogged the streets where possible.

"Well?" Ramirez asked, softly.

Sayers grimaced. "Looks like a gas main blew up. Tore the guts out of the street and demolished the store to boot. There's a nice big hole right where we need to go."

"Not to mention a nice big horde of zombies," Ramirez said. "I count at least thirty of them." She shifted her weight and winced. Sayers noted it and frowned.

"You shouldn't have come. You're only going to slow us down."

"Your concern is appreciated," Ramirez said, drily. But she looked tired. More tired than she should've been. It was clear she was in pain but putting on a brave face.

Sayers bit back her reply and turned away. If Calvin hadn't asked her to look out for the others, she'd have left them to it. But he had, and so here she was. He'd even used his "consider the new people who could make our lives better with their skills" argument. He was so annoying, but in a way that only made her love him more.

It had taken them more time than she cared to admit to navigate the city. Whole blocks had been cut off by stretches of barbed wire and improvised fencing, making their route circuitous. St Cloud had been busy. Sayers could understand his thinking. Push the zombies back, cordon them on certain streets or in buildings, and thin the herd every few days, then tighten the cordon. Repeat ad infinitum, ad nauseum.

From the scorch marks, she figured he'd been rolling lit fuel drums into the crowds and letting the fire do its work. That was what she'd have done, in his place. Even so, they'd been forced to cut through half a dozen of the fences in order to get where they were going.

Sayers looked up. The sun was sliding below the tops of the tallest buildings. Night was coming on and long shadows stretched across the street. "Well, if we're going to get down there in one piece, we need to draw some of them off." She glanced pointedly at Attila. The dog panted amiably; excitedly, even.

"The dog?" Imogene hissed as she joined them, moving as carefully and quietly as possible. "What's the dog supposed to do?"

"Running zombies was his favorite game." Kahwihta scratched the dog on the head. "He can do it. But what happens when he comes back? They'll just follow us down." She adjusted the hang of her hunting rifle.

"We move faster than they do," Ramirez said, with another wince. "Unless there's a runner in that pack, we should be fine." She touched her side as she said it and took a shallow breath. "We'll be fine," she repeated.

"*Some* of us move faster than runners do, anyway," Sayers said, under her breath.

Imogene grunted. "I think we can help out there." She gestured to the survivor in the cowboy hat and gas mask. "Riggs made up some smoke bombs. Gets them confused, at least until the wind shifts."

"Is that why he wears the gas mask?" Kahwihta asked.

Imogene shrugged. "That and he's afraid of airborne pathogens," she murmured, making air quotes as she did so.

"And the Bermuda shorts?"

"Comfort," Riggs said, as he joined them. His voice was muffled by the mask. "Need me to pop some smoke?"

"Let the mutt do his thing first," Sayers said. She looked at Calavera. "We need to be ready to move. Some of them won't chase the dog, either because they don't notice him or because they can't. We'll have to deal with them."

Calavera cracked his knuckles. "When have I ever let you down?" he asked.

"There's a first time for everything," Sayers said. She

glanced at Ramirez and then back at Calavera. He gave a terse nod. If it came to it, he'd scoop her up and ignore her protests. She signaled Coop and the others, letting them know it was time to move.

Kahwihta leaned down and whispered something to Attila. The dog barked and took off, running towards the mass of zombies clustered about the hole. He zipped unerringly between their legs, barking loudly. The walkers turned, groped and, finally, followed. They stumbled after the dog, groaning loudly. Attila bounded away, pausing once or twice to let them get close.

Sayers drew an arrow from her quiver, rose, notched it, and loosed before she'd even counted how many walkers were left at the edge of the hole. She took a headcount as the arrow flew. Seven left – well, six. Her target, clad in a flowing summer dress and tottering on broken high heels, fell backwards into the hole, vanishing beneath the broken street. She readied another arrow and loosed it, even as Kahwihta popped off a shot from her rifle and Coop's silenced weapon joined the party. Three down, and two left now, both in golf shirts and chinos. One wore a stained apron. Fast food workers, once, maybe.

Calavera vaulted over the car and clotheslined the pair of walkers off of their feet. When they were down, he stamped on their heads, finishing the job. Sayers moved up to join him, Ramirez and Kahwihta following her. Imogene and the others trailed behind, spreading out to watch the street and cover each other.

The street had been torn up from below. The fires had long since been put out, but the destruction remained. The building opposite them had collapsed in on itself, leaving only a broken shell. Chunks of pavement had buckled, creating an improvised slope down into the sewer below. The standing water reeked of things she couldn't name, and insects buzzed. A number of broken bodies were visible, floating in the water. On instinct, she sent an arrow whipping into one.

The floater jerked and snapped blindly at the air. One of the others rose, dripping, and made a vain attempt to clamber up towards them. Both Ramirez and Coop raised their weapons, but Calavera stopped her. "Save your bullet." He slid down the broken slope and planted a boot in the zombie's face. His momentum carried him into the water and took the zombie's head clean off. He rose and looked up. "Only two," he called out.

"Is he always like this?" Imogene asked.

"This is positively restrained for him," Kahwihta said. "Uh-oh." Attila's barking was getting louder again. Sayers turned. The dog was heading back their way, and so were the walkers. Riggs pulled a cannister from the pocket of his raincoat and bounced it on his palm. He pulled the pin, wound his arm back like a professional pitcher, and sent the smoke bomb hurtling towards the oncoming horde of walkers.

Smoke spewed across the street, momentarily obscuring the zombies. He sent another smoke bomb after the first, rolling this one underhanded. Then he turned and raced back to the group. "Time to go, we got maybe a minute," he said, bounding past Sayers and sliding down to join Calavera, raincoat flapping behind him like a cape. Imogene and the rest of her people followed him. Coop and Ariadne's people moved to cover the hole.

Sayers looked at the slope and then at Ramirez, but said nothing. Ramirez frowned, as if she'd asked the question.

"I'll be fine."

"If you fall, I will catch you," Calavera said, helpfully. He held out his arms for emphasis. Ramirez muttered a curse and started a careful descent, Kahwihta helping to steady her. Coop looked at Sayers.

"Now you, Rambo."

"I'll go last. Someone's got to make sure the mutt gets down safely." Coop shrugged and went. She took a quick count of her arrows, using only her fingers. Fifteen. She'd have to make more, when she had time. If she had time.

Attila scrambled past her, tail wagging, panting cheerfully. The walkers were left stumbling around in the smoke, too slow to keep up and too stubborn to quit. But no runners in the bunch, thankfully. Maybe they'd all been drawn somewhere else.

Sayers dropped down to join the others, accompanied by the dog. The air stank, but not of gas – just the usual mélange of rotten meat and human waste. The water was high, over the top of her boots, but that was endurable. Ramirez and Coop, flashlights in hand, pointed the beams of light down the tunnel, heading east. "This way," Coop said. "There should be a hatch about ten minutes' walk up the tunnel."

"If it didn't collapse in the explosion," Sayers said, slinging her bow and drawing the Mauser C96 holstered on her hip. The groans of the returning walkers were getting louder. The smoke was dispersing. If they decided to come down into the tunnel, she and the others would be trapped. Shaking her head, she followed the rest of the group into the darkness.

The walk was unpleasant, but not as bad as she'd feared. The tunnel was wide enough that they could move three abreast. They saw rats, but the vermin had better things to do than bother with them, mostly, she suspected, due to Attila's presence. True to Ariadne's word, there was a hatch – a begrimed slab that resembled something you might see in a submarine.

The water was higher here, but there was a raised ledge to either side of the tunnel. The hatch sat to the right, just above the ledge. It didn't look like it had been opened in years. Sayers studied it in the dim edge of the flashlight's beam. "Ramirez, swing your light onto the door, would you?"

Ramirez did as she asked. "What is it?"

Sayers stepped up onto the ledge near the door. "Blood." She touched it and brought it to her nose. "Not fresh. But still wet." She absently wiped it on her trouser leg. She turned. Attila, chest-deep in the water, was growling softly and staring into the darkness beyond the flashlight's beam. Imogene drew one of her knives.

"What's gotten into the dog?" she asked.

Sayers lifted her pistol. "Something is watching us."

Ramirez cursed softly and swung the flashlight, but nothing was revealed. "Zombie?"

"Definitely," Kahwihta said, stroking Attila's back. She looked back the way they'd come. "If that hole has been there long enough, some of them definitely fell in."

"Or they were down here already," Riggs said, eyes wide behind the lenses of his mask. "I heard stories about people looking for shelter underground. Maybe they weren't just stories."

"We should get the door open," Calavera said, climbing onto the ledge and reaching for the hatch. Coop moved to help him. As they wrestled with it, Imogene and the others closed ranks, looking in all directions. From somewhere out in the darkness came a splash. Attila began to bark. Sayers still couldn't see anything, but that didn't mean it wasn't there. Calavera and Coop struggled with the hatch, but it resisted their efforts.

The thing – zombie? – erupted from the water in the center of the group. It swatted Ramirez and Imogene aside and reached out a dripping, gelatinous hand for Kahwihta and the snarling Attila. Ramirez, spluttering and cursing, tried to keep her light on it as it barreled towards the younger woman. Sayers tracked it through the unsteady light, the Mauser bucking in her hand. It was big, not quite a brute, but built strangely – flabbily. It wobbled, dripped and glistened as it moved.

If her shots accomplished anything she couldn't tell. "Little help, anyone?" she cried out, as the Mauser clicked empty. She had a knife, but she didn't trust her chances. Riggs and the others were turning on it now, firing at the menace in their midst. Their shots did little save to chop bits of it off. It kept moving, sloughing meat from its bones as it went.

Kahwihta retreated before it, firing a shot from her rifle with one hand, the other fixed firmly on Attila's collar. At the last moment, she let the dog go, and he flew like a furry missile, striking the zombie on the side. Both dog and dead thing went down with a splash. Sayers briefly remembered watching the zombie near the Villa fight with a coyote, the animal's odds terrible without intervention.

Calavera leapt down after them. The gelatinous zombie spun as Calavera tried to get a grip on it, and his hands came away covered in jellied meat. He staggered back, off balance, and the zombie went for his throat. There was a clang from the hatch, and the boom of a rifle. The zombie's head burst like a blister, bits splashing into the water. It slumped and sank, vanishing beneath the surface without a trace.

"I told you I heard something," someone said, stepping out through the hatch. Whoever it was froze as they realized the zombie wasn't alone. Sayers stepped forward, Mauser leveled, despite being empty. She whistled softly and looked into the astonished gaze of a woman in black riot gear as the latter turned.

Coop, following her example, swung around the hatch, weapon aimed at the second member of the patrol. He gestured curtly. "Step out. Keep your hands where I can see them."

Sayers confiscated the woman's weapon and handed it to Ramirez. "Thanks for the help – and opening the door." She smiled thinly. "Much appreciated."

CHAPTER THIRTY-THREE
Fight Night

Westlake waited impatiently for the guards to bring the weapons, but no one came. His frustration mounted as he realized they were screwed. When the red light in the ceiling started to flash, he looked at Saul. "They're not coming," he rasped.

"Thank you for pointing out the obvious, dead guy," Carter said. She peered at him. "Guess we don't get weapons this time around. I blame you."

"Maybe they decided not to take any chances," Saul said.

"Maybe you two shouldn't have popped that skeezy guy in the nose," Donovan said.

"What do we do now?" Perkins asked, nervously.

Westlake snatched up two pieces of the broken chair and tossed one to Perkins. "It doesn't matter. Find something to use. Anything sharp. Stabby."

"What about the plan?" Donovan asked, as he smashed another chair on the floor.

"The plan has changed," Westlake said. He tore loose

another shard of wood and tossed it to Saul. "The new plan is to survive until we can come up with a better plan."

Saul caught the length of wood and tested the tip with his thumb. "Perhaps we should have expected this," he said to Westlake.

Westlake grunted. "Wisdom is the cousin of hindsight."

Saul looked at him. "And where did you hear that? A fortune cookie?"

"Self-help book." Westlake glanced at the other man, and then at Ruth. She'd been quiet since her brother's death. She hadn't looked at Westlake or anyone else, but she started to rip up the couch cushions her brother died on, yanking out the springs. "She going to be all right?"

Saul shrugged. "Who can say? They were close, as twins often are. But she is resilient. I- oh." Ruth stood abruptly, a hand full of metal springs, took the length of wood from Saul, and quickly crafted a spear-like weapon. Looking at Westlake, Ruth nodded once, and went to stand by the door. Westlake looked at Saul.

"I guess that answers my question."

The door buzzed and popped open, swinging inwards. The roar of the crowd swept in like a cold wind. They seemed even more excited than the previous night. Westlake looked at the others. They were tired. They hadn't eaten in nearly two days. And the only weapons they had to speak of were mainly broken chair legs. He felt a flicker of… anger. He held onto it. He figured he might need it sooner rather than later.

"Maybe we should just stay in here," Perkins said, softly.

Carter shook her head. "They'll shoot us. At least out there we have a chance."

"Stay together, watch out for each other," Saul said, as they stepped out into the arena. "We'll get through this."

The buzzer sounded. A door opened and the crowd cheered. Up above, on his platform, Mondo began his play-by-play. Like the crowd, he was enjoying himself. He punctuated his spiel with gestures, but Westlake couldn't make out what he was saying. It was a garbled mess of noise, merging with the roar of the crowd.

The first batch of walkers were slow and coming apart at the seams. Ten of them. They stumbled into the arena, dead eyes staring hungrily at their prey. It reminded him of a prison exercise yard. He'd felt dead in prison, but nothing like what he felt now. The raw, aching need that twisted and thrashed within him. It had been asleep for a time. But it was awake now, and ravenous. He lifted his chair leg. "Let's get to work."

Westlake did the bulk of the heavy lifting, and the others were only too glad to let him. The walkers largely ignored him or outright tried to avoid him, and he put that to good use. He let the first few stumble past and then put out their lights with several quick thrusts from behind.

More doors opened and more walkers stumbled into the arena. In the stands, people cheered wildly. Westlake wondered whose side they were on. He looked for the others, and saw Carter dragging her shaft of wood free of a walker's cleft skull. Donovan was already charging towards the new arrivals, chair leg swinging like a baseball bat. A walker wearing speedos and a bathing cap launched itself at him, and he slammed it to the ground. Saul hurried to join him, Carter following in his wake. The others weren't far behind.

If they stayed together, they'd make it. That much Westlake was certain of. Every survivor learned that, otherwise they didn't become a survivor. If you could keep your head and watch out for each other, walkers weren't much trouble. At least when they were coming in dribs and drabs like these were.

Another door opened, and a half dozen metal-zombies loped into the arena, clattering like a cutlery drawer in a windstorm. "Shit, not these guys again," Donovan shouted.

"Stay together," Westlake snarled. "Don't let them separate you." Saul and the others fell back and let Westlake take point. Unlike the walkers, the metal-zombies seemed to recognize that he was a threat and zeroed in on him. Westlake sidestepped the first, letting the others handle it. He did the same to the second, but tripped it as it staggered by. He stomped on its neck and heard metal creak. The zombie turned, slashing at him.

He retreated, and then Ruth was there, sliding the tip of her handmade spear through the visor of the creature's crude helm. The zombie thrashed and went still. She pulled the weapon loose, and he nodded in thanks.

Carter, Saul and Perkins handled a third, pulling it off its feet and sending it flailing into the blades of one of its fellows. But that left three, and Saul and the others were tired. Westlake waved his companions back.

He paused to twist a bludgeon off the arm of a fallen zombie and charged towards the remaining three. One went down quick, bludgeoned and stabbed. But a metal-zombie with a mouth made out of what looked like a bear trap as well as a neck and spine reinforced with rebar, clutched at him, clawing the bludgeon from his hand. He drove his chair leg up through its chin, angling the point so that it caught the brain. It thrashed away, yanking the weapon from his grip as it collapsed.

One left. It crashed into him, nearly lifting him off of his feet. Its arms were wrapped in barbed wire, and its chest was armored. But its head was exposed. Westlake drove his fist into its skull, punching through meat and bone, stretching his fingers, reaching. He caught hold of something and gave it a twist.

The metal-zombie slumped over, nearly dragging Westlake from his feet. He tightened his grip on what he guessed was its brainstem and the zombie went still. Above them, the crowd cheered. There were maybe six walkers left, in various states of collapse – too slow to catch the survivors. But Mondo was shouting, punching the air. He looked excited. Westlake tensed. He knew what was coming.

Only one door opened this time. But what came out was worse than any walker. "What in the name of God is that?" Saul whispered.

"El Gigante," Westlake said, wrenching his fist from the walker's pulped face. El Gigante stepped into the arena, bigger than a brute, and slathered in raw, seeping muscle tissue. Music blasted down from unseen speaker, some death metal crap from before the apocalypse. The monster seemed to hate it as much as Westlake did, because it swelled up with homicidal fury and bellowed to the heavens. He'd never heard a zombie make that sort of noise and hoped never to hear it again.

Even at a distance, the force of its fury hammered at him

like a physical blow. Its strangely jointed, clawed feet tore at the arena floor as the beast prowled towards them, sniffing the air. It caught up a half-dismembered walker and studied it before casually biting its head off. Chewing noisily, it fixed its red gaze on the small group of humans staring at it. It tossed what was left of the walker over its shoulder.

"What is that thing?" Saul whispered, staring at the monster in horrified awe. "I've never seen anything like it."

"A zombie. Just a big one." Westlake tried to sound more confident than he felt.

El Gigante roared and charged.

"Split up," Westlake shouted. "Try and stay out of his way!" El Gigante roared again as it cannoned towards them. It was a strangled, wet sound, like a garbage disposal choking on bones. The creature was not just wide but tall. Its legs were crooked, like those of a dog, and it ran in an awkward half-crouch, knuckling along like an angry gorilla. It shouldered aside the slower walkers in its haste, knocking them sprawling without a sideways glance. It wanted fresh meat.

Saul and the others scattered, running in all directions. It didn't matter. El Gigante made its first kill a moment later. Donovan had been too slow. Cop instincts ingrained, he'd been hustling Perkins along, making himself a convenient target.

El Gigante pounced on both men with bone-shattering force. They rolled through the sand and when the creature bobbed back up to its feet, most of what had been the two survivors were smeared across its chest or laying crumpled on the ground. It flung Perkins's body into the air, roaring that same gargling roar.

As Westlake watched, the monster sank its claws into what was left of Donovan's back and hauled the corpse into the air. It grabbed an arm and a leg and tore the body in two, gobbling the stuff that fell out greedily.

"Son of a bitch," Carter howled, dragging her improvised blade out of a fallen walker's back. The outburst caught El Gigante's attention however, and it whipped around, eyes fixed on her. Variables danced in Westlake's mind, weighing the odds. Running wasn't going to help. There was no place to hide. That meant they had to fight.

El Gigante bounded on all fours towards Carter, who backed away but didn't run. She had her blade out. The crowd cheered. Thinking quickly, Westlake reached down and pried a chunk of sharpened metal loose from the arm of a fallen metal-zombie.

Hefting his weapon, he stepped forward and whistled sharply. El Gigante paused and turned. It eyes met his, and he hesitated. There was nothing human in that skull. But it wasn't an animal either. It was worse. Malign. It was enjoying this.

El Gigante started towards him, gaining speed as it neared. It roared, jaws wide. Westlake leapt aside as it pounced, narrowly avoiding its claws. He scrambled to his feet and met its second lunge, driving the length of metal into its midsection as it knocked him sprawling. Black blood spurted and El Gigante shrieked. It snatched Westlake up and drove him face-first into the wall.

It let him go and he stumbled back, world spinning. Another blow knocked him off his feet and he rolled limply through the dirt, synapses sputtering and dying as he tried to regain control of his unresponsive limbs. Flashes of vision showed him Ruth running. El Gigante caught the back of her coat with a talon tip and yanked her backwards. Then Saul was there, a length of wood in his hands. He stabbed it into the monster's wrist, forcing it to let go. It flailed at him, and he scrambled away, grabbing Ruth's hand as he did so. Westlake tried to get to his feet. Failed. He heard Ruth and Saul shout, drawing the monster's attention.

No. He was already dead. No point in saving him at this point.

As El Gigante turned, Carter made her move. She darted forward, slashing at it. El Gigante fell on her like an avalanche, teeth sinking into her neck as it wrenched her off her feet and flung her away, like a terrier killing a rat.

Westlake watched Carter's body pinwheel across the arena. El Gigante followed and fell upon the body with a savage howl. It began to feed, one eye on Westlake and the others. There was a promise in that gaze, but Westlake was beyond caring.

He shoved himself to his feet. "Try and get to the door," he said, not looking at Saul and Ruth. "I'll buy you a few minutes. Make them count." He started towards El Gigante without waiting for a reply, his hands balling into fists. El Gigante heaved itself up as he approached.

"All right, you ugly son of a bitch," Westlake said, loudly. "Time to settle this, zombie to zombie."

CHAPTER THIRTY-FOUR
Diplomacy

The radio on the table clicked. Ariadne glanced at it and then at Ptolemy. "That's the signal. They're here. Last chance to bow out, Mr Ptolemy."

He shook his head. "No. We do this together."

Ariadne sighed softly. Though she hated to admit it, she was a trifle relieved by his presence. Though three of her people, including Eloise, and the representatives from the other camps were scattered across this floor of the pier, they were still heavily outnumbered and outgunned. Not to mention the omnipresent groaning that echoed through the entire structure. Zombies lurched along in the rolling night surf below, buffeted by the tide. Others wandered the nearby streets. If there was gunplay – *when* there was gunplay – they'd home in on the sound like hunting dogs.

She looked around what was left of the restaurant area. It still reeked of smoke, despite the shattered windows. There was glass everywhere, as well as the remains of barricades made from tables and chairs. The bodies of fallen zombies sat, decomposing peacefully wherever they had fallen. The inhabitants of Playground Pier had made their final stand here before being scooped up by her brother's thugs.

The only light came from a halogen camping lantern she'd salvaged from one of her neighbors' yachts during one of her first sorties. It sat on the table beside a cracked glass pitcher of water and a stack of plastic cups, and cast a stark white glow over the immediate area. Her Thompson sat on the table in front of her, and every so often she caressed it, as if it were a pet. She'd found the weapon in the trunk of an abandoned Volkswagen, of all things, and it had served her well ever since.

She could hear the faint echo of voices, rising up from below. The radio clicked again, then a third time. She smiled sourly. "He's brought twenty men with him. Ten downstairs, ten coming up. I don't know whether that's a compliment or an insult."

"A bit of both, perhaps," Ptolemy said, quietly. He was silent for a moment. "Have you thought about what happens after your brother has been dethroned?"

She sighed. "Some." She looked up. "This city – any city, really – is no longer fit for human habitation. The only way any of us survive is by moving on and out." She flicked a piece of glass off the table and listened to it clink somewhere in the darkness. "But I don't fancy hiding in the mountains."

"You could become a pirate."

She looked at him. "Was that a joke?"

"Was it funny?"

"A bit."

"Then yes, it was a joke." He paused, and she could almost

hear the gears turning in his mind. He wasn't a handsome man, but he was an interesting one. He reminded her of Rupert in some ways. But not too much, thankfully. "You knew about the Villa. What else do you know?" he said finally.

"Ah. I was wondering when you'd ask me that." She smiled. "But perhaps we'd best save that for after, eh? I think our guests have arrived." She tilted the light, shining it towards the restaurant entrance. Several forms were illuminated in the glare, and one of them cursed. "So sorry, Rupert," she called out. "Had to be sure it was you and not some opportunistic zombie. Come in, come in. Plenty of seats, as you can see."

St Cloud approached the table warily, Keates at his side. The rest of his people had stationed themselves nearby, spreading out around the restaurant in order to avoid making themselves a packed target. Though they had no way of knowing where her people were, she knew that Keates would have ensured that his gunmen were ready for an ambush.

"Hello, dear brother. You look well."

"You, on the other hand, look like a post-apocalyptic reject from those George Miller films you were so fond of." He looked at Ptolemy. "Who is this?"

"My name is Calvin Ptolemy." Ptolemy didn't offer his hand. "I represent interests outside of the city."

St Cloud frowned and looked at Ariadne. "What is he talking about?"

"The plane, Rupert. It was something in the way of a diplomatic envoy. It seems we are not the only survivors in this benighted world. And you're not the only one building a new empire on the ashes of the old." She gestured to Ptolemy. "He's come from the Adirondacks." She paused. "The Villa."

"Hokum," St Cloud said, as he pulled out a chair and sat. "The Villa is a fairy tale."

Ptolemy's expression didn't waver. Even though St Cloud denied the Villa's existence, it sounded like feigned ignorance. "It is not, I assure you."

Ariadne nodded. They both knew the stories of the Villa, one redoubt among many for the rich, wealthy, and sly. "He's telling the truth."

"You can't mean you believe this?" St Cloud said, but she could hear the doubt in his voice. The fear. She forced a smile.

"I wouldn't have arranged this meeting otherwise." She leaned forward, fixing him with a steely look. He was tense. Coiled and ready – but for what? She decided to poke him and see where he jumped. "The cogs and gears in your brain are turning. Before you consider using your muscle to prematurely end things, consider that I have people of my own, and that I have been here longer than you." She gestured, and a red laser dot flickered to life on the table before him. It slowly rose, sliding up his chest before halting somewhere on his head. She gave silent thanks for Eloise.

Keates cursed, and his people readied their weapons, but St Cloud gestured for them to relax, as she'd hoped. He refused to give her the satisfaction of panicking. "Get to the point," he said.

Ariadne glanced at Ptolemy. "See? I told you. Impatient. He always has been." More poking, more prodding. As calculated as it had ever been. She needed him mad, reacting instead of taking the initiative. It was the only way to beat him. "I wanted to see you again, Rupert – that's why." She paused, considering her next words carefully. "And I wanted to give you a chance to return my property peacefully."

"What are you talking about?"

"The casino. I want it back."

"Back? It is not yours. It was never yours. Have you gone insane?" He laughed. "Silly question. Obviously, you're mad."

She nodded. "A little bit. Mostly I'm just angry." She paused again. "You had a chance to do something truly grand, Rupert. And you pissed it all away because you wanted to play Caesar, just like when we were children. I am disappointed in you."

"Disappointed?" St Cloud said, incredulously. "You have nothing. I have everything. I have you, in fact." He looked around and laughed. "How many people do you have, Ariadne? I mean, really? Because the twenty I brought here are but a small fraction of Elysium's population."

"And how many of them would happily jump ship to me, if the opportunity presented itself?" she asked, softly. "If, for instance, I offered them safe passage out of the city, and to a refuge far from the hordes of the undead?" She nodded to Ptolemy. "That's why the remaining camps in the city have agreed to join forces with me – and give you a swift poke in the eye in the process."

St Cloud tensed. "It doesn't matter. They don't matter."

He leaned towards her. "This isn't about them anyway. It's about you and I, sister. This is all about your spiteful attempt at revenge."

"You mean for trying to kill me?" Ariadne said, softly. St Cloud sat back, a sullen look on his face. She'd seen that look often, as a child. It appeared whenever she managed to beat him at something. "No, Rupert. I forgive you for that."

He blinked. "What?"

"I forgive you. That's why I left you to it all this time. I hoped – I honestly hoped – that you might actually help the people trapped in this concrete wasteland. I was willing to overlook being thrown off my own yacht because I thought you might actually be the leader people needed, especially when I survived only to then survive all of this." She sighed. "I thought, for a while, that's what you were doing. I heard of people going to the Elysium and finding safety. I watched you barricade the zombies and round them up, believing you were doing it all to help save the world. You proved me wrong. Tell me, Rupert, what sort of leader forces his followers to inhabit a hostile wasteland all because he refuses to abandon his shiny castle?"

St Cloud stared at her in incomprehension and what she recognized as mounting fury. It was like watching a shark rise out of the depths. She pressed on, speaking over him – and speaking as much to Keates as to her brother. "You have vehicles, you have fuel, you have supplies and ammunition. You've picked this city clean, brother. And yet, here you are. Holed up in a tottering monument to hubris." She shook her head.

"They don't see it yet, but they will," she continued.

"You've trapped them here. Forced them into indentured servitude, all because you refuse to leave."

"No, no." St Cloud shook his head, like a punch-drunk boxer. "That's not what I'm doing. The Elysium is safe. Strong. That's why you want it… that's why you wanted it before the apocalypse…"

"No. I want it because I can't let you have it anymore. I can't let you force these people to live out your fanciful notion of military conquest." She gestured to their surroundings. "Look at this place. Look at what you've done to people you should have been helping. Why, Rupert?"

"Because someone has to," St Cloud hissed. "Why not me?" His hand dipped into his coat, almost as if of its own volition. She saw the gun in his hand an instant before Ptolemy tackled her to the floor.

Then Eloise and the others opened fire. The table fell over in the confusion and the lantern rolled across the floor, casting erratic beams of light in all directions. She lunged for her Thompson on the floor nearby, and saw Keates dragging her brother behind an overturned loveseat. She hesitated only an instant before firing at them.

"Are you alive, Mr Ptolemy?" she called out.

"For the moment," he replied. He was crouched behind the table, his shotgun in his hands. "I hope you have an exit stratagem in mind."

"Shoot them first and hope we don't attract many zombies?" she said, scooting behind the table beside him. She checked her Thompson's drum and risked a glance around the side of the table. "He tried to bloody shoot me – did you see that?"

"Lucky for you, I did," he said, and paused, cocking his head to the side. "Wait. Do you hear that?"

She did. The sound of a large vehicle backing up. The crash of metal. The floor trembled slightly, and she wondered if St Cloud's people were trying to bring the whole pier down. Then came the thud of many feet, like a stampede. "Oh God, he wouldn't..." she murmured, but she knew even as she said it that her brother would in fact do just that.

"What? What is it?" Ptolemy asked.

"He's unleashed a horde on us!"

CHAPTER THIRTY-FIVE
Inside

Ramirez rubbed her side. The ache of her cracked ribs wasn't getting any worse, but it wasn't getting any better. She'd had worse injuries, but then, she'd also had time to recuperate. Not now. She'd just have to grit her teeth and bear it. She looked around at the tunnel. It was lit by strings of battery-powered lights, and the ceiling tiles sagged or else had been removed entirely, exposing the now useless cabling and junction boxes above.

A thump from behind made her flinch. She turned and regarded the sewer hatch with a frown. "Are we sure that'll hold?" she asked, glancing at Calavera. He nodded.

"There's a lock on it. That's why we couldn't get it open in the first place. Lucky thing they came along when they did, else we'd have had to shoot the lock off. Be no way to keep them out then."

Ramirez shook her head. "We need to finish this quickly. Even with a lock, that door will give way eventually. Especially now that they know about it." The walkers had followed them down into the sewers, and Ramirez and the others had spotted the first of them lurching out of the dark even as they closed the hatch. There was no telling how many of them were on the other side by now. Frankly, one was too many in a situation like this.

The walkers would just keep banging on the door until it gave way, or they did. They didn't get bored or impatient. At best, you could hope for a distraction. She sighed. Nothing for it now. They had to keep moving. Time was at a premium.

Imogene and the other survivors were scattered about the tunnel, waiting for Coop to finish talking to their prisoners. She glanced at the latter, where they sat unhappily under the watchful eyes of Ariadne's people. She watched Coop, crouched before two guards and speaking in smooth, quiet tones. He was a professional; she knew the type. Ex-military operator, probably. A lot of private security personnel were.

She wondered how things were going on Ptolemy's end. Ariadne had taken on the more dangerous task, which was to her credit. It didn't mean Ramirez completely trusted her, however. That was why she'd been glad Ptolemy had volunteered to keep an eye on her. He was a steady hand; unflappable. There was no one she'd rather have at her back. She hoped he'd be able to keep things at the pier under control.

Kahwihta, sitting nearby, said, "You've got that look on your face, Boss."

"What look?"

"Like you're worried about something but don't want to say what."

Ramirez looked at the younger woman. "I'm always worried. That's my super-power." Coop motioned for her attention. "What did they have to say for themselves?" she asked. He frowned and scratched at his unshaven chin.

"From what our friends here have said, the dormitories are upstairs," Coop said. "So are the gardens and the water collection points. The only things on the level just above us are the casino floor, the parking garage and the loading dock. And it sounds like everyone in the building is on the casino floor. They've converted it to an arena of sorts, and apparently, there's something special going on tonight – some sort of zombie fight."

"A what now?" Ramirez asked in disbelief.

"Yeah, they're real annoyed about missing it. Apparently, they're the only ones assigned to tunnel duty, so we don't need to worry about anyone else stumbling over us." Coop glanced at the prisoners. "They're going to be even more annoyed when we zip tie their hands and leave them down here." He looked back at Ramirez. "I'll leave one of our people to watch them – and the sewer hatch. Just in case."

"They said everyone is in the arena?"

"Other than the ones stationed outside and the ones who went with St Cloud." Coop frowned. "Attendance is mandatory at these things, or so they claim. Reminds me of those stupid team building exercises we had to go through, back before the dead rose."

"They told you all this pretty quickly," Ramirez said, doubtfully. Could it be a trap? That felt like overthinking it, but you couldn't be too sure. Even before the apocalypse, bad intel had led her into more than one unplanned gunfight.

"They're scared," Coop said, bluntly. "Not of us so much. Scared of St Cloud, scared of the zombies. Scared of the people they're supposed to be protecting." He paused. "Reads to me like this whole situation is about one bad day from getting real unpleasant for everyone inside this building."

"Yeah, well. Let's take it slow anyway. Just in case." Ramirez gestured for Imogene's attention. The woman joined them. She was carrying one of the guards' rifles slung over her shoulder. "Tunnels are clear. You know what to do?" she asked. Imogene nodded and patted her new weapon. She gave a grim smile.

"We split into two teams. I'll head down the corridor with one, until we get to the entrance to the loading dock. We take the dock, make sure the doors are shut and no one gets in or out that way."

"Good. We'll take the front, shut down the lobby and the downstairs. Follow the plan, and we'll all get out of this in one piece."

"Don't have to tell me twice," Imogene said. She signaled for her people to move, and they started down the corridor. The remaining member of Ariadne's team went with them, to make sure they found the loading dock. Coop left the last member of his team with the prisoners, with orders to shoot to kill or to fall back, if necessary. Seven to the loading dock, seven for the lobby and one to watch their backs. Not great, but not bad.

Getting upstairs took longer than she thought. The utility tunnels ran on forever. Finally, Coop stopped and indicated a door. "Here we are." He took point without being asked and scanned the space beyond. "Clear."

Past the doors was a narrow vestibule, crowded with a stairwell. The stairwell went up in a zigzag. She could hear something echoing down from the top – a sort of low murmur, muffled by the thick walls. "Whatever is going on up there, it sounds like it's exciting," Kahwihta said.

"All the better to keep them occupied," Ramirez said. She gestured, and Sayers took the lead, moving up the stairs two at a time. Coop followed her, and then everyone else. At the top was another door – not locked, thankfully. Sayers signaled that the way was clear, and they stepped into the sterile, white concrete corridors of the back area that connected the loading dock to the kitchen and the counting rooms.

Ramirez paused. She could hear a faint, brief hymn of gunfire from the direction of the loading dock. It ended as quickly as it had begun. Hopefully no one in the lobby had heard. Hopefully no one had managed to radio for help. If they had, things were going to get very bloody, very quickly.

They hurried towards the lobby, moving as quietly as they could without sacrificing speed. They located the double doors that led to their destination easily enough. Through the round, porthole windows at the top of the doors, Ramirez could see immense plywood walls rising up through the lobby to the main floor above.

The lobby had been spacious once. Now, thanks to the plywood, it was mostly just a stretch of floor leading from the main entrance to a set of floating stairs and a bank of elevators. Generators, boxes and pallets crowded the walls. Serpentine lumps of repurposed cable and copper wiring ran up the walls like jungle vines. Sandbags had been stacked near the doors, creating an effective kill zone in the event of a zombie incursion.

Coop opened the doors a crack, peered through, turned and held up two fingers. Ramirez nodded and waved him back. Before he could ask what she was planning, she stepped out into the lobby, her pistol thrust into the back of her trousers, hidden from sight. The two guards were stationed near the doors, but their eyes were on the stairs. They started at the sight of her. "Hey, where'd you come from?" one called out.

Ramirez started towards them, speaking quickly in rapid-fire Spanish, praying neither of them understood what she was saying. She gesticulated to the plywood walls that rose up and kept talking, doing her best to look put out, afraid, frustrated. She hoped they wouldn't notice the whiff of the sewer about her or the fact that they didn't recognize her. She gestured, turned, gestured again, keeping their eyes on her. The guards looked at one another, and one started forward, hand outstretched. "Hey, hey! Who are you? Where did you come from?" he barked, reaching for her.

Ramirez hit him. A low blow, and one meant to drop him. The guy fell with a shrill yelp, clutching at himself and she bounced his head off the floor for good measure. The other guard was already raising his weapon as Ramirez spun, her side blazing like fire, slowing her down as she reached for her own weapon. She knew she'd never get it out in time and cursed herself. Then Calavera's hands gently settled on either side of the guard's head and the big man rumbled, "No. I think not."

Ramirez grinned and pressed the barrel of her Glock against the guard's chin. "Put it down," she said. "Slowly."

The guard did as he asked. "What- what- what are you … ?"

"What does it look like?" She whistled softly, and Coop and the others exited the back, spreading out through the lobby. "You the only two on duty?"

"No. We got a whole army," the guy began, trying to put on a tough face.

Ramirez smiled. "Half of which is heading for the pier, right? So, by my math, that only leaves half an army." She nodded to the plywood. "Are they in there?" A muffled roar sounded from above and she paused. That didn't sound like any crowd she'd ever heard of.

"Everyone is in there," the guard said, after a moment.

There was a sudden crash from above, and the sound of plywood rattling on its nails. Another crash and a section of the upper wall fell away and slammed into the stairs on the way down. An explosion of sound followed: screams, cries, gunfire. Everyone in the lobby looked up in shock. Whatever was going on up there, it sounded like it had gone wrong.

Sayers cursed and pointed. "Look!"

Ramirez looked up and saw a walker teetering in the gap left by the fallen section. It tumbled down with a moan, plummeting to the floor. There was a solid crack as its head connected with the ground, and then it was pushing itself up. She stared at it in shock. It was fresh. She looked up as more walkers followed the first, falling down in ones and twos. She looked down at the guard. "If I give you your gun back, you gonna shoot me?"

"Lady, if you're breathing, you're my best friend," the guard said quickly. The other nodded. She gestured, and the others let them up. Attila was barking to beat the band as Calavera pounced on a denim-clad walker, bearing it to the floor where he cracked its skull like an eggshell. Kahwihta shot another, dressed in a spangly skirt, so that it spun like a berserk disco ball before collapsing. Sayers put down a third and a fourth, her arrows humming like wasps. A fifth charged clumsily towards Coop, who dropped it with a single, precise shot. The guards and the other survivors did the same, putting down the remaining walkers as quickly as possible. "What the hell is going on in there?" Coop demanded. Ramirez shook her head.

"No time to worry about it now. You and the others need to get the lobby doors blocked off and keep any more walkers from getting out of that gap."

"What are you planning to do?"

Ramirez hefted her pistol. "I'm planning to see what the hell is going on in this arena of theirs."

CHAPTER THIRTY-SIX
Best Served Cold

Ptolemy crouched behind the table and racked the slide on his shotgun. The initial shooting had died down, and things were at a standoff as far as he could tell. The horde was coming up the stairs, following the sound of gunfire. It would take them time, but they'd eventually reach the third floor. Then there'd be nowhere to go.

Ariadne's people held their positions, but they couldn't be expected to stand and wait while an unknown number of zombies approached. Then, the same could be said of St Cloud's forces. It had become a game of chicken. Everyone was waiting to see who broke and ran first. He glanced at Ariadne. "Perhaps we should withdraw."

She shook her head. "You can do as you like, Mr Ptolemy. But I'm ending this here and now." She darted a look around the table she was using as cover. "A horde, Rupert? Really?" she shouted. "Bad enough you tried to shoot me, but now you're trying to get me eaten as well?" She added a few obscenities for good measure, some of which Ptolemy had never heard before. He filed them away, planning to share them with Sayers later. She always enjoyed that sort of thing.

"You have only yourself to blame, Ariadne," St Cloud shouted back from where Keates had pulled him. "This wouldn't have been necessary if you'd had the good grace to die when you were supposed to."

Ariadne checked the drum on her weapon. "Oh yes, of course, it's always my fault, isn't it?" she called out. "Always someone else's fault when things go wrong for you, isn't it? It's an old song, brother, and I am oh so tired of it."

Gunfire echoed from outside, but the first walker appeared a moment later, loping stiffly through the open doorway. It was alone, and Ptolemy suspected it had been lurking somewhere in the pier rather than being a member of the horde he heard coming up from below. It hissed, staring blindly at the overturned tables.

A red dot settled over its head. A moment later, it fell, head split like a gourd. "Thank you, Eloise," Ariadne yelled. She glanced back around the table and shouted, "That's just the first of them. There'll be more coming. What do you expect to do when they're pouring in here? Because I guarantee you that they won't see much difference between us!"

"Maybe not, but that's a risk I'm willing to take," St Cloud shouted. Ariadne frowned and looked at Ptolemy.

"He's not bluffing. He's going to be stubborn about this unless we can convince him otherwise." She paused. "Then again, perhaps it's not him we have to convince."

"Keates, you mean," Ptolemy said.

She nodded. "Those are his people, not my brother's.

Rupert left all the hiring and firing to Keates. The only reason Rupert is still standing is because he's convinced Keates to hold him up. But if we can make Keates see reason…" She trailed off, but Ptolemy understood.

He glanced quickly around the table, taking stock. The world wobbled slightly, but his vertigo seemed to have largely passed. Perhaps it was the adrenaline. Whatever the reason, he hoped it stayed that way. "If we move quickly, we can catch them in a crossfire," he said. "We'll just need a distraction."

Even as he said it, several more walkers staggered into the restaurant, seeking fresh prey. These had the look of some that had seen resistance, with bullet holes in their torsos and missing limbs. They spread out as both sides began to shoot at them. "Ask and ye shall receive," he murmured. Ariadne nodded.

"Don't shoot unless you have to," she said, as she rose to a crouch. "We're going to need every gun we can get to escape. We just need to make them understand that."

"And how do you intend to do that?"

She smiled thinly. "The same way I convinced the board of directors to sell me Rupert's casino – I'll appeal to their self-interest. Now, come on."

He rose to his feet and started running, head low, avoiding the attentions of the walkers as best he could in the dark. Shots pursued him along the floor, and he fired blind in response, hoping to make whoever was drawing a bead on him have second thoughts. It seemed to do the trick because he reached the stack of chairs next to the counter unscathed. He glimpsed Ariadne moving on a parallel course.

Ptolemy turned as a shot plucked at his boot. One of St Cloud's gunmen was hunkering behind a stack of cardboard boxes nearby, lining up a second shot on him. Ptolemy rolled onto his back and fired, forcing the gunman to scramble away. He didn't get far.

A runner in stained denim and a puffy vest raced through the restaurant. It crashed into the gunman and bowled him over a table. He heard the grunting of the zombie as it clawed at its prey. The man it had downed was twitching and jerking, preparing to rise again, even as the runner gnawed on his throat.

Ptolemy took aim and put a shot through the corpse's head. The runner turned at the sound, and he fired again. The zombie's head snapped back, and it fell against the table before sliding to the floor. Ptolemy craned his neck, trying to spot Ariadne.

He saw her nearby struggling with a walker dressed in weather-frayed fatigues. It had no arms, but its snapping jaws were close to her throat. It was still wearing its combat vest and a sidearm. Moving quickly, he got behind it, jerked the pistol free of its holster and put a round through the dead man's skull. Ariadne shoved the twitching body aside and nodded her thanks. She pointed towards her brother's position and he nodded, saying nothing.

Keates had dragged St Cloud behind a table near what had been a buffet bar. Ptolemy could just about make them out as he weaved between the tables and tray racks. In the dark, there was little chance they'd catch sight of him. Bright sparks of gunfire lit up the gloom as both sides put down the remaining walkers. But there were more on the way. He could hear them on the stairs, hammering at the doors that were only barely shut.

He heard voices – St Cloud's, Keates – and crept closer, gently easing a trolley out of his way. "Call them. Tell them to come get us," St Cloud was snarling.

Keates gestured with a radio. "I already did. They're cut off. Too many goddamn zombies and not enough people to control them. The horde's loose and there's not a damn thing we can do about it."

"I can think of something," Ariadne said, stepping into the open, her weapon aimed at the pair. Keates froze, but St Cloud swung his pistol up instinctively. Ptolemy stepped forward, shotgun extended. St Cloud paused.

"I believe we can all hear the gunfire downstairs," Ptolemy said, softly. "If you were expecting reinforcements they are most likely not coming."

"I knew this was a bad idea," Keates muttered, his gaze swinging between them. His hand was poised above his sidearm, but he hadn't drawn it yet.

Ariadne lowered her weapon. "That's because you're a practical sort, Harry. A commonsense sort of fellow. Without you, my brother wouldn't have been able to get up to half the mischief he has. Or, I admit, keep as many people alive." She raised her voice. "That goes for all of you. Which is why I do not want to kill you. The world needs people who know how to survive and how to protect others. What it doesn't need is a warlord." She looked at her brother. "The game is up, Rupert. Surrender."

"Kill her, Mr Keates," St Cloud hissed.

Keates's hand dipped, his fingers tapping his weapon.

Indecision played on his face, something sharp like regret. Then he raised his hands and shook his head. "Mr St Cloud, I quit."

St Cloud stared at him in incomprehension. "What?"

"You heard me." Keates turned away, arms draped over his knees. St Cloud bared his teeth and scrambled to his feet, his weapon still in his hand. Ptolemy tracked him. He could hear the sound of the horde getting closer. It drifted on the wind. They'd alerted every zombie on the boardwalk and they were all on the move. Soon, they'd be out of options.

"You hear that, brother? The dead are coming, thanks to you. This place will be overrun in minutes. Unless we work together to get out of here."

"You can't have my casino," St Cloud said. He glanced at the pistol in his hand and then around. To Ptolemy it looked as if he didn't know where he was, or what was going on. "I won't let you take it from me. Not again."

"Do you know why I tried to take it from you, Rupert?" Ariadne asked, softly. "Because you nearly bankrupted our company – the company our parents left us – to rebuild the damn thing. You invested everything we had in that place. If you'd failed, if it had failed, the company would have gone down with it. But you didn't care about any of that; just like you don't really care about it now. You care about winning. About proving that you're right and everyone else is wrong. I even had to hire a group of conmen to steal from you in the hopes you would be ruined enough to see some kind of sense in how fragile your contained casino ecosystem had become! But it didn't do anything. Even now, in the middle of the bloody apocalypse, you only care about your own damn pride."

He looked at her. "And you don't?"

Ariadne shook her head. "Oh, I'm no saint, but the difference between us is I know when I'm wrong and you don't." She paused. "Put the gun down, Rupert."

The sounds of the dead grew louder. Glass crunched beneath shuffling feet. Shots pierced the dark. Bodies fell, but more bodies were on the way. More and more, always more. There was never an end, would never be an end. Sayers was right about that, at least. The dead were here to stay. It was the living who were on their way out.

St Cloud laughed. There was no mirth in that sound, no joy. It was the laugh of a dead man. Ptolemy knew then that there was no way that he was coming quietly. He'd been backed into a corner; a man like him could react in only one way. "No. No I think not, Ariadne. You want what's mine? You'll have to take it over my dead body." His arm swung up, the pistol extended.

Ptolemy and Keates fired as one. St Cloud fell, the gun clattering from his hand. He didn't get back up. Ariadne released a slow breath and looked at Keates. "I am not my brother," she said. He nodded and lowered his smoking pistol.

"Glad to hear it, ma'am." He hesitated. "Orders?"

Ariadne looked at Ptolemy, and he found her expression unreadable. In that moment, he wondered if she had known that her brother would react that way. Or maybe, true to her word, she'd hoped for better. Was that sadness in her eyes? Or satisfaction? It was too late to worry about it now. He gestured. "You heard him. Orders?"

Ariadne took a deep breath and nodded. Around them, her people and Keates's were edging out of cover, watching one another warily. "Right," Ariadne murmured. She looked at Keates. "First things first – where are your trucks?"

"Downstairs at the front entrance."

She lifted her Thompson. "Then downstairs is where we are going."

"And after that?"

"The Elysium." She smiled fiercely. "And God help whatever gets in our way."

CHAPTER THIRTY-SEVEN
Zombie to Zombie

Westlake flew through the air like a bird. His brain fuzzed like a TV signal degrading to static as he tried to reorient himself. Then he hit the plywood and came back to lucidity just in time to hit the ground. He pushed himself up as his opponent bounded towards him. El Gigante caught him up and slammed him into the wall again, hard enough to crack the wood. Again, it let him fall. It seemed frustrated by its inability to kill him.

El Gigante darted forward, its clawed hand looping out. The impact sent him hurtling backwards into the wall, causing it to buckle outwards. He fell to the floor, knowing that if he'd still been breathing, he'd have stopped then and there. He didn't have time to check and see if anything was broken. It charged towards him again as he struggled to his feet. He managed to catch the creature's jaws before they closed over his head. It reared, flinging him over its back like a bull.

It gave a roar as he got to his feet again. "Annoying, ain't it?" Westlake croaked. El Gigante lunged and he punched the creature in the face again and again. He felt no pain, but every impact he received seemed to scramble his brains for longer. Eventually his slowly zombifying brain would turn off completely. Unless he managed to distract the decaying process. He caught El Gigante by the skull and tried a headbutt.

El Gigante dropped him and stepped back, shaking its head. It seemed to have lost interest in him, if nothing else. Instead, it looked up at the walls, at the stands full of cheering people, as if noticing them for the first time. Westlake hauled himself to his feet, using the wall for support. El Gigante looked at him and grinned. Then, with a rancid exhalation, it leapt straight up. Its claws dug into the plywood, rattling it loose as it started to climb.

The cheers were turning to screams. He looked for Saul and Ruth, saw them heading for the door to the green room as he'd hoped. They were being followed by the remaining walkers, but there was nothing he could do about that. He turned back to the wall and reached up for the first claw-hole. The wall wobbled under him as he climbed, and the nails started popping loose. At the last moment, he leapt for the rail and managed to get a hand on it.

As he hauled himself over, he saw that El Gigante had found fresher prey. The creature had launched itself at the nearest set of seats, and had already torn several people apart, even as the guards fired at it. Those it had bitten were already twitching and flopping.

"Fascinating, isn't it?" Brewer said from behind him. "I never imagined he could do that. I estimate there are at least a dozen potential walkers, if not other varieties, in the stands preparing to turn." Westlake turned and saw Brewer and Mondo behind him, a pair of guards beside them. Westlake took a step towards them and the guards raised their weapons. "I wouldn't," Brewer said. "They have orders to aim for the head."

Westlake shook his head. "Proud of yourself, Doc? Your pet is ripping apart St Cloud's workforce. That's not going to look good on the tourist brochures."

"We all make sacrifices for science," Brewer said. He had Pierogi in his arms, and was gently stroking the animal. "I can stop the beast whenever I wish. But I want to see what it can do before then. Think of what such a creature would mean for St Cloud's efforts, eh? A living weapon, capable of turning a dozen people in as many moments. I expect he'll be quite pleased, once he gets over his snit. And the people of Elysium needed a reminder of what we keep from them. Even if they are unhappy, they are safe. Don't you agree, Mr Mondo?"

Mondo nodded, grinning. "Oh yeah, man. St Cloud is going to be real happy. Now hop to it, zombie man. We need to put some distance between us and ugly there before Doc puts it down." He gestured. "Don't want to shoot you, man. You got a long career in the arena ahead of you. Hell, we'll even feed you."

El Gigante roared again and hurled a section of seating at a knot of guards. The guards scattered, save for one unlucky woman who was knocked over the rail. The crowd had fled for the doors, and the guards looked as if they were ready to follow. Their weapons weren't doing much to El Gigante, save perhaps pissing it off.

Westlake whistled. El Gigante turned towards him. "Hey, what are you doing man?" Mondo demanded. Westlake grinned.

"I don't think I'm cut out for this life."

El Gigante snarled and crept towards them. Mondo and the others started to edge back. Westlake tensed, but the thing's predatory gaze slid past him as if he were barely there to fix upon Mondo. With a snort, it started towards him, shoving benches out of the way. "No – no!" Mondo screamed. He drew a gun from under his jacket and fired it until the weapon gave a piteous click. El Gigante flinched as the shots struck home, but did not slow.

With another roar, it launched itself across the intervening distance and snatched up Mondo. His screams spiraled up and up, higher and shriller as the monster tore him into red, wet pieces. The guards fired, but as with their fellows, the guns did nothing.

Westlake spied Brewer making a run for it. A walker stumbled into the old man, knocking him down. His dog fell from his arms as he snatched a revolver from his coat and fired. The walker fell and Brewer turned to retrieve his dog, but Westlake was already there.

"Going somewhere, Doc?" Westlake growled, hefting the zombie-dog in one hand. Pierogi snapped vainly at him. Brewer took a half step towards him, pistol raised.

"Give me my dog, Westlake."

"Give me the doohickey, I'll give you the dog."

"The what?"

"The remote, Doc. The one that controls El Gigante. Toss it to me, and you can have your rotten mutt back. Otherwise,

I'm feeding your little pal here to El Gigante." Westlake held out his hand. Brewer glared at him. Then, almost against his will, he reached into his coat pocket with his free hand. He pulled out the remote and tossed it.

Westlake caught it and let the dog fall. Pierogi scuttled towards Brewer, gurgling oddly. Brewer snatched up the dog – and fired. The bullet caught Westlake in the chest and he staggered back. Brewer fired again as he retreated. Westlake threw himself behind a set of seats. When he looked up, Brewer was gone.

"Good riddance," he muttered. He could settle up with the good doctor later. For now, he had more pressing problems. He turned and saw El Gigante finishing up with Mondo and his guards. All three were down and wouldn't be getting back up. There wasn't enough left of them to do that. El Gigante rose from its crouch as it caught sight of him.

The creature studied him and flexed its claws. Westlake faced it and raised the remote. "Lights out, big fella." He tapped the button. El Gigante stared at him, and he stared back at it. He tapped the button again. Then a third time.

El Gigante took a step towards him. It bellowed again, ready to charge. Then there was a sound like a rubber band snapping and a plume of smoke jetted from under the creature's mask. El Gigante cradled its head and staggered, wailing. Another snap, and Westlake could smell something acrid. It reminded him of the smell of a light bulb popping. Flames erupted from beneath its mask, enshrouding its head.

The beast roared in what might have been agony or

perhaps just frustration. Westlake tossed the remote aside and snatched up a broken chair. It wasn't much, but it would have to do. He charged. El Gigante was so preoccupied that it didn't notice until he drove the broken ends of the chair into its chest and stomach. He put his whole body into it. If he could get the beast down on its back, pin it to the floor, he might be able to finish it off.

Head aflame, El Gigante roared and knocked him flat with a single blow. He kicked out at its knee, connecting solidly. El Gigante stumbled and tried to brace itself on a seat. He made to scramble away, and it caught him around the chest, smashing him back against the floor. He felt a rib crack and something in him turn liquid, but he ignored the sensation, clawing at the monster's wrist as it leaned towards him. Gobbets of burning meat dripped from its head, pattering across his chest and shoulders.

The world seemed to slow and stutter to a halt as he stared up at that burning, malformed head. He'd almost died like this once before, but it hadn't stuck. Maybe this time it would. Maybe that was for the best. Maybe, just maybe, this was how he was meant to die. This was just the universe fixing its mistake. After all, what else could a talking zombie be, but some colossal mistake? "I hope you choke on me," he grunted.

Whatever else, he had El Gigante's attention now. But only for a moment. He heard a gunshot, and then another, and the monster tensed. "Westlake – are you still alive?" Saul called out.

"No," Westlake said, as El Gigante turned towards this new threat, holding Westlake pinned to the floor.

Its burning features twisted as it glared at Saul and Ruth standing twenty feet away, holding weapons they'd gotten from fallen guards.

"Get – out – of – here," Westlake wheezed, startled by their arrival as well as the sheer stupidity of it. Why were they trying to save a dead man?

Bullets caromed off the concrete as Saul and Ruth fired at the creature. Westlake brought both fists down on El Gigante's wrist with as much force as he could muster, and heard bone crack, though he couldn't tell at first whether it was his or the monster's. Either way, it let him go as it advanced on Saul and Ruth. He flailed, catching its leg. His own weren't responding to his commands. "Not so fast, asshole," he rasped. "You and me ain't finished." El Gigante ignored him and kept moving.

Desperate now, he clutched at the back of its boiler suit. Slowly, he hauled himself up, hand over hand onto its back. No weapons but himself. It would have to do. Otherwise, Saul and Ruth were dead. As he reached El Gigante's shoulder, he spotted them retreating before the monster's advance. They were still shooting, even though they had to realize it wasn't doing any good. Maybe they were trying to buy him time.

Reaching up, he plunged his hand into the fiery halo surrounding El Gigante's head, grabbing the back of its skull. Burning meat squelched beneath his grip. Whatever Brewer had implanted in the monster's skull, it wasn't working. So long as its brain was functioning, it would keep moving and killing. So, the obvious thing to do was...

Westlake reared back and drove his fist into the back of

El Gigante's head. The monster stiffened. The fire-blackened bone cracked and gave way beneath the blow, exposing the contents of the creature's head. Westlake felt his stomach roil with hunger even as he stabbed his fingers into the tarry mass and began to rip it out, handful by handful.

El Gigante staggered, clawing at him. He felt its talons in his back and sides but held onto his perch. He sunk his fingers deep into whatever was left of its brain and hauled back as hard as he could. The remnant came away with a wet, tearing sound. El Gigante gave a rattling sigh and fell face-first onto the floor, its momentum carrying it a few extra feet towards Saul and Ruth.

Westlake staggered back, clutching the dripping hunk of black meat in his charred fist. He looked at it, momentarily overcome by a desire to take a bite. Then, with a sigh, he tossed it aside. "Burnt anyway," he murmured. He looked at Saul and Ruth. "Glad to see you're both in one piece."

"We feel the same about you, Mr Westlake," Saul said. He looked around in concern. "Though I fear we are both out of ammunition, and there are still walkers to contend with." Westlake followed his gaze and saw that there were easily a dozen walkers clambering to their feet or limping through the shattered seats towards them.

Westlake was about to reply when an arrow thudded into a walker's head. He heard a dog barking and a familiar voice calling out. He turned and saw familiar faces to go with the familiar voices. Calavera. Sayers. Kahwihta.

Ramirez.

She slowed, stopped. Stared.

"Westlake?"

Westlake gave a rictus grin.

"Hey, Ramirez. What brings you to Atlantic City?"

CHAPTER THIRTY-EIGHT
The Next Job

"You're dead," Ramirez said, staring at Westlake. They were all standing in the casino penthouse staring at him. Still.

Westlake sighed. "For the hundredth time, yes." He shrugged in reply and looked around their surroundings. He'd seen nicer, but he didn't say that. Its new owner looked like she might take offense.

He was sitting on the sole couch in the room, along with Saul, Ruth and Kahwihta. Ramirez, Calavera and the others – including a few he didn't recognize – were also in the room. None of them looked any the worse for wear. Not as bad as him at any rate. His hands were wrapped in bandages up to his forearms, as were the wounds on his side and back. The bandages were mostly to keep the others from having to look at the injuries or letting any part of him infect his friends; he figured he was going to have to stitch them shut the next chance he got.

"How is that possible?" Ariadne asked, as she looked out over the city. Her city, now, Westlake figured. Although, she wouldn't transform it into a kingdom of terror for its citizens. She turned from the balcony. "Zombies don't talk."

"Well, this one does," Westlake said. He was trying not to take offense, but it wasn't easy. He'd expected some questions, but it had been several hours since Ariadne and Ptolemy had arrived at the casino, Keates in tow, and everyone kept asking the same questions.

"Yeah, but why?" Kahwihta reached out hesitantly and touched Westlake's arm. "How is that possible?" She poked him in the stomach.

Westlake batted her hand away. "I have absolutely no idea. Neither did St Cloud's mad scientist. Then again, he wasn't much of a scientist."

"Is this mad scientist dead?" Ariadne asked with curiosity.

Westlake picked at the bandages on his forearm. It didn't itch, but it felt like it ought to. "Probably not, but he's also probably not here. Not if he's as smart as I think he is. Which is probably a blessing in disguise, all things considered."

She was silent for a moment. "I suppose. Though Rupert seemed to think he was a useful sort of man."

"Only if you want a zombie army."

Ariadne shuddered. "No, thank you. We've got enough zombies as it is." She glanced towards the door to the balcony and Westlake followed her line of sight. The balcony was still open, and the sound of the horde that had followed her, Ptolemy, Keates, and the rest from the pier hung heavy on the air. The sound grew with every passing hour, and likely would for several days yet. But the barricades were up and the casino was secure.

At least, for the moment.

"The barricades will hold until we can take stock of our supplies," Keates said from the back of the room. "After that, we can do a few sweeps, thin them out." He paused. "As far as Brewer goes, I've already ordered my people to burn everything in that lab of his. Every rotten sample. No more arena, no more metal-zombies."

Ariadne nodded. "No. Quite right." She sat down in a chair opposite the couch. "Most of my brother's other direct subordinates were killed by that monster. The perils of prime seating, I guess. The ones who survived are all more than willing to help with our evacuation plans. Once we make radio contact with the Villa, of course."

"Of course," Ramirez said. "And once we clear that horde away from the gate, we can send a scouting party to the airport and see what there is to see."

Westlake felt himself drifting. It wasn't boredom but something more insidious. A sort of lethargy. Almost like an adrenaline crash. He shook his head and found Ramirez and the others staring at him. "Are you OK?" Ramirez asked.

"I'm fine. Look, the dog trusts me, why can't you?" He gestured to Attila. The dog whined softly and went to hide behind Kahwihta. "OK, bad example, but I'm me."

"Only dead," Calavera murmured. "And for quite some time by the look of you."

"Since the Villa," Ramirez said, leaning close. Westlake looked up at her and she shook her head and stepped back. He felt a sudden urge to hide his face, but pushed it down. If they wanted to stare at him, that was their business. "You died in that wreck, didn't you?"

Westlake paused. His memories of the crash hadn't fully

returned yet, but he had a vague idea of the sequence of events. "Yeah," he said. "Yeah, I died." He looked at his hands. "I died and got up again, like everyone else these days."

"And then – what? You walked away?"

"Apparently," he said. He ran a palm over his scalp. "Look, everything between the crash and me arriving here is a blank. I doubt I walked, but I don't remember finding a car, or how I wound up here. But I'm here now, and so are you."

"I guess that means you'd like me to wait on that promise of putting you down if you ever turned, is that right?" Ramirez grinned.

"If you don't mind." He tried to smile again. "Maybe this whole thing is kismet. We're fated to be together, you and I. A team."

She snorted. "Yeah, you're more like a bad penny. Turning up when I least expect it."

He shrugged. "Either way, here I am."

"Yes, now what do we do with you?" Ariadne asked. She studied him, but not with fear or disgust. Interest, maybe.

Westlake shifted uneasily. He'd been expecting that, and he still didn't have anything like a good answer. "Why do you have to do anything at all?"

"Because you're a zombie," Sayers said, flatly. "Zombies do two things. They rot, and they eat people." She looked down at him. "I didn't know you well, Westlake, and from what I saw, you were an asshole. I doubt that's changed any. I don't want to wake up one night to find you chewing on my arm."

"What if I promise not to?" Westlake asked.

"The question is not whether you want to, it is whether you can help yourself," Ptolemy said, quietly. He frowned as he spoke. "This situation is new to all of us. We do not know how long you will be like this. We do not know whether you will remain as you are or turn feral, so to speak. With such a risk, can we allow you to roam free?"

Westlake looked at him. "No one allows me to do anything. If I decide to leave, are you going to try and stop me? Are you willing to put a bullet in my head right now? Because that's the only way you'll be able to do it."

"I'll do it," Keates said.

Westlake didn't look at him. "Nobody asked you." He half-rose from his seat but stopped as Saul grabbed his arm. At a look from the old man, he sat back down.

"Here is what you do: you give him time," Saul said, speaking up for the first time. He leaned forward and cleared his throat. "I do not know Mr Westlake well, or what his relationship is with the rest of you beyond what I have observed, but I know a thing or two about redemption. Did not the Lord say: I will bring the third part into the fire and refine them as silver is refined, and try them as gold is tried? This..." He gestured to Westlake. "It is obvious to me that this state of being is his trial. It is his time of purification."

Ruth nodded. "He saved me. Twice." She looked at him. "He deserves a chance to earn his way into Heaven, at least."

"Perhaps Santa Muerte brought him back for a reason," Calavera said. He looked at the others. "If she has given him a second chance, it is not for us to deny it to him."

Westlake grunted. "Look, if it makes you feel better, I give you permission to put a bullet in my head if I so much as look like I'm going to take a nibble out of someone. Will that make you feel better?"

"No, but it's a start," Ramirez said. She winced and touched her side.

She was hurting, Westlake knew. He could almost taste it – no. His hands curled into fists and he rose to his feet. "Good enough. I need some air." He went to the balcony and out. Inside, the others kept talking. Ramirez and Ariadne had come to an understanding – an alliance between the Villa and Atlantic City. He didn't know the details, but he was sure somebody would fill him in eventually.

In any event, it didn't interest him at the moment. Instead, he leaned against the rail, listening to the call of the dead. The groaning below seemed almost mournful from up here. Distance lessened the sense of danger. Maybe that was why St Cloud had thought he could pull off his little exercise in empire building. Or maybe he'd just been crazy. There was a lot of that to go around, these days.

Kahwihta joined him on the balcony. "So. Did I mention that you look terrible?"

"You and everyone else. How's the mutt?"

"Happy and healthy." She gave him a sidelong look. "What about you?"

"Hungry," he said, without thinking. She didn't flinch or draw back.

"Mental or physical?" was all she said.

He tapped his head in reply. She nodded. "Figures. Zombies don't need to eat. They just *need* to eat. Like their bodies are convinced they require something." She looked him up and down and indicated the wound in his side. "So… does it hurt?"

"No," Westlake said.

"What does it feel like, then?"

Westlake hesitated. "It feels like I'm wearing a suit that's too small. I'm worried I'll pop a seam if I move the wrong way. But at the same time, I'm not really worried at all." He shook his head. "Probably doesn't make much sense."

"It doesn't," she said. "You're not as decomposed as I expected."

"Thanks? Everyone else said I looked like I've been baking in the sun."

"Are you stiff at all? Having any problems moving?" She poked his elbow. "How are your joints holding up?"

"Please don't poke me," he said, somewhat plaintively.

"I'm just trying to figure this out."

"Brewer said something similar." He gave a ghastly smile. "You'd have liked him. He had a dog too."

"Yeah?"

"Yeah." He turned, putting his back against the rail, and crossed his arms. "I'm glad you're still alive."

Kahwihta punched him in the arm. "And I'm glad you're still… here." She paused. "I've been doing some research on zombies. Trying to figure out what makes them tick. Maybe I can figure out how to, I don't know, fix you."

Westlake laughed. "You might have better luck embalming me."

She grinned. "We could try that too. It's not like it'll kill you." She looked back at the penthouse and the others. Her eyes lingered on Ariadne. "What do you think about our new partner?"

Westlake ran a hand over his scalp. A strip of flesh came away and he let the wind take it. "Needs must, right? After all, you shouldn't have trusted me either, and that turned out fine." He paused. "Well, for most of us."

"That's not as reassuring as you might imagine," she said, drily.

"I tried."

"Not very good at the pep talks, is he?" Saul asked, as he stepped out onto the balcony. "May I interrupt?"

"Sure." Kahwihta paused, and touched Westlake on the arm. "I really am happy to see you, Westlake."

Westlake watched her go, feeling a numb sort of warmth that must be acceptance, and then turned to Saul as the latter joined him at the rail. The old man looked down. "That's a lot of zombies down there."

"Lot of zombies everywhere," Westlake said.

"Except the mountains, eh?"

"Zombies in the mountains too. Just not so many." Westlake looked at Saul. "Spit it out, Rabbi. What do you want?"

"To thank you properly. For saving my life, and Ruth's. Without you, we would have surely died." Saul held out his hand. "You're a true mensch, my friend."

Westlake looked at the outstretched hand and then took it. "Right back at you, Rabbi. What are you planning on doing now?"

Saul shrugged. "Miss St Cloud has floated the idea of my helping her keep things organized around here. I may take her up on it." He looked out over the city. "This used to be a nice city. Not a good one, perhaps. But a nice one."

"Yeah," Westlake said, wistfully. "Yeah, it did."

Ramirez poked her head out. "Get in here. I want your opinion."

"On what?" Westlake asked as he reentered the penthouse, Saul following him. Kahwihta and the others were gathered around a table. Maps were spread out across it, held in place by strategically arranged books.

Ptolemy looked up from the maps. "We take the airport. With it in hand, we can begin consolidating the remaining fuel and running short haul flights to Saranac Lake. We take anyone who wishes to go."

"So long as our flight plan avoids New York," Ramirez said. She looked at Ariadne. "Zombie birds. Bad on engines. There is room for you in any of our flight plans, if you want."

Ariadne grinned. "Not just yet. You'll need me here to keep the supplies and survivors flowing for the time being. And, if other survivors arrive here from elsewhere, I can funnel them to you. Besides, if I want to leave, I have my yacht."

Ramirez looked at Westlake. "Ariadne, Ptolemy, and I have been talking about maps and blank spaces. About hidden caches, like the Villa."

Westlake frowned. "Yeah? What about them?"

"How many would you say there are?"

He shrugged.

"I know of maybe half a dozen scattered across the country," Ariadne said. "Most of them just safe houses. You know, for powerful personas rather than witnesses that need protecting."

"But there *are* others, aren't there? Bigger ones. Ones like the Villa," Ramirez insisted.

"I think I heard of one in the south," Westlake murmured, but his brain was doing its slippery dance with his thoughts. "Maybe it was Florida? But it was nothing like the urban legend of the Villa. There's no way we're getting to Florida from here, though, if that was the case. Or to any of the others Ariadne might know of." Westlake paused, as he realized what she was getting at. "The airport..."

"The airport," Ramirez said. "Ariadne says there are pilots among the survivors holed up there. If we're lucky, we might be able to get something larger than a private plane in the air. A cargo hauler maybe. Something big enough to transport supplies, survivors – whatever we find out there."

"If we find anything," Sayers said.

"Santa Muerte is with us," Calavera countered. "We will find something. I know it."

"If we are careful, we could simply hop from airfield to airfield," Ptolemy added. "We can avoid the larger airports and stick to smaller, private ones. That will increase our chances of success significantly."

"My people and I will ensure that our airport is always welcoming, at least," Ariadne said. "For a small fee of course. Bullets, maybe a nice brisket, depending. At least until it's time to move everyone to the mountains."

Westlake nodded slowly. The plan was rough; it needed sanding down and smoothing out. Logistics. But he could see it in his mind's eye as clear as if he'd come up with it himself. "It could work," he said, finally.

Ramirez looked at him. "Does that mean you're in?"

Westlake looked down at his hands. They were trembling slightly. Nerve death, he figured. He wondered how much time he could steal for himself – a year? Two? It would have to be enough. After all, Ramirez's voice had followed him in his undeath, urging him to help others. He looked at her.

"Yeah." He smiled. "I'm in."

ABOUT THE AUTHOR

JOSH REYNOLDS is the author of over thirty novels and numerous short stories, including the wildly popular *Warhammer: Age of Sigmar,* *Warhammer 40,000, Arkham Horror* and *Legend of the Five Rings.* He grew up in South Carolina and now lives in Sheffield, UK.

joshuamreynolds.co.uk
twitter.com/jmreynolds